Praise for the BLUE NOTES series

Blue Notes

"…insightful and thoughtful and made me smile most of the way through."

—Musings of a Bookworm

"…a pleasure to read, from start to finish."

—Joyfully Reviewed

"…settle in for several hours of reading enjoyment."

—Love Romances and More

"I pretty much loved this whole book!"

—Booked Up

The Melody Thief

"It's a beautiful struggling story that I would definitely recommend!"

—Confessions from Romaholics

"A romance with a very realistic approach, and a beautiful introduction to the world of classical music."

—MM Good Book Reviews

"A wonderful story, absolutely enjoyable as a stand-alone."

—Reviews by Jessewave

By SHIRA ANTHONY

NOVELS

THE BLUE NOTES SERIES
Blue Notes
The Melody Thief
Aria

The Trust (with Venona Keyes)

NOVELLAS
The Dream of a Thousand Nights

Published by DREAMSPINNER PRESS
http://www.dreamspinnerpress.com

ARIA

SHIRA ANTHONY

Dreamspinner Press

Published by
Dreamspinner Press
5032 Capital Circle SW
Ste 2, PMB# 279
Tallahassee, FL 32305-7886
USA
http://www.dreamspinnerpress.com/

Aria

Cover Art by Catt Ford

ISBN: 978-1-62380-175-5

Printed in the United States of America
First Edition
December 2012

eBook edition available
eBook ISBN: 978-1-62380-176-2

For Lainie.
You were taken from us far too young,
but your spirit lives on in our hearts.

ACKNOWLEDGMENTS

TO THE amazing writers who have made this book and the other Blue Notes books possible: Rebecca Cohen, Michael Halfhill, Venona Keyes, EM Lynley, Thea Nishimori, and Helen Pattskyn. Thanks also to Andrea Speed, Shae Connor, Jamie Fessenden, and the crew from the Inner Circle for their help with Cary and Aiden's tequila party banter.

Special and heartfelt thanks to my wonderful publisher and in particular my amazing editor Gin, for her sage advice, patience, and support.

CHAPTER

THE ashes flew from his fingers the moment he lifted his hand to the wind. Weightless, ephemeral, they caught the stiff breeze and vanished over the water. The sky grew darker; a sunset painted in bands of fuchsia, orange, yellow, and dark purple streaked the clouds. Lady Liberty stood sentinel against the vibrant backdrop as a ferry made its way toward Staten Island.

Goodbye, Nick.

Sam looked down at the now empty tin in his hands. He replaced the cover and sat down on one of the benches at the edge of Battery Park, smiling to see the words *Macadamia Chocolate Chip* printed on the top. How many times had he seen his lover toss his tubes of oil paints into the battered cookie tin as they headed to the park for a Sunday afternoon picnic? Even after Nicholas Savakis had made his name as a rising young painter, he never replaced that metal tin.

"Who needs all the bullshit?" Nick said when Sam suggested they buy him a new box for his paints. "This works fine." So when the funeral director tried to sell Sam a fancy urn, he refused. Instead, he took Nick's ashes in the hard plastic box and transferred half of them to the tin. He gave the rest to Nick's family.

It's what Nick would have wanted.

Sam had decided on this spot even before the funeral, but it took him more than a year to gather his courage to come here. This had been Nick's favorite place to sit and paint. Sam had often met him here after work during the six years they lived together.

Sam loved to watch Nick's dark hair blow about his face as his lean hands moved with careful precision over the canvas, his long brushstrokes capturing the multilayered colors of the water and sky. To someone unfamiliar with Nick's work, his paintings might seem only an enticing blur of paint and texture. But over the years, Sam had come to see the world through the eyes of the lanky, slightly awkward man whose stained jeans echoed the blue and turquoise he favored in his art. The paintings were whispers of Nick's soul, the beautiful soul Sam had cherished. Sam had hoped to spend the rest of his life with that perfect soul.

He inhaled the salty air and closed his eyes. In the distance, he could hear the drone of traffic. The air was warm for mid-November, but as the sun set below the water, he shivered. The lightweight coat over his suit jacket did nothing to stop the biting wind. Sam had planned to do this the summer after Nick's death. Nick would have laughed at him; he'd have told Sam he always took too long to decide things.

"S'only your fault you're sitting here freezing your ass off," Sam could almost hear him tease.

I love you, Nick. Wherever you are.

He opened his eyes once more, realizing he still held the cookie tin in his hands. He stood up and slipped it back into his briefcase, then slung the strap of the case over his shoulder. He needed a drink; he wasn't ready to face the empty apartment yet. Not tonight, of all nights.

CHAPTER 2

London
Five years later

"MR. LIND!" the reporter shouted at him as he walked out the side
door from Covent Garden. "Do you have a minute?"

Aiden had just finished rehearsing for his London debut in a new
production of Mozart's *Don Giovanni*. He was exhausted and looking
forward to a hot shower back at his place. He pulled up the collar of his
wool coat and tucked his scarf a bit tighter around his neck. With all the
insanity that seemed to swirl around him recently, the last thing he
wanted was to get sick and have to cancel a performance. He could see
the headline now: *Lovesick Opera Star Misses Opening Night*.

Deep breath. I can do this. He turned and flashed his best, most
confident smile at the woman. Opera singers never got much press
attention, but ever since he'd met Cameron Sherrington, Aiden had
been on the radar screen. Cam wasn't only the outrageously wealthy
heir to a global hotel conglomerate, he was also a sometime impresario
who financed Broadway-bound productions and even a movie or two
when it struck his fancy.

"Mr. Lind, I'm Janine Thomas, from the *Sunday Press*," the
woman said as he shook her hand. "I was hoping to ask you a few
questions."

"Sure."

He had been expecting the usual "Did you know that the queen
will be attending your debut?" or "Are you and Lord Sherrington
planning another vacation aboard his yacht this summer?" So he was

entirely unprepared when she asked, "Is it true about Lord Sherrington and Jarrod Jameson?"

"What?" He stared at her for a split second, then swallowed hard and fought to regain his composure.

He knew Jarrod. Cam had invited him and about a hundred other guests to a party a few months before at "the castle," as Aiden liked to call Cam's family's sprawling estate about an hour out of London, at which he and Cam sometimes spent the weekend. Jarrod was an Olympic swimmer and recent gold medalist in the European games held only six months before. Lean, muscular body, model good looks. Gay.

The reporter—Aiden had already forgotten her name—thrust a large glossy photograph into his hands. He knew he should hand it back to her, but he was so rattled he couldn't think straight. The photo was grainy, obviously taken at night. It showed two men entwined and kissing behind a tall iron gate. The kiss was not chaste.

Aiden's mouth went dry. He knew that gate—the gate in front of the London home he and Cam shared in Bloomsbury. One of the men looked a lot like Jameson, although he couldn't be sure. And the other man... Aiden was pretty sure he recognized the familiar high cheekbones, the short brown hair that was always stylishly mussed, and the lean, athletic frame that looked so striking in an expensive suit. And well he should. He'd been living with the man for nearly a year.

He shoved the photograph back at her. "No comment." His jaw tensed as he strode quickly over to the curb and flagged down a taxi.

"Mr. Lind!" she shouted as he ducked into the cab and shut the door. He ignored her and gave the driver his address.

AT NEARLY two in the morning, Aiden heard the front door open and close. He had spent the better part of the past three hours making a serious dent in the contents of a cut crystal carafe filled with expensive scotch. He was drunk, but not so drunk that he didn't care. He wished to hell he was. He didn't *want* to care. It hurt too much.

It was still so surreal, living in this incredible Edwardian house in one of the most expensive London neighborhoods. He had grown up in rural Mississippi in a three-bedroom ranch on his grandfather's farm.

The house had been comfortable but small, built in the late 1960s, when his father married his mother. A wedding present. Aiden had always wondered how his mother must have felt, having her front door a few hundred feet from her in-laws' home. But if it had bothered her, she'd never mentioned it. Elizabeth Lind was the perfect wife and mother, attending church, cooking and cleaning and raising her two children. His mother's world was far removed from the one into which Cameron Sherrington had been born—one of wealth and privilege. Aiden still felt like a usurper, a pretender to his current circumstances.

"Waiting up for me, sweetheart? I told you I'd be at the gallery opening late. Lady Billingsley insisted we go out for drinks afterwards, and you know how she is." Cameron laid his coat over the back of the loveseat, walked over to Aiden, and bent down to kiss him on the head.

"I looked online," Aiden said, his voice a monotone. "The gallery opening was last week."

"Checking up on me?" Cam laughed and kissed Aiden again. "I'm sure you're mistaken." He walked over to the buffet and poured himself a glass of sherry. "I hardly imagined the party tonight. And it was a dull one, frankly. If Sarah hadn't been there, I'd—"

"Was he good, Cam?" Aiden got up from the couch and stood in front of the fireplace.

"What on Earth are you talking about? And who is *he*?"

"Jarrod Jameson."

The slight twitch in Cam's cheek told Aiden everything he needed to know.

"Jameson? You mean the swimmer? What would I know about him?" Cam refilled his glass and waved it in Aiden's direction.

"I know you've been fucking him."

Cam raised an eyebrow. "You're drunk."

"Don't change the subject."

"We can talk about it in the morning, when you've sobered up a bit." Cam gave him a long-suffering look that made Aiden feel like he was six years old again.

"Cam. Shit. You promised you wouldn't—"

"Shhh." Cam took Aiden in his arms and ran his hands through Aiden's hair.

Aiden wanted to pull away, but he couldn't do it. Instead he melted into Cam's arms.

"You know I love you. What happens out there, it's not us. *This*," he continued, "here, this is who we are."

The fire spit angrily, and Aiden watched it with calm detachment over Cam's shoulder. Cam was right. This was *home*. He loved this old place with its creaky stairs, wood paneling, painted doors, and beautifully worn oak floors. They had picked out the furniture together, shopping the antique stores of Portobello Road until they found the perfect pieces.

"Cam, I—"

"You're being paranoid, sweetheart," Cam interrupted. He ran a thumb over Aiden's mouth, tracing his lips until Aiden closed his eyes. "You worry too much. You always do."

Aiden took a deep breath. Maybe Cam was right. Maybe he was being paranoid. The photograph had been taken at night, after all. And he hadn't been sure it was Cam.

"Come to bed, Aiden," Cam purred as he licked a line from Aiden's chin to the sensitive spot under his ear. "And let me show you how much you mean to me."

"AIDEN?"

Shit. He had missed his entrance. Again.

"Sorry, David. I don't know what's wrong with me today."

David Somers peered at him over the rim of his reading glasses and frowned. "It's about time for lunch anyhow," the conductor said as he stood up from the piano. "How about it? My treat."

"I… ah… sure." Aiden had eaten with David before, but he still felt supremely awkward around the superstar conductor whose old-world grace and sophistication were so far removed from Aiden's humble upbringing. David was classical music royalty, and Aiden was the hick kid with the incredible voice.

They'd met three and a half years before, not long after he'd arrived in Germany. David had taken Aiden under his wing, gotten him work in the larger European houses, introduced him to the best

European conductors. David was the reason Aiden was making his Covent Garden debut; in the terms of his contract, he had insisted on Aiden singing the title role. David had even sent Aiden to a friend who had his own line of clothing with one of the largest European fashion houses for a "bit of polish," as David had put it. David had taught Aiden about good wine and good food. Aiden's best friend, Cary Redding, loved to tease Aiden that David was his fairy godfather.

When David's driver let them out in front of a small fish and chips place near Piccadilly Circus, Aiden was more than a little surprised. He'd been expecting something a bit more posh. David was clearly amused to see Aiden's reaction.

"Fish and chips is an art form in its own right," David told Aiden in his upper-crust New England accent. "Not everything on your plate needs to be haute cuisine."

Ten minutes later, settled at a table near the back of the tiny restaurant, Aiden nodded in hearty agreement as he bit into a delicately battered piece of fish that melted on his tongue. "This is incredible."

David's response was a knowing but reserved smile. David never laughed, as far as Aiden could tell, and right now, Aiden was thankful for it.

"Something's on your mind, Aiden," David said. He never did beat around the bush.

"It's nothing." Aiden wiped his lips and tried not to blush.

"I've never seen you this distracted."

Aiden was utterly embarrassed. It wasn't as if he was going to discuss his love life with someone like David Somers. Why would David even care?

"I am not entirely oblivious to your situation," David continued, apparently unfazed by Aiden's silence. "I knew Lord Sherrington's parents quite well."

Oh God, Aiden thought. *Can it get any worse?* He waited for the other shoe to drop. David would fire him now, wouldn't he?

"That's interesting," Aiden said, knowing he looked like a complete fool and reminding himself that there were other jobs to be had. Of course, none of the other jobs he'd gotten since coming to Europe were anywhere near his current gig: performing at the best opera house in Great Britain with the best conductor around, singing the title role in *Don Giovanni*.

"I simply wanted you to know that if you need anything," David continued, "I'm here to assist. I have several spare bedrooms at my London flat."

Aiden's mouth fell open. Was the man offering to put him up if he left Cam?

David offered Aiden a warm smile. "I put very little stock in the gossip rags," he said as he tore a piece of fish off with his bare hands, "but I am not so naïve as to believe that there is never a grain of truth to be found between their covers."

"You… you would do that?" Aiden stammered as David's words began to work their way to his fuzzy brain. "Put me up?"

"Of course. Aren't we friends?"

Aiden coughed and choked on a piece of fish until tears appeared in the corners of his eyes.

David handed him an extra napkin with casual aplomb. *Does anything ruffle this man?* Aiden wondered. *Friends? Me and David Somers?*

"It would be my pleasure."

"I… uh… I mean… that's very kind of you and all, but…."

"Aiden." David's face was serious now, his expression sympathetic and kind. "You have far too little faith in your own abilities both on and off the stage. It isn't my place to give you advice as to your private affairs, but I feel it's my duty as your friend to remind you that I am here should you ever need my help."

"I… uh… thanks, David. I'm honored. I mean, I'm—"

"There's no need to thank me. And no need to speak of it further." He gestured to Aiden's plate. "By the way," he continued, "the fish is far better consumed hot."

Aiden nodded dumbly and went back to work on his food, knowing the heat in his cheeks was visible to his companion but unable to do anything about it. There was no doubt in his mind that David's offer was entirely genuine.

David Somers wants to be my friend? It seemed so improbable, so surreal. And yet, there it was.

"YOU were splendid, darling," Cam gushed as he met Aiden in the front entrance of his family's estate and planted a kiss on his lips. "Not that I expected anything else, of course."

Cameron had invited the entire *Don Giovanni* cast back to the castle to celebrate Aiden's London debut. And the orchestra. And the stage crew. *Half of London, really.*

Cam guided Aiden into the grand ballroom of the estate to a round of applause from the guests. Aiden caught David Somers's eye, and the conductor raised his glass and smiled.

The place was magnificent. Glittering chandeliers cast flickering slivers of light on the polished marble floors. The ceiling was painted with tiny stars on a deep blue background, the walls paneled in well-oiled wood that shone and reflected blue and white with the crystals overhead. Toward the back of the ballroom, enormous arched doors led out onto a patio running the length of the room. Aiden was reminded of the dizzying effect of a disco ball, only far more ethereal.

A jazz orchestra played at one end of the high-ceilinged room as women in ball gowns danced with men in tuxedos. Aiden had begged Cam for a little party at their own home. He was entirely out of his element here, amidst the titled guests and local celebrities. Cam, however, had insisted that Aiden deserved the lavish celebration, and Aiden, knowing it was useless to argue, had finally relented.

For nearly two hours, Aiden smiled politely as guest after guest congratulated him on his performance. Finally, at the end of his patience and feeling the usual exhaustion that followed an evening of singing, he walked onto the patio and into the damp evening air. The midwinter chill on the breeze helped clear his mind.

It was quiet here, overlooking the formal gardens. Beyond, Aiden could barely make out the copse of trees he and Cam had often picnicked under. Beyond that were the woods where they'd ridden on horseback—where Cam had taught Aiden to ride. Even now, as winter began to weave its tendrils throughout the countryside, it was still lovely. In spring, the trees and flowers would burst into a frenzy of color, each plant painstakingly placed for maximum visual impact.

Aiden wished his mother could see this. She'd always loved to tend her garden.

Overhead, a plane made its way to parts unknown, but the only thing Aiden could hear was the wind as it moved through the trees and shrubs. He wondered what it must have been like for Cam, growing up in this beautiful but formidable place. They often spent weekends here in the spring and summer, but it never felt like home to Aiden. He couldn't get used to the servants who pressed his clothing and turned down the bed at night, or the elaborate breakfasts that greeted them in the mornings with food enough for ten people.

In all his stays at the castle, Aiden had never once met Cameron's mother. He once asked Cam how often he saw her, but Cam only laughed and pointed out that Aiden hadn't seen his own parents or his sister in more than two years. Funny, thought Aiden, how he still missed his parents sometimes. But then again, John Lind had made it abundantly clear that he wanted nothing to do with his only son. Aiden's mother wouldn't defy her husband, although she wrote to Aiden regularly by e-mail. His sister, Deb, had also made the effort to stay in touch, and he saw her once a year at most.

"Aiden!" he heard Cam call from the glass doors behind him. "You must meet Lord Cook and his wife, Audrey."

With a sigh, Aiden turned and walked back into the ballroom.

AT NEARLY three in the morning, Aiden climbed the back stairs to the enormous bedroom he and Cameron shared. The room, as the rest of the house, was decorated in antiques. The bed was the only compromise in the room. Made of reclaimed wood Cam had told him once made up a wall-sized cabinet, it had been crafted to resemble the other pieces. Mahogany, finely detailed carving. Outrageously expensive. Cam had told him it was French and several hundred years old. Oil paintings of the English countryside hung at perfectly placed intervals on the damask-covered walls.

The party still continued below. It would go on until sunrise, Aiden guessed, but Cam would forgive him for turning in early. Not that Cam would hesitate to tease him mercilessly about being an early bird the next day. Aiden had a difficult enough time keeping up with

Cam's seemingly boundless energy, but after a long day and performance, Aiden knew it was a lost cause even to attempt it.

Aiden shed his tux, slipped into a heavenly pair of silk pajamas Cam had given him as a gift—one of many gifts—and washed his face in the spacious bathroom attached to their room. He reached for the toothbrush, neatly laid out on the glass shelf above the sink, when his stomach rumbled loudly enough for him to hear. He laughed. In all the chaos of the evening, he had forgotten to eat.

He never did eat much before a performance. He was loath to admit it, but he desperately feared burping when he was on stage. Not that he ever had. Still, it was a bit like a good luck charm for him, not eating. But afterward....

Damn. The servants would all be helping out at the party, so it wouldn't be easy to find someone to bring him a snack. He didn't want to get dressed again, he was too comfortable. He'd have to get the food himself without being noticed. Aiden smiled at the thought that he knew his way to the kitchen without descending the main staircase. He and Cam had sneaked down to the kitchen by way of the servants' stairs more than a few times to snag leftovers after a particularly athletic round of sex.

He pulled on a pair of slippers and tied a warm woolen robe around himself. He made his way down the long hallway that joined the east wing of the house with the west, past the enormous staircase that led to the front entry, and toward the back stairs. He had nearly reached the stairs when he heard it—the sound of voices from a sitting room that joined a pair of bedrooms.

"Right... oh, yes... right there. That's it. Just a little more. Oh... fuck!"

Aiden laughed to himself. He wasn't all that surprised that some of the guests had made their way up here for a little added entertainment. The servants had been instructed to make the guest bedrooms available to Cam's "good friends," which in Aiden's experience meant anyone who asked to stay.

He quickened his pace, not wanting to eavesdrop. The door to the sitting room was slightly ajar, so he kept his eyes focused on the stairwell so he wouldn't be tempted to look inside. But then he heard a second voice, and he froze where he stood.

"Damn, but you're tight tonight, sweetheart. Have you missed me? Have you been saving yourself for me? Because that tight little ass of yours is too delicious—"

Aiden's gut roiled. He stormed over to the door and kicked it open with such violence that the sound echoed down the hallway. What he saw inside made him sick.

Jarrod Jameson was bent over an overstuffed settee. Naked. Cam, fully dressed, was ramming him from behind, his hands grasping Jarrod's waist. Later, Aiden would realize that his gaze hadn't focused as much on the men as on the antique sofa, with its beautiful carved scrollwork and hand-embroidered upholstery. Cam had taught him to appreciate the delicate beauty of just such an antique.

"Get the fuck out of here!" Aiden shouted at Jarrod as the two men abruptly separated.

"Aiden, sweetheart, I—"

"Shut up," Aiden snapped at Cam as Jarrod picked up his scattered clothing from the Persian rug and ran out of the room, still naked. It was a good thing Jarrod left so quickly, because Aiden's hands were balled in fists and he was having a hard time restraining himself from punching Jarrod's face in.

Cam opened his mouth to speak, but Aiden didn't give him the opportunity. "Don't fucking try it, Cameron. It won't work this time." He turned and left, slamming the door to the sitting room behind him.

Back in his room—*their* room—a minute later, Aiden threw off his pajamas, pulled on a pair of jeans and a cashmere sweater, slipped on a pair of moccasins and a wool jacket, grabbed his wallet, and headed down the main stairway. He'd get his things later. He couldn't stay a second longer.

Several guests were milling about the front door, drinks in hand, laughing. They barely looked at him in his street clothes. Maybe they didn't recognize him.

Or maybe they don't give a shit.

"I'm taking the Jag," Aiden told one of the servants. The man looked at him with surprise but complied, returning a moment later to let him know the driver would be bringing the car around. Aiden was on the road back to London a few minutes later.

WHEN Cameron returned from the castle the next morning, Aiden had several suitcases spread around the bedroom and was packing his belongings. Aiden had tried to sleep but had given up in the end, deciding instead to get his things together. He couldn't do this anymore. How could he have been so naïve? He had stupidly believed the man the first time. But the second....

What's the old expression? Fool me once, shame on you... fool me twice, shame on me?

God, his chest hurt. His eyes were red from lack of sleep and tears. Ironic that the biggest night of his career would be the worst night for his heart.

"Darling," Cam said as he looked into the bedroom at the array of suitcases on the floor and on the bed, "don't do this."

"Do what, Cam? Because last time I checked, *I* wasn't the one *doing* anything. It was you, doing it to *us.*"

"Darling, please!"

"Don't you fucking call me that! You don't *deserve* to call me that."

"Dar—Aiden," Cam began again, "let's talk about this. We can straighten this out."

"Sure. We can straighten it out. I'll forgive you again and you'll go on doing what you want, won't you?"

"You're jealous. You always were."

"Cam, for God's sake! Of course I'm jealous. We live together, and I just caught you fucking some—"

"Sweetheart. Aiden." Cam walked over to Aiden and took him in his arms. "Don't do this."

Aiden did his utmost not to respond to that touch, to the touch that had once sustained him through the ups and downs of his career. It was one of the hardest things he had ever done, not to melt into Cam's arms as he loved to do.

"It's over, Cam. I can't live like this. It's not what I thought we were about." Aiden's voice cracked.

"I'll never speak to Jarrod again." Cam's tone was reassuring. "I promise you."

"It's not him. Don't you understand? You'll just find someone else. I'm obviously not enough for you."

There. He had said it. And it was true. Because no matter how much he told himself he deserved better, it all seemed to come down to his own failings. He, Aiden Reuben Lind, hadn't been able to keep Cameron happy. It didn't matter how he looked at it. He had failed. It was time to admit it. Time to leave. Time to move on.

"I want *you*."

Aiden pulled out of Cam's arms and walked silently to the bathroom, grabbed his toiletry bag, and tossed it into the suitcase he'd been working on. "It's over, Cam," he said as he latched the case and pulled it off the bed.

"What will you do without me?"

The question scared Aiden to death. "I'll be fine," he said under his breath. He hoped he sounded more convinced than he really was.

"You *need* me, Aiden. You need what I can give you. Money. Better name recognition. Work."

Work. Aiden hoped to God Cameron wouldn't interfere with his work. *Would he do that?*

"I'll be fine," he repeated.

"You'll regret this, Aiden. I assure you."

Was that a threat? He didn't dare ask. "Good-bye, Cam," he said. He picked up the suitcase and headed out the bedroom door. "I'll send someone around to pick up the others."

Cameron said nothing.

"DAVID," Aiden said an hour later as he stood on the doorstep of David Somers's London flat, "it's good to see you. I hope I'm not coming at a bad time."

David smiled and opened the door for Aiden, took the suitcase over Aiden's protests, and led him inside. "The offer to stay here didn't have an expiration date." He gave Aiden's shoulder a reassuring squeeze. "You can stay as long as you like."

CHAPTER 3

Hamburg, Germany
May, six months later

AIDEN rolled over to avoid the light filtering in from the window, pulling the sheet with him. The sun hurt his eyes and his head pounded. He vaguely remembered the closing night party at the opera house, but the raging hangover was enough to tell him he'd had too much to drink. It wasn't as if he drank regularly—alcohol played hell on his vocal chords—but he had let himself indulge.

No one else to blame but me.

He had wanted to forget all the crap for a change. Not that the booze had helped him forget. He'd turned down several offers from attractive men and women at the party. He wondered now if he should have given in.

And let the fucking press have a field day with it? Right.

Naked, he slipped out from under the covers and plodded over to the bathroom. He stood over the toilet and yawned, finished with a tap, and walked to the sink. He splashed cold water on his face and looked into the mirror.

I look like hell.

Not that he didn't usually look like shit in the mornings. Maybe it was the fluorescent lights, but there were more lines around his mouth and eyes than he remembered. Closing night parties were the worst. Or maybe the best, depending on your perspective.

As he headed back to the bed, there was a knock on the door. "Just a minute," he said in German. "I'll be right there."

He pulled a bathrobe from the closet and tied it quickly, then went to open the door. A bellboy held a large vase filled with roses. Three dozen, plus one for good luck. Germans never sent an even number of flowers. Not that Aiden needed to count. He already knew who sent them. He motioned the kid to put the flowers on the table by the window, then handed him a ten-euro bill.

The young man's face lit up at the generous tip, and he left the room with a smile. "Vielen Dank," he said.

Aiden nodded and closed the door behind him.

For a full minute, he leaned on the door, looking at the roses. They were stunning. They always were.

Only the best.

He walked over to the table and pulled the card out of the flowers. He didn't have to read it. He pretty much knew what it said. Still, he found he couldn't help himself. He read it anyhow.

Aiden—

So sorry I couldn't make the performance. I have no doubt you were amazing. I know you're still angry. I hope you'll forgive me. I miss you. Call me, sweetheart. Please. I'll make it up to you. —Cam

He crumpled up the note in his fist and let it fall into the wastebasket. It was progress. At least he wasn't tearing them up anymore.

His cell phone vibrated a few hours later. He tapped it. "Jaz Man, how the hell are you?"

"You tell me" came the rumbling voice through the speaker. "Jules says you're in town next week. We're having a little get-together on Saturday, and we hoped you'd join us."

Aiden smiled. It had been nearly a year since he'd been back to Paris, and he was really looking forward to it after a gray and lonely four weeks in Germany.

"Little, my ass," he shot back. "That guy can't do anything little."

"Nah," Jason said with a laugh. "Not my Jules."

"I'll come by after the concert." He wouldn't miss a party at Jules and Jason's. "What are we celebrating?"

"A good friend of mine is flying in for a few weeks. Thought we'd show him how much he's been missing, living in the States. How long you going to be in town?"

"Four weeks. Concert on Saturday, then rehearsals for a new production of *The Pearl Fishers*."

"Damn. If I'd known, I would've timed it differently. You could've stayed with us."

"Don't sweat it. It's not like you haven't let me crash at your place before. Besides, the hotel's paid for and I'm only a few blocks away. Tell Jules if he feeds me, I'll be over every night."

"Hotels now? Pays to be a big star, huh?"

"Right." Aiden would never have admitted it, but he'd have been far happier to stay on his friends' couch—the three months he had spent at Jules and Jason's when he'd first traveled to Europe had been some of the best of his life.

"So how are you doing?" Jason asked. "Really."

"I've got a full schedule this season and my Met debut next year in New York. Couldn't be better."

"That's not what I meant, and you know it."

Aiden said nothing.

"Cary told me you moved out of Cam's almost six months ago. Why the hell didn't you tell me? You didn't even mention it last time you called."

Aiden felt a pang of guilt. It wasn't as if it were a secret. His moving out of Sherrington Place had been all over the European gossip rags. But then Jules and Jason wouldn't have read about it, and Aiden was on the road so often these days that it wasn't as though he had a real "home."

"Long time coming." Aiden pretended he didn't care. Not that Jason would buy it. And Aiden knew he was rationalizing not telling anyone about Cam. He just didn't want to talk about Lord Cameron Sherrington to anyone right now. Maybe ever.

"What happened, man?"

"It wasn't meant to be. Nothing exciting."

"Aiden, I—"

"Look, Jaz, I need to get going. My flight leaves at one, and I haven't even showered yet. I'll give you a call when I get settled in. I'll come by Saturday after the concert. It'll probably be around eleven. Okay?"

Jason hesitated for a moment, then said, "Sure. We'd like that."

"See you then. Tell Jules I can't wait to see him."

"Good-bye, Aiden."

"'Bye."

Aiden tossed the phone onto the bed. He took one last look at the roses, then went to take a shower.

CHAPTER 4

Paris, France

SAM surveyed the apartment with a mixture of delight and envy. The lively party reminded him of what he'd read about Saturday night gatherings at Gertrude Stein's Paris apartment on rue de Fleurus at the beginning of the twentieth century. A universe away from his Philadelphia high-rise, Jules and Jason's large apartment was filled to capacity with American expats, European artists, musicians, and writers, all chattering away in a variety of languages.

The sound of jazz filled the room—Jules Bardon, violin tucked under his chin, while David Somers accompanied him on the piano. Jason mentioned David's name in passing, and Sam struggled to place the man. From the whispers he had caught when the two began to play, Sam guessed he was a conductor, and a well-known one at that.

"Hey, Sam," came a deep voice from behind him along with a clap on the back, "enjoying yourself?"

"God, Jaz, this is the most amazing party I've ever seen. And the food…. I can't believe you did this for me."

"Jules cooked all week," Jason explained with a wry laugh. "He takes these parties pretty seriously. He also loves an excuse to throw a party, and I love to humor him." Sam couldn't help but notice how Jason's green eyes seem to light up when he spoke about his partner.

Sam had arrived in Paris two days before for a three-week vacation. Although Sam and Jason Greene had met in court several times, they had only gotten to know each other two years before, in a Philadelphia bar. Jason had been raw, reeling from the pain of a broken relationship. They nearly ended up in bed but became friends instead—for which Sam was very thankful in retrospect. Jason had moved to Paris shortly after that, but the two men stayed in touch, and Jason had been trying to persuade Sam to come for a visit ever since.

"I can't tell you how good it is to see you happy, Jaz." Sam followed Jason into the living room.

"Do I really look happier?" Jason grinned.

"Yeah. It's a little sappy the way you look at Jules, though." Sam nodded toward the piano. Jules smiled at them both, and Sam swore he was positively glowing. Jules, for his part, ran a hand through his hair and shot Jason a slightly possessive look. This was the first time Sam had met Jules, and Sam knew Jules still wasn't quite sure of Sam's intentions.

As if he has anything to worry about! Sam repressed a chuckle. Jason was obviously head over heels for Jules. Sam repressed a sigh. *It was like that with you and Nicky too.*

"Glad you came?"

"I am. It's been a long time since I've been to Europe. It's changed a little." *Or maybe you've changed.*

The guests gathered around the piano applauded, and Jason used the interruption to excuse himself to answer the door. A man and woman entered, he in a tuxedo, she in an obviously expensive cocktail dress—both far better attired than the rest of the crowd. Sam thought the man looked vaguely familiar, but when recognition didn't come, he walked over to the drink table to refill his wine glass, then wandered out onto the large balcony.

The late spring evening was pleasant, with the sound of traffic from the boulevard two blocks over providing a low hum of urban music. From here Sam could see the Jardin du Luxembourg and the chateau at the edge of the park. He could smell the flowers on the breeze and hear the voices of people walking by on the street.

You should have come back sooner. But he hadn't been ready before now. He had come to know this city at Nick's side, and even though the memories of their trip ten years before had dulled with time, Sam still saw Nick in so much of Paris.

It's still beautiful, Nick.

"Sam!" Jason called over the din of the guests as Sam stepped back inside. "I'd like you to meet a friend of mine." Sam turned to see Jason standing beside the man in the tux. "Sam Ryan, meet Aiden Lind. Aiden, this is—"

"We've met." Aiden offered Sam his hand. His expression was cold.

"I... of course," Sam said haltingly as he took Aiden's hand and shook it. "It's good to see you again, Aiden."

Someone called for Jason and he was gone a moment later, leaving Sam and Aiden alone.

Aiden Lind. The name jarred something in Sam's brain. New York City. Five years before.

How old would he be now? Around thirty?

Aiden's face was leaner, his shoulders a bit broader than Sam remembered, although perhaps that was the cut of the tux. At the edges of Aiden's mouth and eyes, where the skin had been smooth years before, tiny lines now were visible. His wavy hair was smartly styled, short in the back, longer on top, covering just the tips of his ears. Everything about Aiden seemed to ooze sophistication.

He's a big star. Even Sam, with his limited knowledge of classical music and opera, had seen Aiden, dressed in a tux and hawking an expensive watch, peering up at him from the back page of *Newsweek.*

"So you're the friend from Philadelphia?" Aiden's jaw tensed visibly.

"That's me. Moved there about five years ago, a few months after you left for Europe. Got my dream job." Sam took a quick sip of his drink. It did nothing for his dry mouth.

"Employment law." Aiden smiled, but Sam saw none of the warmth he expected to see in the expression.

"You remembered." Sam wasn't sure why that pleased him.

"Yes." The smile faded from Aiden's face, and he seemed momentarily at a loss for words. Was that hurt Sam saw flash through his eyes?

"Listen, Aiden. I know I was an asshole back in New York. I... I'm really sorry. I had just—"

"*There* you are!" a woman interrupted as she put her arm around Aiden's waist. Sam recognized her as the woman Aiden had come in with. "And you promised me you'd bring me a glass of Pouilly-Fumé. I've been waiting *forever*, Aiden."

"Sorry, Alexandria." Aiden reached past Sam to the drink table, then poured a glass of white wine and handed it to her. "I ran into an old acquaintance of mine. Sam Ryan, this is Alexandria Gilman."

"Nice to meet you." Sam offered her his hand.

She smiled back at him with blindingly white teeth. "A pleasure," she purred in English with a hint of a French accent. The diamond choker at her neck caught the light overhead and glinted. She was beautiful in a cool, calculated way, her dark hair pulled into a tight chignon at the nape of her neck. Her dress followed the curve of her slim body. Sam couldn't help but notice the large diamond ring on her left hand.

"Alexandria's husband's company is one of the benefactors of the Bizet series," Aiden interjected, as if that explained everything about the woman. Sam wasn't so sure he wanted to understand the situation beyond that. The way Alexandria hung on Aiden, she looked like far more than simply a benefactor.

"And what do you do for a living, Sam?" Alexandria took her appreciative measure of him. Something about the way she assessed him made Sam ill at ease.

"I'm an attorney."

"Really? What kind of law?"

"Employment law." Simple, to the point, and more information than he felt comfortable revealing at that moment.

"How fascinating." Alexandria's tone made it clear the topic bored her to no end.

Sam looked around for a way to extricate himself from the conversation. As if on cue, the guests gathered around the piano applauded once more. "Thanks," Jules told the guests as a blush rose on his pale cheeks. "Maybe we'll play some more later."

"That's my cue," Sam said, improvising. "I promised Jules I'd help him with the desserts."

"Sam, I—" Aiden began, but Alexandria interrupted again.

"I'm starving. Shall we get some food?"

Sam shot them both an awkward and apologetic smile. "I better go." He made a beeline for the kitchen, past a group of guests.

Once safely inside the kitchen, he leaned against the counter and took a deep breath.

Oh, that went just swimmingly! Nearly as well as how he'd handled things in New York five years before.

CHAPTER 5

New York, New York
Five years before

THE SoHo bar was crowded when Sam arrived a few minutes after eight o'clock. Some of his friends had recommended the place to him, but he had never been inside. Typical of many establishments in the area, the walls were stripped bare of years of paint. Modern canvasses in various sizes and shapes broke the monotony of the ancient brick. Italian track lighting hung from the drop ceiling illuminated the artwork and the tables. Sam could make out the strains of classic jazz over the low drone of conversation. The smells of alcohol, aftershave, and musk hung in the air.

Sam realized his hand rested on his briefcase. He thought briefly of the metal cookie tin inside, which inevitably made him think of Nick. He and Nick first met in a bar, but Sam had never liked them much. As a couple, they had mostly socialized with friends, alternating hosting get-togethers at their loft apartment and spending weekends upstate in small B and Bs.

Sam felt overwhelmed as he sat down at the end of the bar and ordered a drink. He reminded himself that he was just here for the alcohol, but the Manhattan gay scene loomed frighteningly on the horizon, and he was woefully unprepared. Even now, a year after Nick's death, he wasn't ready, though he'd already received several appreciative looks in the few minutes since his arrival. He wasn't sure he'd *ever* be ready for it again—it had been intimidating enough the first time around.

"Vodka tonic," he told the bartender. Tonight he needed something stronger than his usual beer. Running a hand through his hair, he took a look around the bar for the first time. There was no dance floor, so the action was subtler. Men filled nearly every seat at the long bar, chatting in undertones over drinks. He fought the urge to leave. When the bartender placed a drink in front of him, he thanked the man and took a long, desperate swallow. The comforting effect of the alcohol began to kick in.

What are you doing here?

The man seated to his left got up and threw a twenty down on the bar, then waved to the bartender and the other men at the counter. Sam finished his drink in one long swallow and looked up again, this time into a pair of warm brown eyes framed by long lashes. The newcomer smiled affably at him. Sam managed to return the smile before quickly looking back down at his empty glass.

This was a mistake. He pulled his wallet out of his jacket and rummaged for a twenty.

"I hope you're not leaving on my account," said the man next to him. And, God, what a voice! A resonant, sexy-as-fuck baritone that went straight from Sam's ears to his cock.

"Aiden Lind," he said more formally as he offered Sam his hand.

"Sam Ryan. Nice to meet you." Aiden's hand was warm, his grip firm.

Aiden gestured to the bartender. "Two more. On me."

"I was just about to leave." Sam didn't want to be rude, but he needed to get out of the place. Coming here had been a mistake.

"Sure I can't convince you to stay?"

"No. But thanks, Aiden. It was good meeting you." Sam forced a smile and picked up his satchel before heading for the door. A moment later he stepped out into the chilly night air, taking deep breaths to calm his racing heart.

He wasn't ready. He pulled his jacket collar up, then started for the subway station.

"Sam!"

Sam turned around to see someone running after him down the street. *What was his name? Aiden.*

"Look, Aiden," Sam said as he caught up with him, "I'm tired."

Aiden blinked. "Oh. No. It's not like that." He reached into his jacket pocket and pulled out a wallet. Sam's wallet.

Shit. The guy was being nice, and Sam had tried to blow him off.

Sam took the wallet and their fingers brushed. Sam's cheeks warmed as their eyes met. Uncomfortable, he shifted his briefcase from one hand to another. "Thanks. Damn good thing my head's attached to my body tonight."

"No problem." Aiden shoved his hands back into his pockets.

"It was good meeting you." Sam was hard-pressed not to like the man.

"You too, Sam." Aiden hesitated a second longer, then turned and waved as he headed back toward the bar.

It's only a drink. No strings. It's not like you have anyone waiting at home.

"On second thought," Sam called after Aiden, "I think I'll have that drink."

"Great!" Aiden turned around and beamed at him, and Sam's initial hesitation evaporated in the warmth of Aiden's smile.

A few minutes later, they walked back into the bar. Aiden motioned to a free table. "This okay with you?"

"Sure." Sam set his briefcase back down and settled into one of the metal chairs.

"What are you drinking?" Aiden asked.

"Vodka tonic."

"Great. I'll be right back." Aiden headed for the bar before Sam could offer to spring for the drinks.

Now that they were back inside in the light, Sam got his first good look at Aiden. He hadn't noticed when they were sitting down, but Aiden was nearly as tall as he, probably around six feet. He'd already noticed Aiden's curly hair, high cheekbones, and the strong line of his jaw. Now, Sam couldn't help but notice the black jeans that hugged Aiden's firm ass and the long-sleeved Henley that fit his upper torso tightly enough to hint at the muscle beneath. Casual but undeniably sexy.

Back a minute later, Aiden sat facing Sam, and Sam noticed Aiden's foot tapping the leg of his chair.

He's nervous too. That surprised Sam. The guy was good-looking, friendly. Trying to quell his own anxiety, Sam took a deep breath. "Thanks for the drink. And thanks again for the wallet."

Aiden seemed buoyed by Sam's change of heart. "Long day?" He brushed a stray lock of hair from his eyes.

"You could say that." Sam shook his head and exhaled audibly. *If you only knew....*

A waiter brought their drinks. "Cheers." Sam held up his glass and Aiden touched his beer against it.

"Cheers."

They drank in silence for a few moments until Sam realized he must have been staring, because Aiden leaned in and gazed at him—a gaze that held more than a whisper of lust. For the past year, Sam hadn't even considered how he looked to the world at large. He donned his expensive suits like the uniforms they were, shaved, and combed his unruly hair, but he'd just gone on living, nothing more. He'd had a few blind dates friends had set him up on, but none of them had gone anywhere and he hadn't cared. Now he was suddenly self-conscious, his suit rumpled after a long day bent over piles of documents, his hair undoubtedly sticking up in odd places as it liked to do.

When did it get so hot in here?

Sam pulled off his jacket and draped it over the back of his chair. As the second drink went straight to his shoulders, he felt his old confidence return. "What do you do for a living, Aiden?"

"Musician."

"Really? What kind?"

Aiden seemed uncomfortable, almost apologetic. "I'm a singer. An opera singer."

"You're serious?" *Explains the voice of God vibe.*

"Yeah." Aiden shifted in his seat.

"That's cool," Sam said enthusiastically.

"You think?"

"Yes, definitely."

Aiden laughed—a warm, rumbling laugh that made Sam melt like a puddle into his seat. Aiden Lind was a handsome man, even more so when he laughed. "I get a lot of flak from my family about it."

"Really? Why?" Sam finished his drink and flagged down the waiter for another round.

"They think it's queer. I used to sing rock and gospel. That was okay with them. But opera? And shit, if they knew I liked men *and* women...." He laughed again, but Sam heard an edge to the sound this time and saw a flash of something like pain in Aiden's eyes. "So what do you do, Sam?"

"Compared to singing opera? Just boring stuff. I'm a lawyer for a firm near Wall Street."

"I sort of guessed. Nice suit, briefcase 'n all. Nice tie too." Aiden wasn't looking at Sam's tie, though; his gaze never left Sam's.

Maybe it was the booze, but Sam wasn't in the slightest bit tempted to look away. Instead, he loosened his tie and undid the top button of his shirt.

"So what kind of law do you practice?"

Shit. What was it about Aiden that made everything he said sound like an invitation to do something sexual? The voice. Definitely the voice.

"Personal injury. Not my first choice." Sam had rationalized taking the job for many reasons, but one in particular topped the list: the prospect of going home to Tennessee and back into the same dark and claustrophobic closet he had come out of was too horrible to contemplate.

"What would you rather be doing?"

At that moment Sam could think of a few things he'd rather be doing that had nothing to do with practicing law. "Employment law. Plaintiff's work. You know, the underdogs?"

"Nothing wrong with that, is there?"

"No. Nothing at all." The job had been a compromise: it hadn't been what Sam had wanted, but it hadn't been part of Samuel Stetson Ryan III's "plan" either. It had been a huge disappointment to the old man that Sam didn't return to Memphis to work for his firm.

Sam shifted in his seat, brushing Aiden's foot by accident. At least he *thought* he'd done it by accident. "So." Sam changed the subject and tried to focus on something other than Aiden's foot rubbing against his own. "What's it like, singing opera?"

The waiter came with another round of drinks—Sam lost count of how many he'd downed. Was this three already? It was hard to focus, and Sam was pretty sure it wasn't the alcohol that was turning his brain to mush.

Aiden leaned back in his seat with his legs slightly apart. It was an inviting pose. Aiden held his beer in his right hand and gesticulated with it as he spoke. As Aiden's leg pressed against Sam's, Sam tried to keep his eyes focused on his companion's face. His own face felt warm.

"It's great," Aiden replied. "I'm planning to go to Germany soon, maybe do a few auditions there."

"Sounds exciting. What would you be auditioning for?" Laughter erupted from the bar. Sam moved his chair closer to better hear Aiden's answer, and his leg slid between Aiden's. Sam shivered with the touch. He found it more and more difficult to focus on the conversation, but it had nothing to do with the noise level.

"Most of the larger German cities hire contract singers for their opera houses. It's better than in the States. Here, you mostly just string gigs together to make a living. There, you have a steady job for a year at a time, do stuff in repertory. Beats waiting tables."

"I didn't realize it was that tough getting work." He and Aiden were less than a foot apart now. From this distance, Sam saw the hint of Aiden's hard nipples beneath the close-fitting Henley. He imagined how he might take one of those nubs between his teeth.

"Once you get an agent, it gets better. I only graduated from school a few years ago, and it's hard to get hired for big roles right away."

"Kind of like getting stuck doing the grunt work right out of law school." Sam knew the feeling well. He'd only made partner last year, and he'd done his share of shit jobs before that.

"Yep." Aiden finished the rest of his beer, lingering over the mouth of the bottle before giving Sam a smile.

Sam swallowed hard and tried to ignore the renewed jolt of sexual heat he sensed in Aiden's gaze. He looked down at his drink. It definitely wasn't only the booze talking. He got hard just thinking about kissing Aiden, tasting him. "Are you from around here, originally?"

"Nah. I'm from Mississippi. Little town named Fenton, right outside of Jackson."

"Really? Hell, I grew up in Memphis."

"No shit." Aiden laughed. "I thought I heard a little Tennessee in you."

"You had me fooled. I figured you were from up north."

"Comes with the territory. Good ear. Had to study French, German, and Italian in school. You lose the drawl fast or they beat it out of you."

They talked about growing up in the South for a few minutes. Comfortable, easy conversation. How long had it been, Sam wondered, since he'd had a conversation like this with someone other than Nick?

Too long.

"Listen," Aiden began as he stared awkwardly at his beer, which was now clearly empty, "would you like to get out of here?"

Since Nick died, Sam had said no to anything but casual hints at dating. *This* was much more of an offer.

"I'd like that," he heard himself say.

Aiden looked surprised and pleased, but no more than Sam. Had he really said yes?

"I live over in Alphabet City. It's not much, but…."

"That'd be fine." Sam might be ready to spend the night with someone, but he sure as hell wasn't ready to take a man back to his own apartment—the apartment he and Nick had shared. Not yet, anyhow.

Maybe never.

AFTER a short cab ride, Sam followed Aiden up the stairs of a third-floor walkup off Avenue C and into a small two-bedroom apartment. The living room appeared to double as a third bedroom. Pots, pans, and cooking utensils hung from every inch of the high-ceilinged walls of the tiny kitchen. An electronic keyboard sat atop a cardboard box, and piles of music filled the built-in shelves. In spite of the clutter, the apartment was clean and smelled vaguely of lemon.

"I live with two other singers," Aiden said. "Mark works nights, and Rob is out of town at a gig, so we have the place to ourselves."

Sam put his briefcase down and tossed his coat onto the couch. He turned to find Aiden only a few inches away. In the shadows of the semidarkness, Aiden's high cheekbones were more defined, his body backlit by the light from the streetlamp outside.

A moment later they were kissing. Rough, hungry lips met with equally awkward eagerness, teeth tapping against each other as Sam and Aiden found their bearings. Sam ran his tongue against Aiden's lower lip and gained entry before pressing inward to find the warmth that waited there. Aiden's mouth tasted good, with a hint of dark beer that lingered from the bar.

"Bed?" Sam asked.

Aiden's answer was a low growl with the same deep resonance of his speaking voice. Sam never realized the sound of someone's voice could be such a turn-on. His body thrummed, and he knew there was no going back. He'd waited so long, denying himself in silent penance for circumstances over which he'd never had any control. Now he would let that final piece of Nick go and give his body over to someone new.

You know he would have wanted this for you.

Aiden put his arm around Sam's waist as he led him down the short hallway, then pushed the bedroom door open with his foot. Sam felt the bed at the backs of his knees as Aiden pushed him down on top of the ragged comforter. The bedding smelled clean, though. Sam didn't have a chance to take in the rest of the room before they were kissing again. Sam scrabbled for purchase on Aiden's shirt, reaching to pull it over his head. He needed to feel Aiden's chest, to feel someone else's skin beneath his fingers.

Aiden's body was as finely honed as Sam had imagined it to be back at the bar. Lean—not the overly sculpted abs that graced Times Square billboards—but just the way Sam liked them, with more than a dusting of dark, curly hair between his nipples. He pressed his hand to Aiden's enticing skin. What would it be like to feel that chest vibrate when the other man sang? The thought led him to a renewed jolt of desire, and he pinned Aiden to the bed before pushing down Aiden's dark jeans along with the gray boxer briefs to reveal the purple tip of a sizeable cock. A minute later, Aiden was completely naked on the bed. The fact that Sam was still fully dressed only served to arouse him more.

He didn't need any encouragement to take Aiden's erection in his mouth; he *had* to taste it. God, but the man tasted so good! Sam swallowed Aiden's long cock down, pulling back the foreskin as he went and grabbing the base with his hand, slicked up with saliva. For a man who made his living with his voice, Aiden remained remarkably silent, but the upward arch of his body was tacit reassurance. Sam licked with abandon at the underside of Aiden's hard width, then tightened the suction until he was rewarded with a gasp.

Sam ran his teeth and lips over Aiden's cock as he moved upward to the tip, then nibbled his way around the crown and probed the leaking slit with his tongue, sucking to milk the salty essence there. He could feel his own hard-on pressed against his pants, which only served to intensify the experience. Denial for now. But later….

"Shit, Sam," Aiden murmured in a distant rumble. "So good. So fucking *good*…."

Sam smiled wickedly, happy to have finally coaxed a sound from Aiden's lips. He reached his free hand underneath Aiden's balls, rolled them in his palm, then licked them, all the while fisting Aiden's hard cock. He swallowed it again, skating wet fingers to find the clenched ring of muscles between the tight asscheeks. The press of his finger against the tight opening was rewarded with a low drawn-out groan, so he teased it again.

"Lube?" he whispered as he released Aiden's cock for a moment.

"Don't want any. Just push your finger in."

Sam hesitated.

"Nah, Sam. It's good like that… I like it like that sometimes."

The words shot through Sam like fire. He pressed his saliva-slicked finger inside and felt Aiden's big hands grasp his shoulders and pull him closer, encouraging him to push deeper. Sam hollowed his cheeks and increased the suction, pulling and licking until he could feel Aiden's balls pull tight against his forearm.

"Shit… Sam… gonna… come," Aiden warned.

Sam released Aiden's cock from his mouth but continued to rub his lips and hand over it until he felt the warmth of Aiden's come on his cheek. After Aiden stopped shaking, Sam met his warm brown eyes and smiled.

Aiden reached up and wiped Sam's cheek with the sheet, then leaned back against the pillow and inhaled long and deep. "Good God." His voice was impossibly low and sexy. "That was incredible."

Sam's face warmed at the compliment, and he fought the urge to protest. Even after so many years of living in New York as an openly gay man, he still felt the stirrings of shame from time to time, his conservative Southern roots too well ingrained to ignore. But the moment of embarrassment was short-lived, eclipsed by his own unsatisfied need.

"I want to fuck you," he whispered. "If that's okay...." He had never been hesitant before, but he felt like he was seventeen all over again, doing it for the first time in the woods behind the cabins at summer camp.

"You're joking, right?" Aiden laughed. "Hell, yeah." He reached under the mattress and pulled out a box of condoms and a small bottle of lube, then tossed them within Sam's reach.

The tension in Sam's shoulders relaxed until he felt his companion's hand rubbing at the crotch of his pants. His breath caught in his throat. *Too long. Way too long.* He started to loosen his tie, but Aiden stopped him.

"Fuck me in that suit. It's so damn hot." He rolled onto his stomach and lifted his ass in blatant invitation. "I want you to fuck me in your clothes."

"Damn," Sam hissed as he unzipped his fly and pulled his cock out. There was something thrilling about the way Aiden had taken control, something about the way Aiden's words had sounded almost like an order that made Sam shiver. And, oh God, the globes of Aiden's ass beckoned, tight and smooth. Sam stroked him while he uncapped the lube and slathered his fingers with it, then reached around to press at the hole he had only barely breached before.

"No prep," Aiden rumbled. "Lube it up. I like it when it hurts a little."

What the hell do you say to that?

Sam knew the feeling himself, although he had never admitted it to Nick. He and Nick had been tender lovers—the kind of lovers who explored every inch of each other's bodies with gentle fingers and tongues. Their lovemaking had never approached the rough animal sex Sam had often fantasized about. That hadn't been Nick's style; he had been as laid-back and slow in bed as he was in life, and Sam had loved that about him. The sex had been great. Better than great, but now....

Sam rolled the condom over his erection and greased it well, then leaned over and spread Aiden wider. Aiden's low laugh was an invitation, and Sam saw Aiden's eyes fill with a mixture of need and playfulness. He pressed the head of his cock against Aiden's hole, inhaling sharply as the outer ring of muscle gave way and he felt the warm tightness nip at his sensitive tip.

"Come on," Aiden urged him. "I want it all the way inside."

He pushed harder, Aiden's inner muscles gradually releasing with some resistance until Sam was seated up to his balls. Aiden was half-hard again, and Sam grasped his thickening flesh with one hand as he pulled out. Then he pushed in once more, making sure he brushed against Aiden's prostate. He felt Aiden's shudder and saw the look of pleasure on his face.

"Harder, Sam. Need it harder."

"Oh God, yes. But it's been too long. I won't be able to…."

"I don't care." Aiden's voice was rough, husky with need. "Do it like you know you want to."

The realization that Aiden had guessed at something Sam himself had long denied only served to intensify the urge to pound Aiden senseless. "Fuck," he panted. "You're so tight."

The bed shook as he picked up speed, pistoning back and forth, letting go of all of his repressed desire. His shirt clung to his skin, his pants rode up his ass, but that only increased the pleasure that ran from his cock up his spine and pulled his sac tight. He came with a shout and a series of shudders, then leaned down so his face was only inches away from Aiden's.

Their eyes met. For Sam it was like diving into dark water—he didn't know what he might find, but he was caught in the siren song. Aiden's lips met his, and something deep inside Sam's heart let go. A door he had closed when Nick died opened just a crack. It stayed open for a brief instant before he felt ice in his veins as fear seeped back inside.

"Stay?" Aiden asked hopefully.

"I…." Sam hesitated. "Okay." He knew he should leave, that he wasn't ready for this, but he couldn't do it. He was so raw, so hungry for Aiden's touch. He wanted more.

Aiden smiled at Sam and began to unbutton his shirt.

CHAPTER

Present

AIDEN told Alexandria he'd walk back to the hotel from Jules and Jason's, but she'd insisted on the limo instead. He guessed she'd want to spend the night at his hotel. He'd expected it. He downed a double scotch in the limo as it idled by the hotel entrance.

"I should get some sleep," he told her after he finished his drink. It was true. He was exhausted, but not so exhausted that he'd make the mistake of taking her to bed. He hadn't exactly been celibate since he'd left Cam, but he wasn't so desperate as to think that sleeping with the wife of a major donor was a good idea. "Why don't I call—"

Her lips cut short his words, and she rubbed her hand over his crotch until he grew hard.

"Sorry, Alexandria." He pushed her hand away and opened the limo door.

He didn't look back. He knew she'd been expecting sex; he just hadn't figured out how to escape her grasp after the concert. He also knew there'd probably be hell to pay for turning her down.

An hour later, he was wide-awake in bed. Unsatisfied and thinking of Sam, even though he'd tried to think of anything but. It was bad enough with people like Alexandria, who wanted him because of his voice. He didn't need the drama of a "real" relationship, not after what he'd gone through with Cam. He'd learned his lesson. Hell, he'd learned his lesson with Sam too, hadn't he?

Fool me once....
Five years before

AIDEN woke up with a headache and a sore throat. *Fuck.* He almost never got sick. Not that it helped that he'd spent the entire night worrying about Sam's reaction to news of the possible scholarship. Aiden had gotten a grand total of about three hours of sleep. Maybe.

He wasn't sure what he'd expected from Sam. He knew what he'd hoped for. He'd wanted Sam to tell him not to go. Or at least tell him they could still try to see each other. But what had he expected after only two weeks?

They'd been getting along so well since they'd met at the bar. Aiden couldn't remember the last time he'd been so hopeful about a relationship. And then he'd gone and screwed it up by mentioning the scholarship. Sam was the first man he'd spent time with in New York who hadn't left him feeling insecure about where he'd come from and who he was. Sam was like him in so many ways. No, Sam wasn't from a backwater town like Fenton, but he was still a Southern boy in the big city.

And if he didn't even get the scholarship? Aiden knew the answer. Then he'd be able to stay in New York. Get to know Sam better, if Sam wanted that.

Aiden dragged himself out of bed and wandered out to the kitchen. Mark was asleep on the couch, and Aiden did his best not to wake him up. He clicked on the kettle for tea and shoved a handful of Vitamin C into his mouth, then gagged on the horse pills. A few minutes later, armed with a mug of tea laden with honey and lemon, he retreated to his bedroom.

There was a muffled knock on the door a few minutes later. "It's open."

"Thought you might have company," Mark said with a yawn.

"Oh, shit, did I wake you up?"

"You mean with all the coughing?" Mark laughed and sat down on the edge of Aiden's bed. "Nah. Damn garbage trucks woke me up. I should have worn my earplugs."

"Late night?"

"Not too bad. Closed the restaurant at two. Looks like I got more sleep than you, though."

Aiden shrugged and sipped his tea.

"Sam didn't come back with you, then?"

"No."

"No smartass comebacks this morning? Where's my big-mouth roommate and who is this pathetic slob?"

"Love you too, Mark."

Mark lay back on the bed and snorted.

"Sorry. I've got a cold." As if that would convince Mark. Aiden half wanted him to ask what was bothering him. He needed someone to talk to.

"Right. And?"

"And I'm so fucking confused."

"About Sam? I thought you two were golden. I was thinking a few more weeks and I'd tell Rose she could move in when you move in with him, and I get your room."

"You still might be able to." Aiden tried to sound nonchalant, but he knew he wasn't fooling anyone.

"How's that?"

"I'm a finalist for the scholarship I told you about."

Mark sat up abruptly and put up his hand. "That's great news!" Aiden gave Mark a high five. "If I didn't have Rose," he said, "I'd be jealous. Hell, I *am* jealous of you. That's such a great gig. So where's the problem?"

"I'll probably get it."

"Still not seeing the problem here. This could make your career, right?" Mark paused for a moment, then eyed Aiden warily. "This is about Sam, then."

Aiden nodded and set his mug on the nightstand. "I don't know what to do. I mean, if I get the scholarship, I'm out of here for at least a year. But Sam and I have only been together a few weeks. Shit! I'm not making any sense, am I?"

"Perfect sense." Mark lay back down again. "So have you asked him what he thinks about it?"

"Sam?"

Mark rolled his eyes. "Damn, Aiden. And Rose says gay men understand relationship shit better. Who else would I be talking about?"

Aiden ignored the jibe. "I told him about it and he said he was happy for me."

"You didn't ask him if he wanted you to stay, did you?"

"No."

"Why not?"

"I didn't want him to think I expected it." Aiden faltered, then added, "I mean, we've only been going out a few weeks, and…. Fuck, Mark, what do you want from me?"

"You didn't want him to think you care about him?"

Was that it? Aiden wasn't sure. Maybe. *Or maybe you're worried he'll say, "It's been fun, but…."*

"It's only been two weeks. He'd probably think I was insane if I asked him if he wanted me to stay."

"You like this guy a lot, don't you?"

Aiden did. "Yeah. But this is such a great opportunity."

Mark laughed. "Sounds like you don't know what *you* want."

He's right. I have no clue what I want.

He'd never been so torn in his life. Sure, leaving home to take the full ride Indiana University had offered him had been difficult. But he hadn't hesitated and he hadn't looked back. This time was different. He wanted Sam and he wanted his career.

"Why don't you ask him how he feels?" When Aiden stared at him in openmouthed shock, Mark added, "I know, I know! Rose's been training me. I'm supposed to 'express my feelings'." He imitated Rose's high soprano voice. "But seriously, man, how can you decide what to do if you don't know how he feels?"

"Yeah." Mark was right and Aiden knew it.

"Hey, Sam," Aiden told Sam's voice mail a few hours later. He had called the office, but Sam's assistant told him he was tied up in a meeting. "I was hoping we could talk. I'm around this weekend. Give me a call, okay?"

MONDAY morning came far too quickly and without any call from Sam. When Aiden's phone rang after lunch, right after he'd settled down to practicing, it was not Sam but the woman from the scholarship committee calling to congratulate him.

Aiden left Sam another message. "Sam, hi, it's Aiden. I'm sure you were probably busy this past weekend. I... I just wanted you to know I got that scholarship I told you about. I'll be leaving in a week, and I was thinking that I'd really like to see you... ah... you know, before I leave. If you have a chance, please call me."

Another week went by with no answer. Aiden found himself in a JFK waiting room with a one-way ticket to Frankfurt, Germany. But he had his answer, didn't he? Sam wasn't interested. And who could blame Sam? Aiden was a nobody, a Mississippi redneck who'd barely managed to finish high school and who had only graduated from college because he could sing.

CHAPTER

Present

AIDEN headed out of the hotel before eight o'clock for a run. He hadn't slept much, but the morning was bright and clear and the Luxembourg gardens were already filled with people. He often ran here when he was in Paris, usually with Jason. Today, however, Jason had decided to sleep in since he'd been up so late cleaning up after the party.

The long gravel paths felt good under Aiden's feet, and the smell of cut grass went a long way toward improving his mood. He headed past the enormous fountain with its bronze horses, catching the faint scent of roses on the air as he began to pick up his pace. It had been too cold to run in Germany, and he was a little stiff. Still, it felt good to get out and stretch his legs.

On his second lap around the park, he heard someone call his name. A reporter, he guessed. Ever since Jarrod Jameson had spilled his guts to a London rag, the continental press had followed Aiden with something approaching religious zeal. Aiden was the wronged man, the golden boy of the opera scene, the man Cameron Sherrington had told the press was "the love of his life."

Aiden had tried to stay out of the love triangle the press sought to create, but he was smart enough to know that the sympathy generated as a result of his very public breakup had helped his career. Not that he wasn't a good singer. He was, and he knew it. But when his agent called to tell him Rolex wanted to feature him in an ad, he knew it wasn't only because of his singing. He also knew better than to turn the offer down.

"Aiden! Aiden Lind!"

Aiden kept running. A moment later, he felt someone tap him on the shoulder, and he spun around, ready to tell the reporter to go to hell. But it wasn't a reporter. Sam Ryan was bent over, gasping for air, hands on his knees.

"Damn," he said between wheezes, "are you trying to kill me?"

"What?" Aiden stared at Sam, too surprised to think clearly.

Sam laughed. "I thought maybe you'd like a running partner."

"I was just heading back to the hotel." It was a lie, the words tumbling out of Aiden's mouth before he could stop them.

Sam looked sheepish. "No problem," he said as though he had expected Aiden's response. "I shouldn't have interrupted your run. I thought I—"

"Look, Sam, I accept your apology. Really I do. New York was a lifetime ago. We've both moved on."

"Sure." Sam rubbed the back of his neck and looked very uncomfortable. "I understand completely. No worries. It was good seeing you again. I'm sure I'll see you around." He ran a hand through his hair, managed an awkward smile, then took off down the gravel path toward the park entrance.

Back in his hotel room an hour later, Aiden stared out the window at the busy street below. Why the hell had he acted that way with Sam in the park? He was angry, and he couldn't explain it. They had dated for a whopping two weeks, after all.

Five years ago. What the fuck is my problem?

There was a knock on the door. More flowers. *Call me*, read the note. *I really need to speak with you.* He tore the paper into tiny pieces.

So much for progress.

AFTER Sam left Aiden in the park, he kept running until he reached the banks of the Seine, less than an hour later. He didn't remember getting there. Across the bridge was Île de la Cité and Notre Dame. For nearly an hour, he stood there, leaning on the stone wall above the river, deep in thought.

He hadn't expected a warm reception from Aiden. Not after the way Aiden had acted at the party. So why was he even trying to talk to the guy? He had no one to blame but himself for Aiden's reaction, anyhow. God, he wanted so much to go back, to start over again!

Approaching Aiden today hadn't been easy. In fact, even deciding to take Jason and Jules up on the offer of a visit had been supremely difficult for Sam. Everything about Paris reminded him of Nick. He and Nick had saved up for their trip for nearly two years. They'd come to celebrate Sam's passing the bar and Nick's first gallery show.

Sam stared up at Notre Dame and closed his eyes. He could almost hear the echo of Nick's voice as Nick reached the top of the tower ahead of him.

"Hey, Sammy, check this out!" Breathless, he gazed out at the city below as Sam finally caught up. "Look at the pattern of the rooftops and the way the sunlight reflects off the tiles."

Sam put his arm around Nick's shoulder, taking a quick glance outside before he brought his gaze to rest on Nick's curly hair and admired the corner of his jaw. The word "beautiful" that escaped his lips had nothing to do with the Parisian skyline.

Sam had been to Europe before with his family, but nothing could compare to seeing Europe through Nick's eyes. Sam often forgot Nick was two years older; Nick approached the world in an almost childlike manner. Where Sam looked out over Paris and saw only a mass of buildings, Nick appreciated the innate beauty there—colors, textures, sounds, and smells.

At sunset, they cruised the Seine on a bateau mouche, their dinner simple baguette and brie sandwiches with tiny pickles and cheap wine. It was the best dinner Sam had ever eaten. The view from the boat was spectacular. But years later Sam would remember little of the view. It was Nick he had been watching the entire time, the joy on his face far more interesting than the scenery.

Sam opened his eyes. He hadn't been ready five years ago, when he'd first met Aiden. He could still hear Aiden's voice on the answering machine. *I just wanted you to know I got that scholarship I told you about. The program starts two weeks from today, and I was thinking*

*that I'd really like to see you... ah... you know, before I leave. If you
have a chance, please call me."*

He'd wanted to call Aiden. He'd picked up the phone more times
than he could remember. But in the end, he'd put it off. Too little, too
late. And now, who could blame the guy for wanting nothing to do with
him?

It was noon when Sam headed back to Jules and Jason's place.

Five years before

"SAM?" came the voice of his assistant over the intercom. "Call for
you. Line three."

"Thanks, Yvonne." Sam set down the document he'd been glued
to for the past two hours and picked up the handset. "Sam Ryan."

"You sound damn sexy when you're in lawyer mode."

Sam grinned. "You always sound sexy. It's that voice."

"We still on for dinner tonight?" Aiden asked.

"Should be fine. My late meeting got canceled. Meet you at seven
at Waraji?"

"Deal. My treat this time."

"You don't need to do—"

"Yeah, I do. Besides, I just got paid for my church job."

"Church job? You?"

"Don't worry. I'm only singin'," Aiden shot back with a laugh.
"I'm a soloist at a Unitarian church off Seventh Avenue. Pay's pretty
good, and I only work a few hours a week."

"Guess the Baptists didn't want you."

"They did. But the Unitarians pay better."

Sam laughed right as his computer chimed to remind him of a
telephone conference. "Look, Aiden, I gotta run. I've got a meeting in
five minutes.

"See you at seven, then."

"Looking forward to it."

Sam leaned back in his chair and sighed. He and Aiden had been seeing each other for two weeks. After much soul-searching, Sam had decided he was going to ask Aiden over to his apartment in Brooklyn Heights on the weekend. *Just for brunch*, he told himself. If things worked out, maybe he'd ask Aiden to spend the night.

One step at a time.

"HOW did the audition for the agent go today?" Sam asked that evening over a warm cup of sake.

"Good. He says he's interested in setting up some auditions for me in the spring. He's going to put me in touch with a colleague in their European division."

"So how does that work? Are they looking to hire for specific roles?"

"Some. But they also have contacts who are trying to put together their seasons, so they'll probably set me up for some auditions with conductors. This guy's friends with the conductor of the CSO."

"Chicago Symphony?"

Aiden nodded. "David Somers. The guy's the hottest young conductor on the scene in Europe. He spends the summers in Milan—I hear he's got a villa there."

"I didn't know the music business paid that well," Sam said as he refilled their cups again.

"Recording contracts are pretty lucrative. But he comes by his money the honest way," Aiden said with a grin. "He inherited it. Old money. Mansion in Connecticut, that sort of thing. The guy's amazing, though. If he likes my voice...."

"He'll love your voice."

"Thanks, Sam." Aiden's face flushed.

"No need to thank me. You played me your audition tape, remember?"

"Yeah. But sometimes... I don't know... it's hard to get past the crap. I spent the first eighteen years of my life listening to my dad tell me what a fuckup I was and the last five hearing about how music wasn't any way to earn a living."

"Does he still say that?" Sam thought briefly of his own father's unmet expectations.

"Yeah. Pretty much every time I call or visit. He keeps telling me to come home and study to be a preacher." Aiden's laugh was bitter. "Can you just see it?"

"I would say you could do whatever you wanted," Sam said with a warm smile. "But I think Baptist preacher would probably be pushing the envelope."

"No joke." Aiden ran a hand through his hair. "Oh, I forgot," he added a moment later. "There was something I wanted to tell you about."

"Sure. And when you're done, I've been wanting to ask you something. Don't let me forget." As if he would. He'd been mulling over how to ask Aiden to his place without it sounding like the big deal it was.

"I got a call from this arts organization in Hamburg, Germany. I'm a semifinalist for a scholarship." Aiden didn't look all that pleased with this news.

"Scholarship? I thought you were done with school."

"I am. This is a special deal where they send you to Europe, all expenses paid. Give you a place to stay, a Eurail pass, and some money for food and stuff."

"Really? That sounds great! How long's it for?"

"A year." Aiden met Sam's gaze for a long moment, and Sam immediately understood that Aiden was hesitating because of *him*. Because of *them*.

Sam's mouth went dry. "Wow." He tried to sound enthusiastic despite the sick feeling in his stomach. "That's great, Aiden."

"You think?"

"Sure. I mean, that's a great deal. You've been wanting to go to Europe. It couldn't get any better, right?" It was true. Aiden had told him about Europe the night they'd met. He knew how important this was for Aiden's career.

Aiden's smile seemed forced. "Right. Yeah, I've wanted this."

"So when do you hear if you get the award?" Sam barreled ahead, sensing the larger question that hung unspoken between them and knowing he couldn't begin to answer it.

"Sometime in the next few days. They said they'd be calling my references, you know. Checking to see if I'm the kind of man they want to sponsor."

"Are you worried?"

"Nah. I'm pretty easy to work with. The recommendations will be good."

Sam sucked down another cup of sake to fill the silence. "Then it's a sure thing, right?" he asked after a pause, trying to sound enthusiastic.

Aiden shrugged. "I guess." There was another moment of awkward silence between them, and Sam refilled their cups again.

"How soon would you leave?" Sam tried to focus on pouring the sake. He wasn't sure he wanted to know the answer.

"If I get the award, I'll be leaving in a few weeks. They don't give you much time to think about it." Aiden emptied his cup in one swallow. "So what did you want to ask me?"

Sam had nearly forgotten about inviting Aiden over on the weekend. He had planned it all out. But now.... He took a second to compose himself, then said, "It's nothing, really. I thought you might want to catch a movie after dinner."

Aiden looked surprised, and Sam guessed he hadn't been very convincing. "I... ah... sure. Of course. But don't you have to work in the morning?"

"I'll be fine," Sam lied. He wasn't fine. He wasn't at all sure what he was, but he was sure he wasn't fine.

As THEY left the movie theater a few hours later, Aiden grabbed Sam around the waist and kissed him. "Come to my place tonight?"

"I shouldn't." Sam wanted to be with Aiden, but the Europe trip sounded like a done deal. And Aiden *needed* to go to Europe for his career. Besides, Sam wasn't even sure he was ready to ask the guy to spend the night at his place. What could he possibly say about Europe?

He had no right to ask Aiden to put his career on hold for something that hadn't even started.

It's only been two weeks.

"Something wrong? I mean, if this is about the European thing, I...."

"It's not that," Sam lied. "It's a great opportunity."

"Yeah."

Sam glanced at his watch. "I better go. I've got a meeting in the morning."

"Sure."

"I had a great time."

"Me too." Aiden leaned over and kissed Sam on the lips. Sam knew kissing complicated things, but Aiden tasted so good, and Sam melted into the kiss. If Sam could only forget how attracted to Aiden he was—how much he genuinely *liked* Aiden—they could both move on and call it a night. *Or a life, maybe, as in "it's been great, but...."*

Damn the man for being so fucking attractive! And so... nice. Sam felt like a complete asshole, running away like this, knowing that it was *all* about the European thing, about the possibility of Aiden leaving and Sam's own stupid, fucked-up fear of moving on.

"You need to stop worrying, Sam, and let yourself feel sometimes," Nick had once told him.

Nick. God, he missed Nick so much he ached. Aiden was here. Alive. Real. Why was he going home alone?

"Night, Sam."

"Night." Sam smiled, then headed for the nearest subway stop without looking back.

CHAPTER

Present

AIDEN stood in front of the door to Jules and Jason's apartment. His hands were slightly sweaty and he felt queasy. He'd been dreading this all day long not because he didn't want to see Jules and Jason—he did—but because he'd been dreading seeing Sam again. He'd been a total shit to the man both at the party and, even worse, when they'd met in the park. He'd even tried to call Sam to apologize, but Jules said Sam and Jason had gone out to do some marketing and wouldn't be back until later. By then Aiden was in rehearsals and unable to call. Jules promised to relay the apology to Sam.

What the fuck got into me? And what would he say to Sam—what *could* he say to Sam now so Sam wouldn't think he was the world's biggest asshole? Aiden pressed the bell and took a deep breath. He could do this. *Act like an adult. Cut the hurt puppy dog bullshit.*

"Hey, Aiden! Glad you could make it." Jason opened the door to the apartment and gestured Aiden to come inside before giving him a warm hug. Aiden wondered if Jason realized how long he'd been standing there. He probably did, seeing as though he'd buzzed Aiden into the building more than five minutes before. "How'd the first rehearsal go?"

"Great." Aiden sat down across from Jason on the couch. "The tenor's an old friend of mine from Germany. He and I were at the same opera house for a year. David's conducting, of course."

"Yeah. I'm sorry he couldn't make it for dinner. He said Alex was performing in Rome, and he wanted to be there for the dress rehearsal."

Jason smiled, then added, "He never misses a dress rehearsal or performance of Alex's if he can help it."

"He knows what is good for him" came another voice from the kitchen doorway—Jules, his long hair pulled back in a ragged ponytail, wearing an apron over his jeans and T-shirt.

"Jaz tells me he's been following you all over." Aiden and Jules exchanged the typical French greeting of kissing each other's cheeks.

"Wouldn't have it any other way." Jason chuckled.

The door to the apartment opened, and Sam walked inside carrying several shopping bags. "Hope I'm not too late." Sam glanced over at Aiden and smiled. "Good to see you again, Aiden." He put the bags down and shook Aiden's hand. "And thanks for calling."

"You're welcome. I'm sorry I snapped at you in the park." Aiden tried to ignore the familiar jolt of heat in that contact.

"I know." Sam's smile appeared quite genuine.

Aiden tried to pretend as though seeing Sam again didn't have him on edge and unable to focus. He realized he was still holding Sam's hand and pulled away, feeling awkward and uncomfortable. He wondered if Sam felt the same, because he noticed the bob of Sam's Adam's apple as he swallowed. Aiden tried his best to silently communicate that he was no longer angry. He hoped it worked. Whatever had happened with them in the past, he'd moved beyond it. Or so he kept telling himself.

"I brought you a little something, Jules." Sam pulled a bottle of wine out of one of the bags and handed it to Jules.

Jules's eyes widened. "*Château Margaux?* Have you been talking with David Somers?"

Sam laughed. "No. But I wanted to thank you both properly for letting me stay here and for the party the other night."

The pleasure in Jules's eyes belied his stern expression. "You shouldn't have. It's far too expensive." He put his hands on his hips and glared at Jason, then added in French, "You had something to do with this, didn't you?"

Jason winked at Sam but said nothing.

"Give it up, Jules," Aiden chimed in. "You know you can't win this one. Besides, even I know it's your favorite."

Jules threw his hands up, then gave Sam a big kiss on the cheek and went to uncork the bottle.

A short while later, they were all seated around the dining table, drinking the wine and enjoying Jules's cooking, the smells of fresh bread, garlic, and butter hanging in the air.

Dinner conversation was easy and comfortable, though Aiden had to force himself not to stare at Sam from across the table. It was difficult not to look—the intervening years had been good to Sam. Aiden couldn't help but notice how sure of himself Sam seemed—the tension and sadness he had once sensed in the other man had been replaced by a quiet calm that Aiden found surprisingly appealing. Once or twice Aiden thought he caught Sam's gaze, as well, though Aiden dismissed the look as one of simple curiosity.

After dinner Jason excused himself to help Jules do the dishes, refusing Aiden and Sam's offers of assistance. "Balcony?" Aiden suggested.

"Sure." Sam followed Aiden outside. "Makes me wish I had a view like this," he added as they looked out over the park. "Not that I don't have a good view of downtown Philly from my place, but it's nothing compared to this."

"I almost ended up putting down roots here." Aiden's expression was wistful.

"Why didn't you?"

Aiden's face fell. "It didn't work out. I ended up in London instead."

"Oh. Sorry. I didn't mean to pry."

"You're not."

There was a brief moment of silence; then Aiden added, "Look, Sam. About the other day—"

"No need to apologize."

"I thought you were a reporter. I overreacted. I was a jerk."

The look on Sam's face was sad now. "Funny, how we seem to do a lot of apologizing to each other, isn't it?"

"Yes. We do, don't we?" In spite of himself, Aiden smiled. "Maybe we just need to stop." He turned to lean on the iron railing.

"New York was a long time ago. Maybe we can move on from that. Be friends?"

"I'd like that. A lot."

Aiden's chest tightened at Sam's response, and he forced back memories of five years before. *Let it go.*

"There is something I'd like to tell you, though," Sam continued. "Something I should have told you five years ago. And then I promise I won't say another word."

"Sure. Of course."

Sam took a deep breath. "You were the first... the first man I'd been with, since my partner, Nick, died. I mean, I had dated a little, but I hadn't slept with anyone since then."

Aiden did his best to mask his surprise. Sam had never said anything about a partner in the short time they dated.

Although it's not like we shared life stories in the two weeks we spent together.

"I'm so sorry. I didn't know." God, why did he sound like such an idiot? The guy had just told him someone he cared about had died, and that was all he could come up with?

"Of course you wouldn't have. I should have told you."

"What happened?" Aiden saw Sam stand a bit taller, his shoulders set back as if he were steeling himself. Aiden immediately regretted asking the question. "I mean, if you're okay talking about it, that is."

"I'm good with it. Really." He paused for a moment, then continued, "His name was Nick. He was twenty-seven when he died. We met at Columbia when we were both undergrads. He was an art student, I was pre-law. We lived together for about six years."

Aiden nodded, unsure of what to say.

"About a year before you and I met, I got a call. They said he'd had a massive stroke. An aneurism. He lived for about a week. I had to...." Sam looked down at the street and his jaw tensed visibly. "That night... at the bar... it was the first time I'd been out since Nick died."

Shit. It was all Aiden could do not to say it out loud. If he'd known.... *If I'd known, then what? It wasn't only Sam who was confused back then.*

"I didn't expect to meet anyone, Aiden. And I sure as hell didn't think I'd meet someone I actually *cared* about." Sam ran a hand through his hair as if trying to collect himself. "And when you told me about the scholarship… dammit! I knew why you were telling me, but I didn't know what to say."

"You said you wanted to tell me something that night," Aiden said in an undertone. "It wasn't about the movie, was it?"

"You remember that?" Sam looked directly at Aiden, and Aiden could see surprise and pleasure in the other man's eyes. Aiden smiled and nodded. "I was going to ask you to come over to my place," Sam explained. "The place I'd shared with Nick. But when you told me… shit. I could barely get up the nerve to ask you over. What right did I have to ask you to stay in New York? And when you called to say you'd gotten the scholarship, I hesitated. When I finally called, you were gone."

Aiden did his best to smile. "I didn't know what I wanted either. I don't know what I would have said if you'd asked me to stay. In the end, that scholarship made my career. Maybe that's just the way it was supposed to work out."

"Thanks."

"For what?" Their eyes met for a brief moment, and Aiden was tempted to take Sam in his arms. To kiss him.

"For not punching the shit out of me when you saw me again." Sam laughed. "But seriously, I appreciate it. Giving me a chance to explain, after all this time."

"I'm glad you told me." He *was* glad, although Sam's admission left him more unsettled than before.

"Friends?"

"Friends," Aiden repeated. "So maybe we can get together. Do some sightseeing while you're here?" He hadn't planned on asking, but he wanted to see Sam again, even if it was only to walk around Paris.

"I'd like that."

"I don't have rehearsal tomorrow. Why don't I stop by around eleven? We can grab lunch if you'd like."

"Sounds great."

AIDEN walked back to his hotel a little after one, tipsy and thoroughly exhausted. It was a "good" kind of tired. He hadn't realized how much he'd been hurt by Sam's silence when he'd left for Europe five years before. How much he *still* hurt. It felt like an enormous weight had lifted. He was looking forward to spending time with Sam.

He opened the door to the hotel and headed for the elevator.

"You've been hiding from me," he heard Alexandria say from behind him. Before he could respond, she wrapped her arms around him and kissed him, moving one arm up his shoulder to comb his hair with her fingers. She wore a short dress with silver sandals that accentuated her long legs.

"I told you I was having dinner with friends." He pulled away from her and struggled to mask his irritation.

"Of course you did." She imitated his serious expression. "But I thought you'd be back by now." She pushed him into the elevator and pressed a button.

"Alexandria—" He forced the elevator door back open with his foot. "—this isn't going to happen."

She reached for him again and he pushed her away.

"Alexandria." He tried to keep his voice down, but he was at the end of his patience. "I don't *fuck* married women. Go home. Please."

There was cold fury in her eyes, but Aiden didn't flinch. He expected her to yell at him, but instead she simply laughed as if she didn't care. She flicked her long hair with one hand and she strode out of the hotel without looking back.

Aiden released the elevator door and leaned against the wall of the cab. It would be another long night; he was sure of it.

CHAPTER 9

AIDEN finally fell asleep around four that morning. When he awoke with the sunrise, he lay in bed with a particularly stubborn morning erection and thought about Sam. He weighed his options: jerking off or getting some exercise. Since he was pretty sure he wouldn't get Sam Ryan out of his head with just his hand, he decided on the exercise. He'd work out and clear his head. He didn't need to be a basket case when he went to meet Sam. He'd be nervous enough anyhow.

God, but he'd made so many mistakes. He pulled on sweatpants and a T-shirt and headed out the door a few minutes later. It had all seemed so black and white back then. He'd either have Sam or his career. But it hadn't been that simple, and it stung to realize it now. Who was to say they couldn't have found a middle ground for their relationship to survive?

When Aiden returned to his room an hour later, breakfast was already on the table, along with the morning newspaper. He opened the window to the cool morning air and peeled his sweaty shirt off, then sat down to read. He'd never been a big fan of newspapers, but he made a point of reading them in French to improve his command of the language.

He sipped his coffee as he read through the arts section, smiling at the interview with David Somers on the front page, which discussed the opera Aiden would be performing in a few weeks. Not surprisingly, the reporter made it a point to compliment David on his impressive career successes. David, of course, was charmingly dismissive and steered the conversation back to Aiden and the other singers as well as the modern sets that had been painted by a popular French artist.

Aiden had just poured himself a second cup of coffee when he saw it. A photograph, toward the bottom of the society page. A photograph of him and Alexandria, locked in a passionate kiss. Well, at least it looked passionate. His face was mostly obscured by hers.

Oh fucking hell!

He stood up and gritted his teeth, stormed over to the window, and looked outside. The photo had been taken the night before, when he'd come back from dinner at Jules and Jason's. He struggled to recall the hotel lobby. He hadn't seen anyone when they'd walked in, but then again, he hadn't been paying attention.

His cell phone rang, and he pulled it out of his pants. Alexandria. *Great.* She'd obviously seen the photograph too. He let the call go to voice mail.

Not like there's anything I can do about it. He'd just have to wait until it blew over. On the bright side, though, he was unlikely to be seeing much of Alexandria. *Silver lining.*

His phone buzzed again. His agent this time, with a text. *Remember—any publicity is good publicity.* Aiden laughed and shook his head. Chuck Ritter was a great agent and pragmatist. Still, the fact that the photo had not only ended up in print, but had already hit the web, unsettled Aiden. How many other people would see it? He didn't want Sam to see it. He tossed the phone onto the bed and headed for the shower.

SAM sat on the couch drinking a large café au lait, computer on his lap. He had surprisingly few e-mails to respond to—his partner, Stacey Atkinson, had managed to put out most of the fires at the office, and the two new hires were pulling their weight. He answered the remaining e-mails to clients before reviewing the latest draft of a motion to compel in a race discrimination case. But he wasn't seeing the document. He was thinking about Aiden.

His hand strayed to the touchpad on the laptop and moved the pointer up to the search box. He typed "Aiden Lind" and clicked Search. The Wikipedia entry read:

Aiden Lind. Opera singer. Born August 29th, Jackson, Mississippi. Baritone, known for roles such as Scarpia in Puccini's Tosca, *the title role in Mozart's* Don Giovanni, *Renato in Verdi's* Un Ballo in Maschera, *among others. Recent performances in London, Milan, Rome, San Francisco, and Chicago have been met with critical praise.*

Impressive. All of it. But it said nothing about the man except that he was going to turn thirty this summer and was quite successful. Sam followed a link for an article from an American gossip magazine, entitled "Aiden Lind's Silent Agony."

Rising young opera star Aiden Lind, in Milan for rehearsals of a new production of Verdi's La Forza del Destino *at La Scala, has been seen on the arm of Italy's favorite pop singer, Sylvia Trattorina. The two spent the evening at Disco 90, a new dance club. However, rumor has it that Mr. Lind left the club by himself. Since his much-publicized breakup from London billionaire Cameron Sherrington, Lind has rarely been spotted in public other than at the usual opera galas and fundraisers. Sources close to Mr. Lind say he is still heartbroken over the split. Says Luigi Ferri of* Eurostyle Celebrity Magazine, *"It's a classic story of heartbreak. He's single, gorgeous, and a paparazzo's wet dream. It's a terrible tragedy to see him suffer so." Ferri went on to say....*

Sam felt his jaw clench and he closed the window for the article. The man in the article was nothing like the Aiden Lind he had known in New York or, for that matter, the man he'd spoken to last night. Sam knew Aiden was bisexual, but he could hardly see him dating pop divas or crying his eyes out in an empty hotel room.

Friends, he reminded himself. And if they ended up in bed together, would that be so terrible? He'd be heading home in a little over two weeks.

Home. Five years after he left New York, the fabulous apartment with the killer view of Philadelphia still didn't feel much like home to Sam. Home for him was the Brooklyn loft, with the pipes running along the ceiling and the easel in the corner covered with blotches of paint, the futon bed, and the rice-paper light fixture. The only trace of Nick that inhabited the Philly apartment was in the paintings he had left behind.

Sam remembered the first time Nick had seen the loft and how he'd been fascinated by the slate roof on the old brick fire station across the street. Sam had gone apartment hunting without Nick and had hesitated to put a deposit down on the apartment without Nick's approval.

"I trust you, Sam," Nick had told him. "You know how hard it is to find a cheap place in Brooklyn Heights. Go for it."

And when Nick gathered Sam into his arms, he told him, "It's perfect." Sam agreed.

They lived in that apartment together for more than five years. The loft was the first place Sam ever considered home, a place where he could be himself and where he was loved unconditionally.

Sam closed the computer and set it on the coffee table.

CHAPTER 10

AIDEN led Sam back from the Louvre through the Jardin des Tuileries toward Place de la Concorde. Aiden had been to the Louvre many times before, but he'd enjoyed it more this time than any of the others. They'd spent most of the time wandering around the museum, not stopping for long in any of the exhibits, but chatting comfortably throughout their tour.

As they walked on through the park, the obelisk rose high above the trees and the gravel crackled beneath their feet. Aiden felt a bit giddy as he watched children on bicycles weave in and out of the paths, laughing. He loved Paris this time of year, with its flowering gardens and trees. The smell of freshly cut grass caught the breeze and reminded him of the first time he'd come here, not knowing what to expect and entirely overwhelmed by the beauty of the city.

"Last time I was here," Sam said, "I spent two whole days at the Louvre. Nick brought his sketchbook, and I wandered from gallery to gallery, taking pictures. I'm pretty sure we closed the place both days."

Aiden couldn't help but notice how Sam's demeanor changed when he spoke of Nick. Sam wore a wistful expression and his voice was warm. Aiden felt a pang of something himself to see the look on Sam's face. Envy, perhaps? Not that Aiden didn't still think of Cam sometimes, but then again when he *did* think of Cam, the memories weren't always good ones.

"So Nick was an artist?"

Sam nodded. "A painter. Oils, mostly, although sometimes he worked in watercolor. Abstract modern paintings. Lots of color and texture."

"Have you been to the Orangerie?"

Sam laughed. "Spent an entire day there. Nicky was fascinated by the colors of Monet's paintings. I think I fell asleep on one of the benches. Just about got kicked out by one of the museum guards."

"I take it you're not an artist, then?"

"Hardly. But I learned to appreciate modern art. I'm always amazed by people like you."

"Like me?"

"Artists, I mean. Musicians. People with talent."

Aiden's face warmed. "We're not so special, really."

Aiden always felt he didn't deserve the attention. When he graduated from Indiana University, his father refused to come see him receive his diploma. "It's not like you did anything but open your mouth," he'd told Aiden. It was true. He'd sung his way through school while so many of his friends had worked their asses off.

"It's a gift, Aiden."

The statement was unequivocal, and Aiden smiled in response.

"Do you enjoy singing?"

"I love it. But not the applause or the fans." Realizing how this sounded, Aiden added quickly, "I mean, I appreciate all that. Don't get me wrong. But what I love the most is the music."

"Really?" Sam stopped walking and looked at Aiden with obvious surprise.

"The best part is the first time I get to sing through the opera with the orchestra."

"You mean in costume?"

"No. Usually in a pair of jeans." When Sam looked uncomprehendingly at him, Aiden explained, "It's called a *Sitzprobe*. The singers all sit in chairs on stage and sing through the music with the orchestra. There aren't any costumes or sets; you don't have to worry about blocking—where to move and when—you just sing. It's a little like being in the middle of a recording, where the sound seems to come from all around you and you feel like you're part of something amazing."

Aiden blushed at the realization that he'd gotten a bit carried away with his description. "Sorry. I sound like an idiot, don't I?"

"Never. It makes me wish I could feel that. Not that I know anything about music, but the way you describe it, I can almost imagine what it would be like."

They began to walk again, talking and stopping from time to time to look in various shops along the route. "What do you think of that?" Sam leaned over to point to a hand-loomed scarf in a store window, accidently brushing against Aiden's shoulder. Aiden's pulse quickened. He tried his best to focus on the scarf, but the scent of Sam's crisp cologne had him remembering their first night together in New York, years before.

"For you?" It was a silly question. The scarf was obviously made for a woman.

Sam laughed. "For my mother. I need to pick up gifts for her and my sisters."

"I like it. Why don't we go inside?" Aiden clapped Sam's shoulder. Aiden meant it as a friendly gesture, but Sam's mouth parted with the touch. Aiden's hand lingered for a moment longer than he'd intended. He didn't want the contact to end.

"Sounds good." Sam's gaze met Aiden's, and Sam, too, appeared to hesitate. Then a patron exited the store, and the moment was gone just as quickly.

By the time they left the store, Sam having purchased several scarves and a sweater for his youngest sister, it was now early evening, and the sky was overcast.

"Looks like rain." Sam stared up at the sky.

"You've been lucky so far. Usually this time of year, it rains a lot more. Do you want to take the Métro the rest of the way?"

"Nah. I don't mind getting a little wet."

Neither of them had thought to bring an umbrella, so they picked up their pace. But as they neared the Seine, the intermittent drops of rain soon became a torrent.

"Follow me." Aiden pointed down one of the narrow streets. He held his hand out to steady Sam over one of the small rivers that had formed on the cobblestones, and stepped into the water up to his shin. "Shit." He brushed a soggy lock of hair from his eyes.

Sam jumped over another mini torrent, holding Aiden's hand a bit tighter. A taxi snaked through the pedestrians running for cover, and

Sam and Aiden stepped backward to avoid the ensuing splash of water. Sam lost his footing, managing to keep his balance only because Aiden grabbed him around the waist. Aiden laughed and looked down at his soggy shoes, socks, and pants.

"Sam," Aiden called over a clap of thunder, "I know a nice café right down the block. Why don't we duck inside and wait until this passes?"

"Sounds great," Sam ran down the sidewalk after Aiden, still holding his hand.

They reached the café a few minutes later, but not before they were both soaked to the skin. Aiden took two napkins from a waitress and handed one to Sam. They wiped their faces and made their way over to a table by the window. Outside the storm had worsened.

They ordered a light meal and chatted comfortably for several more hours. They both took off their shoes to let them dry, and their stocking feet brushed beneath the tiny table. Rather than pulling his feet away, Aiden pressed them more deliberately against Sam's. The hint of color in Sam's cheeks was reassurance enough that it wasn't just Aiden feeling the heat between them. If anything, their physical attraction had grown in the intervening years.

Aiden didn't notice the rain had stopped falling until the sky grew dark and faint bands of color appeared on the horizon. Sam texted Jason to let him know he would be late returning to the apartment. Their clothing finally dry, they ventured back out onto the wet streets in search of Aiden's favorite tea shop. "Best hot chocolate in Paris. And the pastries are incredible."

"I'm going to need to run an extra mile tomorrow," Sam said with a rumbled laugh.

"I promise I won't chase you off."

This time it was Sam's hand on Aiden's shoulder. "I'll hold you to that."

They turned a corner down rue du Fouarre. "This is the place." Aiden's excitement at finding the tiny shop was immediately replaced by disappointment. The shop was closed. "Sorry. I didn't realize they closed early."

"I'll make sure to come back before I leave. Promise." The edges of Sam's mouth turned upward.

"My hotel's about a block away.... Would you like to get something to drink in the bar before you head back to the apartment?" Aiden hadn't meant for it to sound like a come-on, although he knew it was. He didn't want the day to end.

"I'd like that." Sam's smile faded, his expression now intense, searching. He took Aiden's hand, his thumb brushing Aiden's palm. It was all Aiden could do not to lean in and kiss Sam. Then again, he'd never made any bones about his attraction to Sam. This time, though, he would let Sam take the lead.

It started to rain again. "We'd better get going," Aiden said, "or we're going to melt."

Sam laughed and they took off down the street at a healthy run, still holding hands.

SAM hadn't planned on going back to Aiden's hotel, but he wanted to. His attraction to Nick had been a low, steady thrum, but the sexual need he felt when he was near Aiden was a palpable thing. Like sitting too close to a fire, it burned, but he didn't want to move away for fear of the cold.

The hotel was a hybrid: small, like most European hotels, but with the conveniences of its US counterparts. Sam was surprised to find that the bar in the lobby featured a jazz trio, and even more surprised to discover that the live music was quite good. He and Aiden lingered over their drinks, alternately listening to the music and continuing their conversation.

"I had no idea it was so late," Sam said in stunned surprise when he finally looked at his watch and saw that it was nine o'clock. "I should get going. Jules and Jason will be expecting me back."

Aiden, who was sipping his third or fourth vodka tonic, smiled at him and, with one practiced movement, put his hand over Sam's. Their eyes met as he said in an undertone, "Come up to my room? I can order us some dinner."

Aiden waited patiently, his earnest gaze focused on Sam. The easy conversation and Aiden's relaxed charm were so damned enticing, and the candle on the table seemed to bring out the amber in Aiden's eyes.

Sam inhaled slowly and swallowed.

"Sure." His voice sounded confident, but his gut clenched in anticipation. He wasn't exactly nervous—the alcohol had dulled most of that—but he wasn't quite convinced that it was the right decision either.

Stop analyzing. This is a vacation. You're supposed to enjoy yourself.

Aiden flagged down the waiter, insisting over Sam's protests that he pick up their tab. They rode the elevator upstairs in silence as Sam texted Jason once more to let him know that he might not be back until morning. He could imagine Jason's expression as he read the text, but the only response he received was a simple *Enjoy yourself.*

Aiden's room was far nicer than anything Sam had imagined, a suite with a separate sitting room and a bathroom that was larger than any he'd seen before in a European hotel. Aiden had moved up in the ranks of opera singers if the price tag for a room like this was any indication.

"Nice." Sam looked around appreciatively.

Aiden smiled. "When I first came to Europe, I slept anywhere I could. David introduced me to Jason and Jules... I got intimately acquainted with their couch." He chuckled.

Sam thought of Aiden's earlier comment that he'd once thought of settling in Paris. "So London's home?" He wouldn't ask about Aiden's ex. Not yet, at least, although he was curious after reading the article on the Internet.

"I guess you could call it that." Aiden's expression betrayed nothing, but Sam swore he saw a hint of pain in his eyes. "I'm not there very much. I've been so busy singing, I don't have time to put down any roots."

In some ways, Aiden was much like Sam had been before he'd moved to Philly. Nick's death had left him without a place to call home. Nick had *been* his home. There was something familiar in the emotions Sam sensed in Aiden. He seemed unsettled.

No. He seems lonely. Sam walked over to Aiden, stopped a foot or two away, and met Aiden's eyes. Even with the buzz of the alcohol, he still felt nervous this close to Aiden. He hoped his hands weren't shaking as much as he thought they were. "I know we said just friends," he began, "but I'd really like to kiss you."

Sam knew it was silly—neither of them believed this was about being "just friends" anymore. But the look of pleasure on Aiden's face was needed encouragement. Sam stepped forward and put his hands on Aiden's face to draw him closer. Aiden smelled of musk and rain, and his jaw was rough with stubble.

Sam brushed his lips over Aiden's, a feather's touch, taking his time to linger and inhale the other man's scent. Sam's cock filled in response, and he felt Aiden's shudder as their bodies pressed together. Aiden was hard too. Sam could feel his erection as surely as he felt his own against Aiden's thigh. He linked his hands behind Aiden's head and slipped his tongue past the willing lips. He closed his eyes and reveled in the feel of Aiden's body, the warmth of him.

God, he'd missed Aiden! He hadn't realized until now just how much. For five years he'd rationalized their relationship away. He'd convinced himself that he'd been getting over Nick, that he needed Aiden because he craved the warmth of another person after being alone for so long. But now, as he ghosted his hands over Aiden's shoulders and back, he understood that Aiden had offered him much more than warmth all those years ago. Sam just hadn't seen it. He hadn't been *ready* to see it.

Aiden untucked Sam's shirt and pulled it over his head before licking a line up to Sam's neck. Sam's breath came in ragged gasps as Aiden tossed the shirt aside and began to nip and suck on Sam's nipples.

"Harder." Sam spoke in a hoarse whisper.

Aiden growled as if he'd been holding himself back, waiting for Sam's approval. He took Sam's left nipple between his teeth and Sam hissed his response, shuddering as the sting melted into pleasure.

He had never let himself go sexually, never shown anyone the side of himself he kept hidden. He had always been the one with the power. But with Aiden, he wanted to take the chance. He wanted to give up control.

"Fuck me," he moaned. "I've never let anyone do that to me. I want you to fuck me like I did to you when we first met."

It seemed to take Aiden a minute to fully comprehend Sam's words. But Sam could tell he understood. He could see the hunger as well as the pleasure in Aiden's eyes, and he knew it was reflected in his own.

"Get undressed." Aiden's tone wasn't harsh, but there was no mistaking the command.

Sam's body thrummed with both excitement and apprehension. He took a deep breath, forced back his fear, and did as Aiden asked. He kicked off his still damp shoes and socks, not caring where they landed. Then, his eyes on Aiden's, he unbuttoned the fly of his jeans and pushed them down over his hips. He stepped out of them, wearing only his boxers.

"All of your clothes."

Sam was already painfully hard. He pulled the boxers off, his face hot with embarrassment at his jutting erection, his shoulders tense. He felt vulnerable, but he couldn't remember ever being so turned on. Perhaps sensing Sam's anxiety, Aiden walked behind him and began to massage his shoulders, working his fingers into the muscles until it hurt.

"Turn around and put your hands on the bed," Aiden ordered.

Sam complied, bending over so that his ass was displayed. He ached to know what Aiden would do to him. Then he felt Aiden's hands on his buttocks, squeezing and manipulating the muscle there. Aiden nipped at the skin, then licked and kissed the pain away. At each tiny bite, Sam moaned until Aiden spread his cheeks and Sam felt the warmth of his tongue at his hole.

No one had ever touched him like this. He felt momentarily uncomfortable. But Aiden's soft moans of pleasure soon had Sam forgetting all about his embarrassment. He closed his eyes and just let himself feel.

"Oh... damn... Aiden...." Colors flashed beneath his eyelids and his breath came in gulps.

"You taste so good." Aiden's voice was impossibly low and a bit rough to Sam's ears. Aiden spread him even wider and pressed his tongue inside him, past the tense muscles Sam fought to relax, deeper still. Sam growled, the alcohol and the intensity of the sensation making him feel as though he were floating.

Aiden withdrew and said, "Lick your hand and rub yourself."

Sam willed the room to stop spinning around him. He spit on his hand, although he didn't need much since he was already leaking so badly. His cockhead was so sensitive that he had to squeeze himself a few times or he'd have come right then and there.

By the time Aiden had replaced his tongue with several lubed fingers, Sam was coming hard all over his hand and the sheets. It was almost painful, he was so stimulated. From a distance, he heard Aiden rip open the foil condom packet. He felt Aiden press against him, then ease himself past the clenched ring. It burned.

"Relax, baby," Aiden purred near his ear. "It's going to hurt a little, but I promise you it'll be worth it. Just relax."

Sam let his mouth fall open and leaned his head forward on the pillows. He stopped fighting the intrusion, imagining himself opening to Aiden's cock.

"That's it, Sam. Let me in."

"Oh, fuck!" Sam shouted as Aiden seated himself fully inside. The burn intensified and faded as Aiden slowly pulled out, then pushed back in, using Sam's hips as leverage. Three or four thrusts, and Sam's spent cock reawakened. His single thought—*why the hell didn't I do this before?*—dissolved into a blur of sensation. Sam didn't think, he let himself *feel*.

"You good?" Aiden asked.

"God, yes. It feels…." Sam couldn't finish the sentence. The sensations were too overwhelming. It was as though he had discovered a completely different part of himself hiding under the veneer of control he'd worked so hard to master.

Aiden's throaty laugh echoed about the room. He reached around Sam's waist, pulled him up a bit from the bed, and fisted Sam's cock. "Come with me, Sammy," Aiden whispered in Sam's ear. "Let me hear you come when I come inside you."

"Yes. Please. More. Make me come again."

The next thing he knew, Sam was coming into Aiden's slippery hand. A heartbeat later he felt Aiden's body shudder his release. Aiden bent over him so that his chest was tight against Sam's back. Sam felt Aiden's heart pounding and heard Aiden's gasps against his sweaty neck.

"So good," Sam said. "God, that was so good." He turned his head and met Aiden's gaze.

Aiden kissed him.

"So fucking good."

AIDEN awoke to moonlight seeping through the half-drawn drapes, Sam's arms wrapped around his waist, Sam's head on his chest. It wasn't that he couldn't sleep; he didn't *want* to sleep. He'd guessed at what lay beneath Sam's controlled exterior years before. But tonight had been a revelation. He wanted to remember this night and the sound of Sam's voice as he came, the look of surrender in Sam's eyes. He wanted to remember how he felt when Sam ceded control. Completely.

His mind wandered back to New York City and to their brief time together. *Nothing's changed. In two weeks, he goes home and I'm still here.*

And that's how it should be. He wasn't interested in giving up his career, and Sam had made his feelings about long-distance relationships clear five years before.

CHAPTER *11*

AIDEN glanced at Sam as they ran, side by side, down the path that led by the upper lake in the Bois de Boulogne. They'd spent the better part of the past two days together, exploring the city when Aiden hadn't been in rehearsals. And the nights—Aiden almost grinned to think about the past few nights in his hotel room. They'd made love, they'd fucked, they'd slept spooned together like lovers who had been together for far longer. Sam felt so damn familiar, sometimes Aiden imagined the intervening years had been more like a few weeks.

"This place is incredible." Sam's voice brought Aiden back to the here and now. "Reminds me of Central Park."

"When I was doing auditions years ago, I'd come here every chance I got. Take the subway and spend the day. I had a lot of downtime."

"Seems like you don't anymore."

"A few weeks here and there. Every once in a while, I get more than a week. I've got two weeks off in August."

"Anything special planned?"

"I rented a place on the beach in Alabama. Nothing exciting. I thought it'd be nice to chill somewhere out of the spotlight." Aiden's family had never been able to afford vacations. He'd grown up envious of the other kids whose families had rented houses on the Gulf Coast, so when he'd made enough money to take a vacation, Aiden hadn't thought about Monte Carlo or the French Riviera. Besides, those places reminded him of Cam and the days they'd spent aboard the Sherrington family's yacht.

"Seriously? I used to go there with my folks. Where do you stay?"

"Fort Morgan, not far from Gulf Shores." Aiden warmed with the reminder that Sam had grown up so close to his own home in Mississippi.

"We stayed in Gulf Shores a few summers. We'd all pile into the minivan. My dad would fly back up to Memphis to work during the week, but my mom would take us to play miniature golf and to the beach."

Aiden wondered—in that vague, dreamlike way he'd begun to wonder about Sam since they'd reconnected—if maybe someday he and Sam might spend some time there together.

They headed back to Jules and Jason's a few hours later and arrived around lunch.

"Meet you at the hotel lobby in about an hour?" Sam pushed a stray lock of hair from his eyes.

"Sounds great. One of the other singers told me about a new place near Étoile that's supposed to be good. We can do some shopping afterward if you'd like."

"Perfect. I'd like to pick up a few gifts for folks back home."

Aiden couldn't resist leaning over to kiss Sam lightly on the lips. "See you soon."

Aiden walked backward and waved as Sam punched the code on the outer doorway and slipped inside. It had been a great morning. He had rehearsal at five, so there'd be plenty of time for a quick lunch and a trip to Galeries Lafayette or one of the other big department stores.

Jules had invited Aiden for a late dinner that night after rehearsal, back at the apartment. Aiden felt slightly guilty that he'd been monopolizing Sam for most of his Paris visit, but neither Jason nor Jules seemed particularly concerned. In fact, it was quite the opposite. Both men would disappear when Aiden showed up at the apartment to meet Sam, then claim to have something to do. This was usually followed in short order by Jules biting his bottom lip to keep himself from smiling or a text from Jason saying *Have fun.* Or both.

Subtle as a freight train. Both of them.

Aiden loved them for it.

SAM showered and dressed quickly, choosing a pair of dark jeans and a lightweight linen sweater Jason had picked out for him from Jason's sister's line of menswear. It fit the contours of Sam's broad chest and was slightly translucent. Rather than try to tame his wavy hair, he let it dry naturally. After a quick glance in the mirror, he decided he looked about as good as he could. He hoped Aiden would notice.

Aiden. God, but the past week had been a surprise. Sam knew he would have to leave in less than two weeks, but he was having such a good time with Aiden he'd pushed the thought from his mind on several occasions, focusing instead on the here and now.

Sam walked into the hotel lobby to find Aiden speaking to a young woman. Aiden's back was to Sam, so Sam, not wanting to interrupt, waited patiently a few yards away. He didn't intend to listen in, but the sound of their voices carried through the room.

"But certainly you can understand that my editor needs more than just a 'no comment' for this story, Mr. Lind," the woman said in a clipped British accent. "Your public wants to know about Madame Gilman. Especially after Lord Sherrington suggested that you two might have been seeing each other behind his back."

Aiden's body tensed at those words. "He said that?" The shock in his voice was evident.

"What's your response, Mr. Lind? If it's a lie, this is your opportunity to set the record straight."

"I never cheated on Cam. Never."

The woman tapped the screen and scribbled something onto her tablet. She looked back up at Aiden and asked, "Why would Lord Sherrington suggest it, then?"

"I have no idea. Look, Miss Evans, is it?"

The woman nodded.

"I have nothing more to say. I think—"

"Mr. Lind," she said with a knowing smile, "I know Lord Sherrington still sends you flowers every few—"

"How the hell would you know *that*?" It was more than simple irritation now. Aiden was obviously angry.

"All I'm asking is whether you and Madame Gilman are still together."

"We're not," Aiden replied. "We never *were* together. It wasn't anything like that."

"Tell me why I should believe you, Mr. Lind, and I promise I'll leave you alone." Her expression was unforgiving. "Give me something my editors will be happy with, and I'll hop the next train back to London."

"I can't give you—" Aiden began, his voice raised.

"Aiden," Sam interrupted, striding over to them and kissing a very surprised Aiden soundly on the lips. "I thought we had a lunch date." He spoke in a thick Southern drawl. "Or were y'all planning on keepin' me waitin' all afternoon?" He embraced Aiden, put his lips to Aiden's ear, and whispered, "I've got your back." Sam sincerely hoped he hadn't overstepped by intervening. But Aiden looked so uncomfortable, and Sam hadn't been able to stop himself.

"Excuse me," the reporter said as Sam finally released Aiden. "Are you a friend of Mr. Lind?"

Sam ran his fingers through his hair, making sure to look the woman directly in the eyes. "A friend? I'd say we're much more than friends, wouldn't you, baby?" He snaked his other arm around Aiden's waist and pulled him close.

She had her tablet poised as she asked, "What's your name?"

"Beau McKenzie." Sam didn't hesitate. "And I'm afraid Mr. Lind here is late for lunch. If y'all will excuse us, maybe we can talk sometime later."

Without another word, Sam led a speechless Aiden into the elevator and pressed the button for Aiden's floor. The door closed as the woman shouted, "Wait! Mr. McKenzie, I'd like to ask you a few—"

A moment later, Aiden was doubled over, laughing. "Beau McKenzie? Where did you come up with that one?"

Sam grinned tentatively. "My oldest sister married him. Only name I could think of on the fly." He shoved his hands in his pockets and glanced down at the floor. "I hope you don't mind."

"Are you joking?" Aiden licked his lips and laughed again. "That was priceless. But you didn't need to—"

Sam kissed Aiden, relieved that Aiden wasn't angry and even happier that Aiden seemed genuinely pleased. "Nah, I didn't need to. You'd've handled it fine, I'm sure. But it was *damn* fun."

The elevator door opened and they stepped out. "But seriously, Sam," Aiden said, "I'm sorry. I shouldn't have said anything to that woman, I should have just told her to get lost."

"No need to apologize. Remember? We said no more apologies."

"But that stuff about Alexandria. We were never—"

"Old news." Or Sam hoped it was. He hoped he hadn't misjudged Aiden, that the articles he'd read online hadn't been the "real" man. But he knew he had no right to ask Aiden not to see other people. He brushed aside his discomfort and changed the subject. "So how about lunch?"

"We could slip out the back of the building and grab a taxi. She's probably gone by now."

"I was sort of thinking we could have lunch in the room," Sam said with an impish smile. "You know, in about an hour or so."

Aiden laughed. "All right, Mr. McKenzie. Just don't tell Sam, okay?"

"You got it."

CHAPTER 12

OPENING night of the opera, and Sam's departure was approaching far too fast. Aiden couldn't remember being happier, what with spending his free time with Sam and doing what he loved. The fact that David Somers was conducting made it all that much more enjoyable, and he enjoyed dinners with Jules and Jason twice as much with Sam at his side.

David's partner, Alex Bishop, flew in for a few days between performances of his own. The four of them had dinner at a three-star restaurant on the aptly named rue Beethoven, in the sixteenth arondissement. Afterward, Sam and Aiden spent the entire night making love, and they slept in late the next morning, bodies intertwined.

The performance was a resounding success, and Aiden headed from his dressing room to the opening night party to meet David, Alex, Jules, Jason, and Sam. Showered and dressed and once more in his tux, he strode into the main entrance of the theater. The high-ceilinged atrium had been transformed to accommodate partygoers with a lavish buffet, a fully stocked bar, and large floral arrangements. The opera's board of directors had invited the lively mixture of opera patrons, cast, and orchestra members more as a fundraiser than as a purely social gathering.

This too was part of Aiden's job—to mingle with the crowd and thank them for their continued support, knowing that the health of the opera house and his future engagements depended upon their continued donations. He had learned to take full advantage of the adulation and chat comfortably with men and women alike in spite of his lingering insecurities. In the end, though, it was only an act. Beneath the sophisticated veneer, he was nothing like his public image, and he feared that one day he'd be recognized for the pretender he really was.

Alexandria, blessedly, had not come to opening night, although she had called several times over the past two weeks. Aiden had not answered. Alexandria's husband most likely had told her not to make an appearance, fearing more publicity.

Making his way through the crowd seemed to take ages. After forty minutes of stopping to speak to the guests and smiling in response to their compliments, he spotted Sam standing with Jules, Jason, and David in the far corner of the room.

"Excuse me," he told the platinum blonde who still clasped his hand in hers. "I need to congratulate Maestro Somers." He had no real interest in speaking with David—they had discussed the performance after the final curtain as they usually did—but he wanted to talk to Sam. He knew it shouldn't matter what Sam thought, but he wanted to know Sam had enjoyed the performance. He also wanted this part of the evening to end. Sam would be leaving the next morning for the States, and Aiden wanted them to spend as much time as they could together.

Aiden caught Sam's attention, and Sam beamed. Was that pride Aiden saw in those clear blue eyes? None of the compliments he had received that evening meant as much as Sam's smile and the way Aiden felt in that moment.

He'd kept telling himself it was just a rebound thing or maybe some adolescent fantasy—going back to the way things had been in New York, before Cam and all the bullshit. But no matter how he tried to dismiss the thing with Sam, he knew he was fooling himself. It had been more than a fling before, and it was more than a fling now. He genuinely cared for Sam.

I need to ask him if I can see him again.

He'd be traveling to LA in a couple of months. He could spend a few days in Philly before rehearsals started—maybe longer. It'd be easy enough to change his ticket. He made up his mind to ask Sam if he'd like him to visit. What was the worst that could happen, anyhow? The guy would say no and they'd go their separate ways.

He was only about twenty feet from Sam when he felt a hand on his shoulder. He shot Sam the hint of a smile, as if to say, *I'll get there—just a minute longer*. He caught Sam's understanding nod, then turned around to greet his admirer.

"Cam?"

Aiden's surprise and confusion must have been easy to read, because Cameron laughed, then embraced Aiden, lingering far too long on each cheek. "I didn't mean to give you a shock."

Aiden thought that was *exactly* what Cameron had intended. And the gambit worked. Stunned and caught off guard, Aiden didn't immediately tell Cam to go to hell.

"What are you doing here, Cam?" Aiden's throat felt dry, so he snagged a glass of wine from one of the passing waiters and took a long drink.

Cam looked offended. "I came to hear you sing. Why else would I be here?"

Aiden took another swallow of his wine. "You shouldn't have come. Especially for me."

"I've missed you, sweetheart." Cam leaned forward so that his lips nearly touched Aiden's ear.

Aiden backed away far less gracefully than he had intended and bumped into one of the waiters. The sound of breaking glass turned heads.

"I'm so sorry." Aiden was mortified. He had hoped to leave the room quietly, without anyone noticing, but all eyes were now on him and Cam. Including Sam's. Aiden's cheeks burned with embarrassment. "Excuse me, Cam," he added, heading for the doorway without looking back.

AIDEN sat in front of the lighted mirror in his dressing room, staring off into space, rubbing his right shoulder. God, had he really reacted like that? He'd had a hard enough time trying to forget about Cam. He clenched his jaw at this thought, and his gaze caught the huge vase filled with roses that Cameron had sent for the performance. There were at least four dozen, all a deep red.

He knew he wouldn't—he *couldn't*—go back to Cam, especially since things had been going so well with Sam. But the memory of Cam's betrayal still hurt like hell. He closed his eyes and blew air between his lips, trying to clear his mind.

The door to the dressing room opened almost silently. If it hadn't been for the mirror, he might not have even known he was no longer alone.

"I don't want to talk about this, Cam." Aiden watched Cameron in the mirror, unwilling to look at him directly.

"I want you back, Aiden." Cameron looked genuinely distressed, as if he didn't understand what he could have done to alienate Aiden so completely. "We simply need some time together. Alone. The yacht's in the Mediterranean. When you finish here, we can spend a few weeks, just the two of us. Maybe stop in Cannes or—"

"You can't buy everything, Cam." Aiden kept his voice low, measured. "It's over."

"Don't say that." Cameron put his arms on Aiden's shoulders and kissed the top of his head. "You know how sorry I am for what I did. I really am. I can't live without you."

"You don't know how to live *with* me, Cam." Aiden stood up abruptly and faced Cameron.

"I won't ever do it again. I told you he meant nothing to me."

"You lied to me. You promised you'd never—"

Cameron grabbed Aiden and kissed him, then snaked his arms around Aiden's waist and pulled him close. For a split second, Aiden allowed himself to be drawn in by the kiss. But then reality reasserted itself and his brain took over from his body.

"No," Aiden nearly shouted. "I told you, Cam. It's over. It's time for you to go now. Go back to your little fuck buddy."

"But it's so lonely in that big old house without you. Damn, Aiden, it's *your* home too!"

"It *was* my home." Aiden felt tears threaten and fought them off. He'd cried enough over Cameron. "It was the hardest thing I've ever done, leaving. But it was all bullshit. All of it."

"You don't know what you're saying."

"I know *damn* well what I'm saying, Cam. I want you to leave now. And if I ever see you again in public, you're going to pretend you haven't even seen me."

"You can't mean that. You need me, Aiden. You need what I can give you. You—"

"I'm doing fine on my own. I get hired because I'm *good*. Because I work hard." Aiden's heart pounded in his chest and his throat burned.

"Don't mess with me, Aiden," Cam hissed. "You don't know what you're doing."

"Get the hell out of my dressing room." Aiden struggled to maintain his composure, his anger mixing with genuine fear.

"Not until I—"

"Leave, Cameron."

"Don't you dare—"

"You heard the man" came a steely voice from the doorway. "He asked you to leave."

Cameron raised his chin and sneered. "Who the hell are you?"

"The guy who's going to punch your face in if you *don't* leave." Sam's voice was restrained.

"As if," Cameron snorted, but he backed away from Sam and moved toward the door as Sam walked into the room. Then, stopping for a moment, he turned toward Aiden and said, "I meant what I said, Aiden. You need me."

Aiden said nothing but stood his ground and tried to school his face to something hard, immutable. Like granite.

Sam gestured to the door. Cameron stormed out, slamming it as he left.

Aiden drew a long breath. "Thanks."

"My pleasure." Sam's eyes twinkled with mischief. "Lord Sherrington, I presume?"

"Quite." Aiden's nervous laugh filled the room. "I'd love to say that's the last I'll see of him, but I doubt it. He doesn't give up easily."

"You okay?"

Aiden nodded. "That wasn't nearly as difficult as when I found him…." Aiden stopped himself and began again. "Sorry. It's over. No need to rehash all the gory details."

"No need to. Jules told me." Sam's expression was sympathetic. "He was about to go after the man and tear him limb from limb. Jaz had to hold him back."

Aiden shook his head. This time the laughter was more genuine. "Sometimes I wonder how I managed to deserve the two of them."

"Not much to wonder about. You're a good man, Aiden."

"I've made a lot of mistakes."

"Who hasn't?" Sam slipped his arm around Aiden's waist. Aiden took a long, slow breath and leaned his head against Sam's shoulder and lost himself momentarily in the warmth of Sam's body. Aiden relaxed with the soothing contact.

"Let's get out of here," Aiden said finally. "Do you think Jules and Jason will mind if I monopolize your last evening in Paris?"

Sam chuckled and planted a sweet kiss on Aiden's lips. "I already told them I'd be back in the morning to say my good-byes."

Sam and Aiden took a cab back to the hotel from the opera house. They barely spoke in the taxi, although the silence was far from uncomfortable. As they walked through the lobby to the elevator, they held hands. The scene in the dressing room had left Aiden feeling a little off-kilter, and the contact was reassuring. Aiden knew it was more than only the encounter with Cam, though, that left him feeling that way.

Sam squeezed Aiden's hand as the elevator reached their floor. A few minutes later, they were kissing, Sam pressed against the inside of the hotel room door. Aiden unbuttoned Sam's shirt to find the smooth skin beneath and lick one of Sam's nipples.

"More." It was more a gasp than a spoken word, but Aiden didn't need anything else to understand what Sam wanted. He took the pink flesh between his teeth and nipped at it, then licked it until he heard Sam's hiss.

"What do you want?" Aiden realized the hidden meaning in the words as soon as they were out of his mouth. He didn't care. It wasn't as if he didn't know the answer.

"I want to remember this."

The words both pained and encouraged Aiden. He pushed Sam's jacket and shirt off, then began to nip at Sam, just enough to mark the pale skin. Sam's breath was audible, stuttered, as Aiden worked his way down, getting to his knees, not caring if the expensive tux got wrinkled. Who gave a shit about that?

"Aiden."

Aiden closed his eyes and tried to calm his racing heart. And, oh God, what was that pain in his chest? It was exquisite, this combination of need and impending loss.

"Come." He took Sam by the hand and waited a moment until Sam stepped out of his pants and boxers. He didn't look back as he led Sam to the bedroom. He wanted to prolong the anticipation for both of them.

The look of surprise on Sam's face as Aiden flipped on the light and caressed Sam's body with his gaze was perfect. Sam was beautiful like this. Vulnerable. Still slightly awkward in his own nakedness, and yet craving that discomfort almost like an addiction. Aiden had never found anything so enticing as he did Sam's need to give himself over to Aiden.

Aiden turned Sam around so he could lave the back of Sam's neck as he tweaked Sam's pinkish-brown nipples. Sam leaned into Aiden's embrace, his head on his right shoulder, allowing Aiden access to the sensitive spot under his ear. Aiden knew what Sam wanted, but he withheld the touch, instead squeezing Sam's nipples harder and rolling them around in his hands.

"Aiden. Please."

Tell me you want me, Sammy.

Aiden released a nipple and ghosted a line down Sam's chest with his fingers, stopping above Sam's cock and biting Sam's neck hard enough to make him shudder.

"Please."

Not yet. I'm going to make you remember this. I'm going to remember this. I'm going to make you remember me.

Aiden pinched Sam's right nipple between his thumb and forefinger as he pressed against Sam's back so that Sam would feel his hard cock against the small of his back. On any other night, he might have fucked Sam like this, still fully dressed. Tonight, he would feel Sam's skin against his own skin.

He released Sam's nipple and pulled Sam's head back farther, turning it so he could steal a kiss as he finally touched Sam's cock. Aiden slipped his tongue into the corner of Sam's mouth—he couldn't kiss him deeply from his position behind Sam, but that was what Aiden wanted. Sam tried to turn around to meet Aiden's tongue, but Aiden kept Sam firmly against him.

"I want—"

"I know what you want." Aiden squeezed Sam's cock and brushed a thumb over the weeping slit.

"Aiden... please...."

This time Aiden turned Sam, snaked his arms around Sam's naked body, and pulled him tight before slipping his hands downward to cup Sam's bare ass. Sam's hard cock ground against Aiden's thigh, and Aiden felt his self-control begin to erode. No, it was more than that. He was turned on by Sam's submissive side, but he suddenly realized he didn't want to be completely in control tonight.

He wanted to be with Sam. To *really* be with Sam. To hold him close more than just one more night. And with that thought, the memory of New York resurfaced with such force that the pain in his chest spread to his arms and his legs.

Fucking hell. What's wrong with me?

"Aiden, is there something wrong?" Sam must have noticed the change in Aiden's demeanor, because Sam was now looking directly at him with a strange expression.

Aiden forced a smile. "Nothing. It's been a long night." It was a lie, of course. Aiden knew what he was feeling had nothing to do with performing or even Cam.

"Then let me make it better for you." Without waiting for a response from Aiden, Sam began to take Aiden's clothes off. His fingers brushed Aiden's neck as he loosened and tossed away the black silk bow tie. Sam undid the black studs of Aiden's tuxedo shirt, pausing with each stud to feather kisses at each inch of flesh he revealed. He kissed Aiden on the lips as he slipped the silver-and-black cufflinks from Aiden's wrists.

Throughout all of this, Aiden watched in silence, pulling his thoughts back from the reality of Sam's impending departure to the reality of the here and now. He would not waste the time they had left together; he would cherish it.

Perhaps Sam felt the same, because he took his time to acknowledge each bit of skin revealed as he continued to remove Aiden's clothing.

"Christ... it feels so good." Aiden's legs shook as he stepped out of his pants and boxers.

Sam held out his hand and led Aiden to the bed. "Make love to me, Sammy." *Slow. So I can remember you.*

Damn. Aiden didn't want this to end. Why the hell did it have to end? He was almost foolish enough to raise the subject with Sam, but then Sam kissed him again—and thank God for that. Aiden wouldn't spoil the time they had left.

AIDEN said good-bye to Sam the next morning, standing on the sidewalk in front of Jules and Jason's apartment building. He had wanted to go to the airport with Sam, but with an early makeup call for the afternoon matinee performance, he just didn't have the time. The taxi driver had already put Sam's bags in the trunk and now sat patiently, her eyes focused straight ahead, as Sam and Aiden held each other. Rain began to fall, creating a light mist as it hit the warm pavement. The smell of asphalt mingled with the crisp scent of the rain.

"Sam, I'd like to see you—"

"Shhh." Sam kissed Aiden. "This was the best vacation I've had in years. I'm so glad I got to see you again. And the opera was wonderful."

It wasn't what Aiden had expected to hear—or maybe it simply wasn't what he *wanted* to hear. *I knew all along it was just going to be a fling. He has a life in the States, and my life is here. Let it go.*

"Thanks." Aiden hoped he sounded convincing.

The taxi driver honked the horn and glared at them.

"I'd better go. Can't miss my flight. Stacey's probably tearing her hair out managing things at the firm by herself."

Aiden forced a laugh. "We wouldn't want that."

"Thanks again, Aiden. This was great."

"It was." The truth, although not the entire truth. Aiden fought the urge to ask Sam if they could see each other again when he was back in the US in July. But he wouldn't. He could sense the distance Sam was already creating between them. Subtle but undeniable. And yet....

"Take care of yourself."

"You too, Sam."

Aiden kissed Sam briefly on the lips; then Sam turned and slipped inside the cab. A moment later the car had pulled away. The rain began to fall harder as Aiden headed back to his hotel.

CHAPTER *13*

Connecticut
November

A STRING quartet played softly in the background. Beethoven, Jason had told him, although he could have said it was The Who and Sam would have believed him.

Sam hadn't planned on flying up to Connecticut for David Somers's fortieth birthday celebration. When Jules and Jason called to invite him a few months after he returned from his Paris vacation, he tried to bow out gracefully, saying he'd be happy to meet them in New York City afterward. But then David himself called—Sam guessed the conductor hoped to reassure him that it wasn't just Jules and Jason's idea that he come to David's family's estate. Sam had been hard-pressed to turn David down. He honestly liked the man, and although they hadn't spent much time together in Paris, Sam couldn't think of a good reason to turn him down.

The trip was hardly a disappointment. Sam spent two days skiing in Vermont with Jason (Jules watched them from the warmth of the ski lodge), then headed down to David's palatial estate. There, he'd spent a day shopping for antiques in a nearby town with Jules, Jason, and David's sister, Rachel. Still, as he mingled about the guests— musicians, mostly—he couldn't help but think about Aiden and the party at Jules and Jason's apartment months before.

He'd known Aiden wanted to see him again after Paris. And yet, as he stood on the Paris street with the taxi idling a few feet away, he hesitated. He didn't know why. The weeks he spent in Paris at Aiden's side had been wonderful. The sex had been a revelation. He'd watched Aiden's face as the taxi pulled away. He saw the look of disappointment there, but he'd told himself it was unrealistic. Their lives were so completely different. He couldn't have asked Aiden to come to Philly for more than a quick visit any more than Aiden could ask him to come to Europe.

No, if he were being honest with himself, he'd call his hesitation what it was: fear. Pure and simple. The kind of paralyzing fear he hadn't felt since Aiden mentioned the scholarship years before. And he'd given in to it, knowing what it was but helpless to do anything about it. But what was he so afraid of?

"Is something wrong?" Jules asked. Sam guessed that Jules had been standing next to him for a minute or so, but he simply hadn't noticed. He'd been too busy looking around, trying to see if Aiden had come.

"Nothing at all. It's a lovely party, and the music is wonderful." *Only it'd be better if Aiden were here.*

"I'm glad you came." Jules took his hand and led him over to the enormous glass doors that opened onto the patio.

It was too cold to go outside, and the snow lay thick on the ground, but Sam could see the lake shimmer in the moonlight. The snow had stopped falling nearly an hour ago, and he was happy he'd planned to stay a few more days. Apparently the blizzard had paralyzed the entire eastern seaboard. Jason suggested they go cross-country skiing around the estate tomorrow.

Jason, Alex, and David stood by the doors, sipping champagne and chatting about Italy. David flagged down one of the servers, and Sam soon acquired a glass and joined the conversation. Somewhere between the third or fourth glass of champagne, Sam caught Jules looking over at Jason, who glanced briefly at his watch. In retrospect, Sam should have realized something was up, but the champagne had gone straight to his head, and he wasn't thinking clearly enough to put the pieces together.

"Excuse me." Jason handed his still full champagne flute to a passing server. "I'll be back in a few minutes."

It was nearly one in the morning when Sam saw Jason again. Sam was heading to his room, having danced until his feet hurt. His head was spinning from the alcohol, and he yawned as he reached the large landing on the main staircase.

"Tired?" Jason asked as they passed each other on the stairs. His hair looked damp, as if he'd been outside, and his cheeks were ruddy from the cold.

"Rachel just about wore me out on that last dance. I figured I'd call it a night. You going back down to the party?"

Jason smiled. "Had to run an errand. I promised Jules we'd play a little once the crowd thinned."

"I could come back down." Sam didn't want to be rude.

"Don't sweat it. David's planned a small dinner tomorrow—you'll get to hear us play then."

"You sure?"

"Sure. Besides, you look beat."

"All right. Tell Jules good night for me."

"Will do."

Sam climbed up the last flight of stairs and headed down the long hallway toward his room. He had almost reached the door when he nearly walked headlong into one of the other guests.

Except that it wasn't just one of the other guests. Sam's heart rate accelerated when he saw who it was.

"Sam?" The look of pleasant surprise on Aiden's face appeared genuine.

"Aiden? I didn't expect to see you here." Sam couldn't help but stare. Aiden wore a tuxedo that skimmed the planes of his body. His cheeks were slightly pink, and his hair, which had grown longer since Sam had last seen him, was pulled back at the nape of his neck in a short ponytail and was damp.

"I wasn't going to come," Aiden admitted. "I was singing at City Opera and I figured that with the snow delays on the train lines, it'd be so late when I finally got here, it wasn't worth it. But Jason said he'd pick me up at the station with David's Jeep, and...." His voice trailed off and then he laughed.

"This isn't a coincidence," Sam said, finally putting the pieces together. "Is it?"

"Nope. Not if I know Jules and Jason."

Sam shook his head. "You'd think, knowing them like we do, we'd have guessed they'd pull something like this."

"I'm sorry, Sam. If I'd realized—"

"I'm not sorry," Sam interrupted. "I'd been sort of hoping you might come. I was disappointed you hadn't shown."

"Really?"

Sam smiled. "Yeah."

The color on Aiden's cheeks deepened as he said, "I'm glad."

"So how about I join you for a dance, then?"

"Would you?" A hint of a smile played on Aiden's lips.

"Damn straight. Besides, we wouldn't want to disappoint Jules and Jason, would we?"

Sam grinned. "Hell no."

Aiden put out his hand, and Sam took it. Together, they descended the stairs to the party below.

"*EVERY good Southern boy needs to know how to dance,*" Aiden's mother had told him when he'd balked at his lessons at Miss Felicity's Dance Studio. In the end, dancing had been a skill that served him well in his career, although he'd never liked it much. At least not until tonight. With Sam at his side, he silently thanked Miss Felicity. Sam, too, was a good dancer, equally comfortable with a Carolina shag as with a waltz, it seemed.

"What are you grinning about?" Sam asked as they moved together for a slow dance.

"Just wondering what Miss Felicity would say about my choice of dance partners." When Sam raised an eyebrow, Aiden explained, "You know, the big-boned lady who rapped you on your hand when you stepped on the girls' feet?"

Sam laughed. "Mine would have approved. Mr. Simpson. Twenty-nine. Retired from the local ballet company. First man I ever realized was gay. He taught me to samba. I caught him and Mr. Marsden, my gym teacher, making out in the back room one night before class."

"Sounds a lot nicer than Miss Felicity."

"You could say that." Sam's expression was one of unadulterated mischief.

"You *didn't!*" Aiden swung Sam around and stared at him.

"I learned about more than dancing that summer," Sam admitted with a sly grin. "I wonder if my mother knew about me being gay and was trying to steer me toward role models even back then."

"Better than learning about sex behind the convenience store. Somehow I never figured my first sexual experience would be shoved up against a dumpster with my sister's ex-boyfriend." Aiden closed his eyes briefly as he leaned on Sam's shoulder. "Last I heard, Eddie was married with three kids." He wondered if Eddie was happy.

"You ever think about having kids?"

"Sometimes. Then I look at some of my colleagues and I remind myself what a stupid idea it would be. I've got a friend—a soprano—who has a ten-year-old son. He traveled with her when he was young, but once he started school...." Aiden shook his head.

"Seems like that would be a great experience for a kid, traveling around the world."

"She was lucky. Her husband was a pianist and vocal coach, so he traveled with them sometimes." The music ended and Aiden gestured to a table at the far end of the room, away from the band. "I heard they'd gotten divorced a few years ago."

"I'm sorry to hear that."

"So was I." Aiden had always seen Grace and her family as a ray of hope that maybe someday, he'd be able to find someone and settle down. "Not that I could blame her husband." He didn't add that Grace admitted she'd cheated on her husband with her costar in the production of *La Traviata* Aiden had also sung in. It was too close to home.

AT FOUR o'clock in the morning, the band finally packed up. Aiden and Sam had danced some more. After a few more drinks, Aiden volunteered to sing a few arias with David Somers on piano, though Aiden admitted to Sam that he didn't much like performing at parties.

"For David, though," Aiden told him, "I'd sing an entire opera in my underwear, standing on my head."

They paused alone on the stairs to the guest bedrooms. "Come to my room?" Aiden asked.

"I'd like that." Sam's cheeks were ruddy from dancing and alcohol. He leaned forward and touched his lips to Aiden's. "I've missed you, Aiden." Aiden could hear the strain in Sam's voice at the admission. "Seems like I always miss you when I leave."

"Then don't leave." Aiden hadn't meant to say it quite that way— he'd only meant to reassure Sam—but he realized he was talking about more than spending the night together. He took Sam's hand and led him to his room, then pulled him inside and closed the door behind them.

THE sun rose as they lay in bed, bodies still intertwined from their lovemaking.

"I'm not really good at this." Sam combed his fingers through Aiden's damp hair. "Relationships. Not since Nicky. I shouldn't have let you go again in Paris."

Aiden's breath caught in his throat. "It's not like I can offer you much." Aiden believed the words but still wished they weren't true. "My life's pretty crazy, with all the traveling I do." He knew they were both thinking about Grace and her family.

"I know. But does that mean it would never work? We're not kids anymore. It's not like we're expecting things to be perfect. Besides, my work's hectic too."

Aiden took a slow, steady breath, then said, "I've got the place in Alabama again in April. You could come down. We could spend some time together. Even if it's only for a day or two."

"Seriously?" Sam kissed the top of Aiden's head. "I'd love to. And maybe you could come to Philly for a visit between now and then. Only if you're in the States, of course," he added quickly.

"I'm back in the US at the end of December. You have any plans for New Year's?" He knew he sounded like an overly excited kid, but he couldn't help himself.

"None. That'd be perfect." This time Sam leaned down and caught his lips.

God, but Sam tasted so good! In spite of his exhaustion, Aiden smiled and said, "How about a shower before sleep?"

"It's a snow day, right? We can sleep as long as we want."

CHAPTER *14*

Philadelphia
Four days later

IT WAS late afternoon by the time Sam arrived back to his Philadelphia apartment. On Thursday Aiden had returned to New York City, where he'd be for the rest of the three-week run of the production of *La Bohème*. There was snow on the ground here too, although it was hardly as pristine as at David's. Sam set his bags down in the front entrance before walking over to the balcony. He pressed his nose against the glass like he used to as a kid, feeling the cold against his skin.

More than ever, the apartment felt empty. Cold and sterile but for the colorful canvasses that hung on the walls. In that moment Sam envied Jason, that Jason had been able to leave his life in the US behind and travel the world with Jules. But Sam knew he could never do the same for Aiden. In spite of everything, he loved his work and the law firm he had built from scratch. Now, in the afterglow of the past few days spent at Aiden's side, he knew it was probably wishful thinking that he and Aiden might be more than sometime lovers. *But what's wrong in giving it a try?*

His phone chirped to signal a text message. *Don't forget*, it read, *give me a call when you get home.*

Sam smiled. He'd be more than willing to take whatever time he and Aiden could find together.

He tapped the phone. "Aiden?"

"Sam. It's good to hear your voice. I didn't mean to be a pest with the text, but—"

"I'm glad you texted. I got in the door about five minutes ago. I was thinking about you. How was the matinee today?"

"Really good. We've hit that middle of the run stride, where everyone knows their stuff and they can sit back and enjoy the ride. Not as exciting as opening night, but you can start to play around a little with interpretation, emotions, that sort of thing."

"I never thought of it that way," Sam replied, fascinated by this bit of information. "I guess I always thought you were aiming for a perfect performance."

"It's why I like the longer runs. If you only perform something two or three times, you're hitting your stride when the show closes. It's a luxury to have more than just a few performances, but David insists on it when he conducts. Another reason I love to sing with him."

"I'm definitely going to have to go to more than one show, then, the next time. Not that my ears are that sophisticated, but maybe if you tell me what to look for, I'd hear the difference."

"I'll look forward to it, then." Aiden's breath was audible through the speaker. "I had a great time at David's," he said after a brief pause.

"I did too." It hadn't hit Sam just how much he missed Aiden until he walked into the empty apartment. He'd been lonely for so long, he'd nearly forgotten how nice it was to have someone in his life. "I'm looking forward to Alabama. I'll check my trial calendar tonight and shoot you an e-mail, but I'm pretty sure I've got enough coverage in April. Most of my associates take vacations in the winter to get away from the snow. And we've just hired two new lawyers."

"Great. You get yourself some rest. We'll talk again soon, okay?" Aiden paused, then added, "Listen, Sam?"

"Hmm?"

"About New Year's. Are you still free?"

"Yes. Why?" Sam held his breath. He'd been looking forward to April, but five months was starting to feel like an eternity.

"I'm in Miami Beach for a fundraiser. It's only for a few days, and I know it's a bit far from Philly, but—"

"I'd love to come."

There was a moment of silence on the other end of the line before Aiden said, "Really?"

Sam couldn't help but smile to hear the surprise in Aiden's voice. "Really."

"That's great. I'll shoot you an email with the dates. Talk to you in a few days?"

"Sounds good. Take care of yourself Aiden." Sam wondered if Aiden could tell he was grinning.

"You, too, Sammy."

Four weeks later

"MR. LIND?" The stage manager poked her head into his dressing room. "There's a Mr. Ryan to see you."

"Thanks, Carla." Aiden guzzled the rest of his bottle of water and went to the door. "Sam. Damn, it's good to see you." He pulled Sam inside and shut the door, then kissed Sam, lingering lightly over his lips before embracing him. There hadn't been any earlier flights from Philly to Miami, and they hadn't seen each other before the concert.

"You were wonderful." Sam put down the small overnight bag he was still holding and swept two fingers over Aiden's lips, a gesture that made Aiden shudder with pleasure.

Aiden smiled the same pleasant smile he always gave when someone complimented him. It mattered little that the reviews of his performances were universally good; he still felt uncomfortable with the praise. Even a little undeserving. "Thank you."

He'd worried that the weeks apart might have made their reunion a bit awkward, but as usual, Sam set him at ease with another kiss.

"So what's on the agenda to celebrate the New Year? You promised you'd let me know what you were up to when I got here."

"Did I?" Aiden did his best not to smile.

"Is it something I'll like? Because I'm thinking spending the night in a hotel with you would be fine with me." Sam laughed against Aiden's throat as he feathered kisses there.

"My lips are sealed." Aiden pushed Sam playfully away, then grabbed a small duffel from off the lighted table. "I think you'll like it, though. Just the two of us. Romantic."

Sam put an arm around Aiden's waist and pulled him back, this time to claim his lips. "*This* is just the two of us." There was a mischievous twinkle in Sam's eyes.

"Do lawyers always argue?"

"Of course."

Aiden pulled away and straightened his bow tie and cummerbund. "Mr. Ryan, we're on a very tight schedule here. The limousine is waiting outside and"—Aiden pushed up his sleeve to check his watch—"we have four hours to midnight. I'll hold you in contempt if we're late."

Sam held up his hands. "I'm throwing myself at the mercy of the court."

"You'll behave?"

"You might have to make me behave." Sam's eyes glittered with lust.

"Shit. You're incorrigible." He aimed Sam in the direction of the door, giving him only a minute to grab his bag before pushing him into the corridor. "This way," he said as he gestured to the entrance to the street. A moment later they were outside, and Aiden was leading Sam over to a limousine. There, the driver took Sam's suitcase and held the door for them.

Once settled inside, Sam looked at Aiden with a raised eyebrow. "Nice. So are we headed to some swanky party that only the rich and famous are invited to?"

Aiden only shook his head. "My lips are sealed." Okay, so Sam proved him wrong on that point pretty quickly with a deep kiss. But he wouldn't give up the secret. "Keep trying. I'm liking this."

"Clearly I've miscalculated. I should be withholding my affections. Then maybe you'd come clean and tell me where we're headed."

Aiden bit his lower lip before opening a panel to reveal a bottle of chilled champagne and two crystal flutes. Then, without missing a beat, he said, "Something to drink?"

"Isn't it a few hours too early?"

"It's past midnight in London," Aiden pointed out as he opened the bottle and filled their glasses.

A few minutes later, they were settled in each other's arms. "I missed you, Aiden." Sam's voice was soft in Aiden's ear. "More than you know."

"Oh, I think I know." Aiden's heart felt as though it were going to burst.

THE limousine stopped about twenty minutes later. Sam looked out the window. They were in a parking lot illuminated by several lights. There was what looked like a small building at the edge of the lot, but other than a single light at the entrance, there was nothing to identify it. When Sam looked to Aiden for an explanation, he just took the champagne flute from Sam's hand, placed it alongside his own on the console, then pulled something out of the same cabinet in which he'd found the bottle and glasses.

"Gonna tell me what that is?"

Aiden held the object out so that Sam could see it. A flashlight.

"What are you up to, Lind?"

The driver opened the door and Aiden illuminated their way, leading Sam across the parking lot and down a paved walkway. The faint scent of the ocean wafted on the breeze, and the air was cool. "You're not very good with surprises, are you?"

Sam shook his head and chuckled. "Depends." He snaked an arm around Aiden, nearly knocking him off balance before pulling him tight to claim Aiden's lips. "As long as it involves you and sex, I'm good with it."

"Could be." Aiden slipped out of Sam's grasp and continued to walk and point the way. "Watch your step here."

A band of metal met the pavement, and the path beyond was wood. The smell of salt water was powerful here. A dock. "Aid—"

"You might want to take your shoes off." Aiden was already slipping out of his patent leather oxfords and rolling up the legs of his tux pants. Sam did the same, unable to suppress a grin. Wherever they were going, he was having fun. He felt like a kid again. "You can leave them here. Ralph will pick them up when he comes with the bags."

"Bags?"

Aiden took Sam's hand, and they walked to the end of the dock until they reached a large white wall. A restaurant, perhaps.

Then the restaurant's lights went on, illuminating the surface of the wall. "Holy shit." It wasn't a restaurant. It was an enormous yacht—at least a hundred feet long. "Where did you…?"

"Mr. Lind?" A man wearing a crisp white uniform, complete with captain's hat, walked toward them down the gangway at the end of the pier.

"Richard?"

"That's me. So good to have you joining us tonight. And this is Mr. Ryan?"

Sam offered the man his hand. "I'm Rich Cowan. Captain of the *Prelude*. Good to meet you."

"The *Prelude*?"

Rich looked to Aiden, who nodded.

"She belongs to David Somers."

They climbed aboard and Sam tried not to stare as a young woman dressed in white pants and a white polo greeted them.

"This is Amy. She'll be attending to you gentlemen. We'll be getting underway for the Bahamas in a few minutes. We'll arrive by morning. Maestro Somers sends his compliments and says you should enjoy yourselves. We'll arrive back in Miami in time for your flights on Monday morning. Enjoy your evening, gentlemen."

"Dinner will be ready in about an hour," Amy told them after Rich left. "Would you like to dine on the foredeck?"

"Sounds wonderful." Aiden turned to look at Sam, who nodded his approval.

"Do you need me to show you the stateroom?" she asked.

"I know the way. Thanks, Amy." Aiden turned to Sam after she left. "Well? How did I do?"

"Not bad." Sam did his best to keep a straight face. But then Aiden smiled, and Sam grabbed him and crushed his lips against

Aiden's. "Better than that," he said after the kiss broke. "Amazing, really."

"We have an hour. How about thanking me up close and personal." Aiden took Sam's hand once more and led him down a set of stairs to the cabins below.

THEY sat on the foredeck, having finished one of the best meals Sam had ever eaten. *Not that the starry sky and the company had anything to do with it.*

"Remind me to thank David next time I see him." Sam stood up and began to massage Aiden's shoulders.

"My fairy godfather."

Sam laughed.

"David's been too good to me." Aiden's voice was slightly wistful now. "Not only this, but he helped me out of a bad situation."

"Cam?"

"I'm not sure I'd have had the guts to move out if it hadn't been for David. Hell, I tried to find a place of my own in London and he told me to stay. Said he didn't spend much time there anyhow." Aiden leaned into Sam's hands, and Sam kissed him on the top of his head.

"You sound almost like you don't think you deserve his friendship."

Aiden's shoulders tensed beneath Sam's fingers. "Am I that obvious?"

"No."

"Sometimes I worry that I can't even begin to give back what he's given me."

Sam moved in front of Aiden and drew him up off the chair with a hug. "You don't give yourself enough credit, you know."

"You think?" Aiden's laugh was bitter.

Sam traced a line over Aiden's lips. "I think I could kick myself for letting you go. Twice."

Aiden's smile looked strained. "Are you sure you want this? I mean, there's a reason you let me go before. My lifestyle isn't exactly the best for long-term relationships."

"It was never about your lifestyle." Sam wasn't exactly sure how to explain his hesitation. "I just wasn't ready."

"You don't need to justify it, Sammy."

"I know. But I wish—"

"Here and now. That's what matters. Fuck the rest of it."

"Right." Sam inhaled a long slow breath and looked over the bow at the moon rising on the horizon. And yet he couldn't help but think of New Year's past. And of Nick. "You're right. Fuck the rest of it."

"Happy New Year, Sammy."

"Happy New Year, Aiden."

CHAPTER 15

Four months later

AIDEN teetered dangerously on the Windsurfer, having dropped the sail yet again. The water was cold, and he was glad he'd borrowed Sam's wetsuit. He'd fallen in more times than he could count. "Remind me why I'm doing this?"

"Because when you get the hang of it, it's a blast."

It was good to have Sam on the shore, cheering him on. Aiden would have given up an hour ago without Sam's encouragement. Aiden rolled his eyes and reached once more for the knotted rope to haul the sail out of the water.

"Bend your knees!" Sam shouted.

"Right." Aiden's back was killing him, but the sun felt good on his shoulders and the breeze off the water was warm.

"Pull it up slowly so that the water runs off as you pull. It's easier without all the water to weigh it down."

"Got it." Aiden bent his knees and pulled, more deliberately this time, and the sail lifted out of the water. It immediately caught the wind, and the board began to move, picking up speed.

"That's it!" Sam clapped his hands together. "Now grab the boom. No, not the mast, the boom!" He laughed and took off down the beach at a jog to keep up with Aiden as he moved over the water. "That's it! You got it!"

Aiden grinned and turned to wave at Sam. The board shifted under his feet as the boom swung wide, and, as he caught Sam's eye, he promptly lost his balance and fell into the water with a splash.

"You make it look so easy," Aiden moaned as they lay on the beach an hour later, wrapped in a blanket, back in dry clothing. "I'm going to be sore for a week after that."

"Next time, you won't be half as sore."

"*Next* time? You think there's going to be a next time?" Aiden rubbed his aching shoulder and silently told himself that there *was* going to be a next time. Sure, they'd only seen each other three times since David's party, but with each time they had spent together, his fear that Sam would disappear from his life again faded a bit more.

"Wimp! You just need to get the hang of pointing the sail."

"I'd rather watch *you* sail it around." Aiden rolled over and laid a sandy arm over Sam's stomach. "Where'd you learn to sail like that?"

"My folks sent me to a sailing camp not too far from here. Bought my own rig when I was in high school. It was a piece of crap, but I didn't care."

"I'd've taken you more for the football type."

"I played on the varsity team. Hated it with a passion. My dad played for Central too, when he was a kid. He didn't give me a choice."

"I tried out for the school team," Aiden said. "They told me I wasn't good enough. It's why I ended up signing up for drama club. It was a good thing—I figured out I could act. The drama teacher got me an audition for the opera program at Indiana University."

"How did you convince your parents to send you there? I thought they were against your singing?"

"I was eighteen, and IU offered me a full ride. My parents—my dad—never really forgave me for it."

Sam planted a sloppy kiss on Aiden's cheek. "Funny," he said, pulling Aiden against him, "how we spend our lives trying to please our parents and never quite manage to succeed in their eyes."

"I don't know. Seems like you've done okay for yourself. Your dad's a lawyer, right?"

"Yeah. But he wanted me to stay in Memphis."

"Jaz says your firm's one of the best in the Northeast for plaintiff's employment law. Isn't he happy with that?"

Sam sighed and held Aiden tighter. "It doesn't work that way. It took my folks almost two years to forgive me for not coming home after law school. I'm not sure my dad's ever forgiven me for not going to work for his firm. We've gotten to the point that we avoid talking about it."

"Did they know about you and Nick?"

"I came out to them my first year of law school. They really liked Nicky. Even came to his funeral. We used to spend Thanksgivings with my folks and Christmas with his."

Aiden had always assumed Sam's background was the same as his—that Sam's family either didn't know he was gay or didn't approve. "I thought your folks were Baptist."

"Methodist. Not that it matters much. Our church was pretty conservative. But my dad's from Michigan originally, so they were a little more open-minded."

"My dad and I don't get along. Last time I was home for Thanksgiving, we got into a huge fight. I haven't been back since."

He hadn't planned on sharing that with Sam—he didn't want Sam to think he was bitter—but he felt so comfortable talking like this. Still, he wasn't exactly going to explain what he and his father had fought about, either. Maybe someday, but not now.

"Sorry." Sam kissed Aiden's cheek. "Sounds bad."

"It's okay. I had pretty much figured that once I'd settled in Europe, I wouldn't see much of them."

Sam seemed to consider this, then asked, "It's not a problem, being openly bisexual? For your singing career?"

"Nah. Not really. I guess some folks have an issue with it, but there are so many gay men in the business.... It's crazy, but the breakup with Cam mostly helped my career."

"Must've been exciting, hanging out with royalty."

Aiden sat up and looked down at Sam, making sure Sam could see he was dead serious. "No. It wasn't. This—" He bent down to kiss Sam. "—is much better." More than anything, he wanted Sam to understand that.

"I'm glad." Sam smiled and Aiden knew he *had* understood.

"I'm done with that, Sam. I know we haven't talked about it, but I'm not seeing anyone else. I don't want to." He realized that it sounded like he was asking the same of Sam, and he added quickly, "But I don't... I mean, with all my traveling, I know I can't expect the same from y—"

Sam kissed Aiden into silence. "What would you think about making Philly your home port?" Aiden wasn't sure he'd heard correctly. "You don't have a place of your own right now, do you?"

"No. But—"

"I'd understand if you don't want to. I'm probably rushing things. And it's not like Philly is comparable to Paris or London."

"It's not that. It's just... are you sure?" Was Sam asking him to move in with him? After Sam's hesitation in Paris, Sam's offer that he move to Philly was the last thing he was expecting.

Sam's laugh was warm as he pulled Aiden on top of him. "Yes. I'm asking you to live with me—when you're not working, that is. I've been thinking about this since New Year's. You don't have to commit to anything long-term. We can call it a trial run, if you'd like."

Aiden forgot how to breathe. "I... yes." He laughed too. "I'd love that."

Their lips met in a tender kiss, and Aiden could see the truth in Sam's eyes. Sam really wanted this. *And so do I.*

CHAPTER *16*

Philadelphia
July

AIDEN returned to the States nearly three months later. He'd shipped a few things from David's apartment, at Sam's suggestion. David, of course, had wished him well and told him he always had a place to stay if he needed it.

Sam had depositions the day Aiden arrived from Italy, so Aiden took a cab from the airport and let himself into the apartment before Sam got home. It felt strange to think that he might call this place home. His last visit, he'd been a guest. But now....

Aiden set his suitcases down by the front door and walked across the living room to open the blinds on the sliding doors to the balcony. The late-July afternoon was warm, but there was a nice breeze, and he opened the glass doors. The sounds of traffic below felt familiar, comforting even. For a few minutes, Aiden looked out over the city, trying to get his bearings, more nervous than he ever remembered being about performing.

It's more convenient like this. Neither of them had confessed their love, although Aiden was pretty sure he already loved Sam. But this way they would have more time to explore the possibilities. It wasn't like with Cam, Aiden reminded himself. They weren't buying a house together or furnishing it. If Sam got tired of him, Aiden could just go back to Europe and move on.

Aiden wondered what Cam was up to. There had been a few more deliveries of flowers backstage at performances, but otherwise Aiden hadn't heard from Cam since Paris. The press had let up on trying to get more details of that too-public confrontation, and Aiden was happy he didn't have to work so hard to avoid them. Alexandria, too, seemed a thing of the past. There had been one very prominent article in one of the French magazines in which Alexandria's husband had been photographed at his wife's side, denying rumors of her involvement with Aiden. But the furor had died down, and Aiden was more than grateful.

Aiden's cell phone buzzed, and he smiled when he saw the caller's identity. "Hi, Sam."

"Got in okay?" Sam sounded tired. Aiden guessed the depositions had been particularly grueling. He made a mental note to make some dinner for them after he'd showered and changed.

"About ten minutes ago. The doorman was fine. Told me he was happy to hear I was moving in and said I should ask him if I needed anything."

"Great. I should be finished in about an hour. Make yourself at home."

"Thanks, Sam. See you then." Aiden tapped the phone and set it on the sleek glass table by the couch.

He liked this apartment, with its high-end Italian furniture and lighting. He liked the floor-to-ceiling windows of the living room and the way the diffuse sunlight seemed to dance over the walls and artwork. The place was so different from the Edwardian home he'd shared with Cam, and he was thankful for that. He needed a fresh start.

One of the clouds overhead shifted, and a brilliant ray of sunlight settled onto one of the abstract paintings on the wall. Nick's paintings. Aiden walked over to that one and studied it for a moment, noticing the textured surface. The oil paints had dried in peaks and valleys, giving the painting a feeling of movement and life. Even with as little knowledge of art as he had, Aiden knew Nick had been supremely gifted. He wondered what Nick had been like.

I wonder what you'd think of me, Nick.

Aiden knew Nick had never lived in this apartment, and yet he could feel the man's presence here as surely as if he had. It wasn't only the paintings or the photographs of Nick and Sam that stood next to those of Sam's family. He could sense Nick's presence in Sam, and it frightened him. Or perhaps it wasn't Nick's presence, but his *absence* Aiden felt in Sam. Nick was there in the photographs and the paintings, and yet Sam had barely mentioned Nick since he'd told Aiden about him months ago.

"You need to be patient with him," David told Aiden after he'd shared the news that he was moving in with Sam. "It takes time to let go."

"It's been seven years since Nick died."

"You never forget the pain of losing someone you love. You simply move on and accept things. It's even more difficult when you lose someone so young."

"I understand." Aiden's words were whispered, almost reverent. How many times had he tried to put himself in Sam's shoes and try to understand his pain? "I can't imagine how hard that must have been for him."

"Talk to him about it. People are often afraid it will make things worse, but it doesn't. He'll want to talk about Nicholas. I myself wanted to speak of Helena after her death. I simply didn't realize it until much later."

Aiden had almost forgotten that David had been married to a woman. It was hard to think of David with anyone but his partner, Alex. Helena, like Nick, had died far too young.

"I'm so sorry, David. I forgot."

"There's no need to apologize. I'm happy to remember her now. But it wasn't always that way for me. It takes time."

Aiden picked up one of the photos of Sam with the smiling Nick. He recognized New York Harbor in the background and guessed it had been taken at Battery Park. He traced Sam's strong jaw with his thumb and studied Nick's eyes. Warm, full of life, loving. He could see it in the photograph, the love Nick had for Sam.

Aiden sighed. Of course he would give Sam time.

THE door to the apartment opened a little before seven and Sam walked in carrying a large paper bag, his briefcase slung over one shoulder.

"Welcome home!" Aiden took the bag from Sam and gave him a brief kiss.

The smell of Chinese food wafted into the apartment as Aiden set down the parcel on the table by the door.

"You cooked dinner?"

Aiden chuckled and shook his head. "I should have told you. I'm sorry, that was stupid of me."

"No harm, no foul. Takeout Chinese tastes ten times better the next day, anyhow."

"I'll go put it in the fridge." Aiden felt like a complete idiot. Of course he should have told Sam. What was he thinking? "The chicken will be done in about ten minutes, if you want to change. Or if you want to shower, I can turn down the temperature and—"

Sam kissed Aiden, lacing his arms around Aiden's waist before Aiden could scoop up the Chinese food. It was an awkward gesture, but it took the edge off Aiden's discomfort. "Damn, Aiden," he said a moment later. "It's so good to have you here."

"It's good to *be* here."

"I'm sorry I couldn't meet you at the airport."

"I don't mind. Besides, if I'm going to be living here, there'll be plenty of times when you won't be able to meet me. I don't want you worrying about it."

Sam's smile was warm. "You're right. It's only that I wanted everything to be good for you."

Aiden had been feeling as though he'd already managed to screw things up, but relaxed at these words. "It *is* good. I mean it. It's funny, but coming here by myself today made it feel more like home. You know, using my own key to let myself in, cooking dinner."

"I'm glad."

The oven timer began to beep. "You go get comfortable," Aiden said, picking up the takeout, "and I'll get dinner on the table, okay?"

"Okay." Sam kissed Aiden on the cheek and headed for the bedroom.

DINNER was a resounding success. "This is so much better than Chinese," Sam told Aiden. "I rarely have time to cook. I think I could get used to home-cooked meals after a long day at the office."

Aiden thought he could get used to someone to cook for. "I don't miss having a regular job. I still practice every day, but it's so much better than having to drag myself into work." He took a sip of his wine and smiled. "Not that I ever had a job like yours, where I was the boss."

"It's a nice change of pace. The first couple of years were tough, though. I spent most weekends in the office doing the billing. I hired a bookkeeper and office manager a few years ago, once I was sure we'd survive. Now the business end of things basically runs itself." He put his hand over Aiden's and added, "Which gives me a little more time to spend at the beach."

As always, Aiden and Sam found plenty to talk about—Aiden's latest contracts, Sam's race discrimination case that seemed headed for trial, despite offers to settle. News from Jules and Jason, Sam's family.

"Let me do the dishes," Sam said after they'd cleared the table, nearly two hours later.

"I can do it."

"House rule. Whoever cooks gets a pass from cleaning up."

Aiden's shoulders tensed at the words. "Sure." He did his best to look as though it really was fine. Still, he couldn't help but wonder if it had been a house rule when Sam and Nick had lived together.

"I'll meet you in bed in a few minutes." Sam gave Aiden a quick kiss on the cheek and turned on the water.

"Sounds good."

Aiden undressed, put his clothes away, and stood in front of the bed. Strange—he didn't know which side of the bed to sleep on. He hadn't thought about it before, the little things that he'd taken for granted with Cam. He knew it shouldn't matter, but he didn't want to screw this up. It felt almost comical, worrying about something so inane. They'd have plenty of time to work things out.

In the end he decided on the side that was not next to the alarm. If it was a problem, Sam would tell him. He bunched up the pillow under his neck and shifted around a few times, trying to get comfortable, wishing he'd shipped his pillow with the other things he'd sent ahead. He'd slept in so many hotel rooms—why was it so difficult to feel at home here?

I'm tired and I'm jet-lagged. I need to relax and stop worrying. It's going to be fine.

He closed his eyes, figuring he'd rest until Sam got into bed. He knew he wouldn't be up for strenuous sex, but he was looking forward to something slow and sensual. It had been too long since he'd seen Sam. He needed the added reassurance of Sam's arms around him, Sam's body next to his. He didn't plan on falling asleep, but the next thing he knew, it was morning and Aiden was left with only the memory of a sleepy kiss before he woke up alone.

CHAPTER 17

"HEY." Aiden looked up from the newspaper as Sam walked into the apartment, carrying half a dozen grocery bags.

"Here, let me help you." Aiden took a few of the bags from Sam and set them down on the kitchen counter. He peered inside one of the bags. It was filled with an assortment of fruits. "These look incredible."

"Farmer's market on Saturday morning. I try to get there early, before the good stuff's gone."

Aiden wished Sam had woken him up so he could have gone as well, but he said only, "When I lived in Hamburg, I used to go to the open-air market every week. Of course, I had an apartment there, so I could cook."

"You'll have to come next week." Sam set some of the vegetables in a basket on the counter.

"Thanks." Aiden walked up behind Sam and slid his arms around Sam's waist, kissing him on the back of his neck. "You're welcome to wake me up the next time."

Sam shivered in response, then turned to face Aiden.

Aiden shifted his balance from left foot to right, trying to get up his nerve to say what had been on his mind since he'd woken up alone. "I'm sorry about last night. I didn't mean to fall asleep. I guess I was more jet-lagged than I realized."

"Honestly, I was so exhausted myself, I don't think I'd have been able to stay awake, either. But we do have the entire day together, without interruptions...." He trailed off, and Aiden saw more than a hint of lust reflected in his eyes.

Aiden pushed away the lingering anxiety and pulled Sam roughly against him, claiming his lips, claiming him.

"Oh, fuck," Sam hissed.

Aiden led Sam into the living room, then pushed him until the back of his knees hit the edge of the leather sofa. "When's the last time you had sex in the living room?" Aiden pulled Sam's T-shirt over his head.

"Never?" There was a breathless quality to Sam's laughter.

"Good." Aiden shoved Sam playfully onto the couch. He was already hard in anticipation. It had been too long, and the thought of taking Sam here…. "Because I'm tired of jerking off in the shower, thinking about how hot it would be to fuck you."

"Glad I wasn't the only one having those thoughts," Sam said as Aiden grabbed his sweats and yanked them off along with his briefs. "And you know I like the naked Sam, fully dressed Aiden thing."

Aiden knelt down by the couch and, starting with Sam's toes, slowly licked his way over Sam's skin. He could taste a hint of soap along with the slight saltiness there. Sam smelled good, with no hint of cologne or aftershave: just an unadulterated masculine scent. Subtle. Distinctly Sam's. Aiden had tried to imagine that scent when they'd been apart with little success.

Sam's legs were covered in fine hairs, softer than Aiden's. They tickled Aiden's upper lip as he slid his tongue over the side of Sam's calf. He bent and lifted Sam's knee to lick behind it. Sam rewarded him with a low moan. "Damn. Do they teach you that in music school?"

"You wish." Aiden chuckled as he parted Sam's legs and moved inward. Teasing Sam but not claiming the prize of his erection. Circling. Biding his time.

Sam arched toward him in a silent plea.

"Not yet, baby. I want you begging." He could sense Sam's control beginning to falter. *That's it, Sammy. Let me see what's underneath that calm personality.* He opened Sam's legs wider and moved so that he knelt between them before tasting Sam's inner thighs, coming oh so close to Sam's balls but not touching them. He slipped his hands under the globes of Sam's ass, wedging them between skin and leather. His own cock ached beneath his pajama bottoms. He felt the small bottle of lube and the condom he'd stashed in one of the pockets, and he couldn't help but grin.

"What?" Sam had clearly noticed Aiden's smug expression. "You know something I don't know?"

"I might." Aiden pulled out the lube and turned it from side to side, imitating a twisted version of a spokesperson on late night TV. "But I'm not going to use it unless you beg me to."

"You're cruel."

"Nope. Just practical."

"God, Aiden. I want you."

Aiden nipped at Sam's thigh, then leaned over and licked his abdomen, flicking his tongue and pressing it into Sam's belly button. "What do you want, Sammy?"

"I want you to fuck me. Please. Fuck me, Aiden."

"That's better."

Sam grabbed Aiden's head, guided him upward, and claimed a kiss in blatant rebellion. "Two can play at this game," he said with a growl.

"Are you this hard to beat in court?" Aiden turned Sam's head and nipped at his earlobe.

"Worse. You should have seen what happened when I—"

Aiden squeezed Sam's cock as he leaned down and took one of Sam's nipples between his teeth.

"Oh. Shit."

"Beg me again."

Sam canted his hips up into Aiden's hand. "Fuck me, Aiden. Please. Make me come with you inside me."

"See? That wasn't so hard, was it?"

"Stop talking, Lind," Sam teased, "or I—"

Aiden turned his attention to Sam's other nipple, biting a bit harder this time. Then he uncapped the lube and poured it into his palms. He rubbed them together until the liquid warmed. He took Sam's cock in one hand while he continued to nip and suck. Sam's moans echoed through the living room.

"Aiden," Sam warned. "Gonna come. It's been way too long."

But Aiden had already released his grip. He slipped a lubed finger inside Sam's hole, stretching him. "Good?" he asked.

Sam only nodded and gasped in response as Aiden worked two more fingers inside. Aiden was at his limit now. He withdrew his fingers long enough to slip on the condom. A moment later he was moaning and buried inside Sam, reveling in the feel of Sam's tight passage. He moved with slow, deliberate strokes, stopping from time to time to catch his breath.

"It's been too fucking long." He loved it this way—face-to-face, so he could see Sam's expression, hear his stuttered inhalations, watch his body as it shook each time he thrust.

Sam bit his lower lip and reached between them to stroke himself but never broke eye contact. Aiden shifted slightly to change the angle and Sam cried out as Aiden brushed his prostate with his tip. "Aiden. Oh, yes… I…."

Aiden let out a half laugh, half sigh. He watched as Sam finally gave in, closed his eyes, and made the face Aiden remembered when they'd had sex in Alabama. Sam opened his mouth and sucked his lower lip in, holding it in place with his teeth. Some of his blond curls had fallen onto his forehead, and tiny beads of sweat were visible there, pinning the curls in place.

Aiden pushed back inside, nailing Sam's gland again and again with each thrust. He could feel Sam's legs tremble, pressed against his chest as they were, wedged between them. He snuck one hand down and pinched Sam's nipple so hard he cried out.

"What do you want, baby?" Aiden asked. "What do you want me to do to you?"

"Fuck me harder. Make me come."

"Say my name when you come, Sammy. Say my name." He thrust harder, faster. "Come on, baby."

"Fuck. Oh, fuck! Aiden! I'm coming." Sam convulsed beneath him and shuddered.

Aiden kept moving, but it didn't take him long, not with the heat of Sam's release between them. "God, Sammy! So fucking good!" He pushed all the way inside and threw his head back. He came with a shout, then nearly collapsed onto Sam, stopping himself at the last minute and helping Sam straighten his legs. He pulled Sam close and rolled them onto their sides so they both fit on the couch.

Sam sighed audibly. "God, Aiden. I missed you so much."

"I know." Aiden's voice was barely a whisper. "I missed you too."

"YOU sleeping?" Sam liked the idea that he might have had something to do with the peaceful, sated expression on Aiden's face.

"Nope. Basking." Aiden rolled over and ghosted his lips over Sam's.

"Basking?"

"Like a snake." He laughed and began to lick a line up Sam's jaw, found his ear and nibbled at the lobe.

"God, Aiden, you're going to wear me out!" Sam didn't really mean it—another round of sex sounded fine to him. Better than fine. He could get used to this.

"You complaining?"

"Shut up and kiss me." Aiden straddled him and leaned down to nip at his chest, looking up from time to time with a wicked grin.

"You're going to make me beg for it again, aren't you?"

"Why not?"

"*Please* kiss me." Sam took a deep breath and waited.

Aiden laughed, then obliged, his chest pressed against Sam's, pinning Sam beneath his body.

"Better?" Aiden asked.

"Better."

Aiden gazed down at him with a strange look in his eyes. Then, as if gathering his courage, he drew a long breath and said, "I think I'm in love with you, Sammy."

Heat rushed to Sam's cheeks. "Glad to hear it"—Sam tried his best to lessen his discomfort—"because I think I love you too."

CHAPTER *18*

Akron, Ohio
August

"MR. LIND! Mr. Lind!"

Aiden turned around, nearly knocking over one of the stage crew. The space backstage was supremely narrow; the old theater was simply not built to accommodate the number of performers moving about during the scene change between acts. There was only one reason the venue had never been torn down and replaced with a new one: there were few theaters around with the acoustics of the Frank George Theater.

Aiden made his way over to his costuming assistant, a round woman with pink cheeks and the patience of a saint. She wasn't a professional by any means but volunteered at the theater when she wasn't working as a curator for the local county library. It had been years since Aiden had sung in such a small venue, but he'd taken the job as a favor to a director friend who was trying to garner financial support for a new production of *Prince Igor*, a seldom-performed Russian opera.

The opening night performance, in spite of many technical glitches, had been well received, but Aiden was happy tonight's performance would be the last. He was looking forward to leaving southern Ohio behind and flying back to Philadelphia to spend a few days with Sam before rehearsals for his next gig in Rome.

"Sorry, Charlene, did I manage to step on my sash again?"

She laughed and followed him back to the dressing room, which wasn't much larger than a closet. "No," she said as she busied herself trying to straighten the multitude of medals pinned to the front of his jacket. "But Mindy says she's got a delivery out back with your name on it. Flowers. I wasn't sure, you know, if you might be allergic, and I didn't want to take the chance."

Aiden smiled and thought once more of Sam and how he might thank him for his thoughtfulness. "You can put them in here, if you can find a free spot."

She returned five minutes later with an enormous vase filled with red roses, and handed him the card.

> *Sweetheart—*
> *You're quite a difficult one to catch up with these days. David tells me you've moved to Philadelphia, but he wouldn't give me any more information. I daresay he's angry with me after my pathetic performance in Paris last year. He's right to be. Let's talk soon. I miss you. I was an idiot.*
> *Call me,*
> *Cam*

Aiden balled the card up into a wad. Disappointment mingled with guilt at the realization that it hadn't been Sam who'd sent the flowers. *It doesn't matter. I don't need him to send flowers to know he's thinking of me.*

Still, he'd been happy for just a moment to think it *had* been Sam who'd sent them. He *wished* it had been Sam for so many reasons, not the least of which was that he still felt insecure about their fledgling relationship and being gone again so soon after moving in. Sam and he had talked nearly every night since he'd been gone, but the conversation had been stiff, and Aiden couldn't help but wonder if Sam was having second thoughts.

Charlene stuck an extra pin in his wig, which had slipped backward on his forehead a bit. "I'm flying out tomorrow." He managed to smile back at her in the mirror. "Why don't you take them home so someone gets to enjoy them."

She beamed. Aiden wondered how Cam might react to the knowledge that a middle-aged woman from a small town in the

Midwest would be enjoying the outrageously expensive flowers. Charlene could scarcely afford them.

That's not fair. Cam meant the gesture, even if it's lost on me. Which led Aiden back to the thought that he'd have been okay if Sam had called before the performance to wish him luck.

AIDEN arrived back in Philadelphia around noon the next day. Sam was folding clothes on top of the dryer and gave him a quick peck on the cheek when he rolled his suitcase into the bedroom. Aiden dropped the bag on a chair and lay back on the bed, kicking his shoes off and closing his eyes.

He didn't mean to fall asleep, but he'd been too wound up—and too nervous about seeing Sam again the next day—to sleep much the night before. He awoke to Sam unpacking his things and setting his shoes in the closet.

"You don't need to do that," Aiden said. "I can put that away." To call Sam a neat freak was an understatement. Not that Aiden was a slob, but he didn't feel the need to put things away the second he got home, either.

"No problem." Sam carried Aiden's dirty clothes over to the washing machine. "I can toss these in the wash with my stuff. There weren't enough whites to do a full load. Better for the environment."

Aiden watched as Sam disappeared. He took a deep breath and stared up at the ceiling. There was no dust on the ceiling fan, he realized with another stab of guilt. Since they'd been living together, Aiden had yet to dust or vacuum. Not that he'd been "home" all that much. He hauled himself out of bed and joined Sam in the hallway, where the washer and dryer were normally hidden behind a louvered door. Sam was pouring detergent into the washing machine.

"Can I help fold?"

Sam looked a bit surprised but shrugged and said, "Sure."

"I always wanted to help my mom do the laundry," Aiden admitted as he took an undershirt from the basket and folded it neatly. "She wouldn't let me. Said it was woman's work. My first college roommate taught me. I think he got tired of how bad I smelled."

Sam shook his head and chuckled. "We were supposed to wash our own, growing up. But we all wanted to do it on the weekend, so we'd trade off weeks. Then I washed one of my sisters' white dresses with a red T-shirt. Savannah nearly strangled me. After that my mom ended up doing laundry for all of us."

"Were you close to your sisters, growing up?"

"I guess. We're probably closer now. We see each other a few times a year. Which reminds me," Sam added quickly. "I usually go down to Memphis over Thanksgiving. I'd like you to come with me. Only if it's okay with you, of course... I mean, I know you're in town, but if you don't want to—"

"I'd love to," Aiden interrupted. It wasn't true—it scared him half to death. Still, he knew how much Sam's family meant to him, and he figured the "meet the in-laws" rite of passage wasn't something he could avoid forever.

At least he wants *me to meet them.* He figured that was a good thing.

Sam's response was to take him in his arms and kiss him on the lips. "They're good people." Sam's tone was reassuring, although Aiden sensed that Sam, too, was nervous about the prospect of introducing him to his family. "I've told them a little about you. My mom loves opera. I think she's been telling the entire neighborhood about you."

Aiden wasn't sure this made him feel any better, but he said nothing, instead hugging Sam and pressing his lips to Sam's neck.

It'll be fine if he's with me.

Sam turned back to the pile of socks in the laundry basket and grinned. But before Aiden could ask Sam what was so funny, Sam had taken a handful of unpaired socks and tossed them at Aiden. Taken by surprise, Aiden raised his hands and managed to catch several of them. Two others landed on the floor, and a third landed on Aiden's head.

Aiden raised a quizzical eyebrow and bit the inside of his cheek. "You are so going to pay for that one, Samuel Ryan."

"I don't know. I think you look very sophisticated with a sock on your head." The challenge in Sam's eyes was obvious.

Aiden feinted right, pretending to aim for the basket full of socks. Sam moved to block him, but Aiden slipped around him on the other side, grabbed the basket, and proceeded to launch socks in Sam's direction.

"You lied when you said you couldn't play football." Sam brushed one of the socks off his shoulder as another hit him square in the face.

"I'm multitalented." Aiden threw three socks at once, but this time Sam was ready. He launched himself at Aiden's waist, tackling him and pulling him down onto the carpet. The basket of socks tumbled out of Aiden's hands and fell on top of them. Laughing harder than he could remember, Aiden pulled a sock off the floor and placed it over Sam's eyes. Sam grabbed Aiden's head and ignored the sock blindfold until he'd thoroughly kissed Aiden into submission.

"Okay! You win, you win!" Aiden's words were punctuated by another kiss, this one rougher, more demanding than the last.

Sam reached down and pulled Aiden's T-shirt over his head. "Need to wash this." Sam held up the offending shirt with a smirk. "And we need to get you out of those sweats too. Really dirty."

Aiden reached beneath his ass and held up a white sock. "Missed one."

All thoughts of Memphis and Sam's family vanished as Aiden helped Sam out of his clothes and they both walked naked through a trail of socks into the bedroom.

CHAPTER 19

Philadelphia
September

"YVETTE," Sam shouted as he strode through the waiting room doors and down the hallway, "I need you!"

A woman dressed in a pin-striped suit poked her head out of one of the offices. "I'm here, Sammy. What's up?"

"Judge Sheridan needs an order on our motion to compel. Gave me until after lunch to hand it up to him. He said he'll let me inspect ShareCo's documents in camera this afternoon."

"No continuance?" Yvette Sarandon rolled her eyes. "Bastard. He really hates you, doesn't he?"

"Yvette—"

"Don't tell me you don't know why he treats you like this. He may be a federal judge, but he's still a homophobic, bigoted, pompous...." She took a deep breath.

Sam shrugged. "At least he's letting me look at the documents. That's an improvement. Tell the new intern—what's her name, Sherri?—that I need her to tag along this afternoon. Make sure you give her the court library copy card. I'll need her to make copies."

"No problem. I'll draft the order for you."

"Thanks. I'll need your eyes. Jim too, if he's free." Sam motioned to his assistant before he walked into his office. "Peggy, can you order us a few sandwiches? Looks like it's going to be a long night. You don't need to stay if you've got plans."

"I can stay if you need me, Mr. Ryan," Sam's assistant said brightly. "I could use the OT, and Bob's out of town, anyhow."

"Thanks. And it's Sam," Sam corrected.

She just smiled back at him and shook her head, then picked up the phone.

SAM left the courthouse around midnight, bleary-eyed from poring over documents. "Thanks again, guys," he told Jim and Yvette. "We'll regroup in the morning. Jury selection probably won't happen next week, but we'll need to prepare for trial, anyhow." With what they'd discovered in their review of the defendant's files, Sam guessed the case would be settling, and quickly.

By the time Sam finally made it back home, it was one in the morning. He hadn't checked his cell until he walked in the door and thought about Aiden. He'd called when Sam had been eating.

Shit. You said you'd call him back.

He exhaled audibly, then tossed his jacket onto a chair, loosened his tie, and tapped the icon on his phone.

"Sam? Are you okay?" Aiden sounded half-asleep and very concerned.

"Oh, crap. I forgot about the time difference. I'm sorry. I woke you up, didn't I?"

"S'okay. I was going to get up in an hour, anyhow. What the hell time is it there?"

"One. I just got back from court."

"*Court?* At one in the morning?" Aiden yawned into the receiver.

"Long story." Sam proceeded to tell Aiden about the attorney for the corporation Sam's client had sued for sexual harassment and how Sam had finally gotten the judge to intervene to force the corporation to turn over documents it had been withholding. Throughout the long explanation, Aiden grunted in acknowledgment from time to time, although Sam was left with the distinct impression that Aiden wasn't listening.

"How about you?" Sam figured he'd best change the topic before he lulled Aiden back to sleep.

"I'm good."

Sam waited for Aiden to say more, but he yawned again. "Listen"—Sam cradled the phone between his chin and shoulder as he poured himself a scotch—"I should probably take a shower and head to bed. We have a conference in the morning with the judge."

"Sure." There was an uncomfortable pause before Aiden added, "Thanks for calling."

"Love you."

"Love you too."

Sam set down the phone and leaned back on the couch, swirling the thick liquid around in the glass and watching the legs run down the sides. Damn, but he wished Aiden were here. Not that he'd have seen much of him, but the thought of climbing into bed alone wasn't all that appealing. It wasn't about the sex—not that he'd have turned down an offer to fuck Aiden into the sheets or vice versa—but he missed the companionship after a long day. It had been something he'd loved when he and Nick were together: falling asleep in each other's arms.

He ran a hand through his hair and yawned, then kicked off his shoes and lay back on one of the pillows, feet dangling over the end of the couch. He awoke the next morning with the sunlight streaming in from the balcony and a crick in his neck, still fully dressed.

Three weeks later

AIDEN unwrapped his philly cheesesteak and inhaled the scent of onions and beef. "Smells amazing. Now if I can only figure out how to get the thing into my mouth without dribbling all over myself, life would be perfect."

Sam laughed and looked back at him with that warm, fuzzy expression that made Aiden want to both hug him and rip his clothes off. They were standing at a wobbly metal table barely big enough to put their sandwiches on, their shoes touching on the rough concrete floor. However tempting the thought, though, Aiden figured he'd better hold on to it for now.

It was Saturday, and they'd gone sightseeing in downtown Philly, spending the morning at the Franklin Institute and then heading over to Ninth Street for lunch. Aiden had arrived the night before for a three-day layover—it was too short a visit to call it anything but—before he left for a three-week stint in LA as Iago in Verdi's *Otello*.

Aiden had been struck by how tired Sam looked, but Sam reassured him that preparing for a big trial always wiped him out. Even the apartment, usually immaculate, was a bit less well-kept. For the first time since Aiden had moved in, Sam hadn't put away his shoes the minute Aiden walked through the door. The place felt a lot more like home than it had on the last few visits.

"Still trying to get those documents?"

"I got most of them. At some point, it's not worth fighting over. Just pisses the judges off, and I think we've got what we need." Sam reached across the table and swiped a bit of dribble off Aiden's chin with his thumb. The heat in Aiden's cheeks was from a mix of embarrassment and the usual thrum of desire he felt when Sam touched him. "It's good having you home."

Aiden's chest tightened with Sam's words. "It's good to be home." And damn. It really was.

CHAPTER *20*

Memphis, Tennessee
November

AIDEN took a deep breath as he stepped out of the rental car and followed Sam up the front walkway to the Ryans' Memphis home. It had been a chilly forty degrees when they'd left Philly that morning. Here it was nearly sixty already, and it was barely noon. The grass in front of the single-story brick house was still green, and pink flowers clung stubbornly to a tall crape myrtle in the center of the half-moon drive. A single electric candle shone, perfectly placed, in every window. The red double door at the entrance to the house was already hung with festive greenery in anticipation of the Christmas season. Aiden saw a huge fully decorated tree through the front bay window, as well as the corner of a mantel draped with more pine swags and perfectly formed velvet bows in a deep red.

The East Memphis neighborhood was reminiscent of Aiden's parents' neighborhood in Mississippi, though it was obviously more expensive with its well-manicured lawns, bushes trimmed to a millimeter's precision, and driveways lined in brick. Aiden caught a glimpse of a shiny BMW sedan and matching SUV in the carport. These observations did little to quiet his already jittery nerves. The Ryans clearly were more than several steps up from the Linds on the economic ladder.

Sam must have sensed Aiden's renewed apprehension, because he met Aiden's gaze and smiled, squeezing his shoulder in a tacit gesture of reassurance. It helped. It always helped to know Sam was there with him. Still, Aiden couldn't help feeling as if this performance was far more important than any appearance he'd ever made singing, and yet it was the only one he hadn't been able to prepare for.

"Just be yourself," Sam had told him as the plane landed. Aiden wasn't sure if that meant he should be Aiden the hick or Aiden the opera singer. He hadn't wanted Sam to worry, so he hadn't pressed the issue. He was sure Sam was a little nervous too. He could tell by the way he kept running his hands through his hair as they drove the twenty-five minutes from the airport. They'd barely spoken in the car.

"Samuel!" A graceful woman with silvery blond hair neatly pinned back in a bun peered out of the now open doorway.

Sam let go of Aiden's shoulder and planted a graceful kiss on his mother's cheek. "Mother, you look wonderful. You always do."

The formality of both the greeting and Sam's words surprised Aiden. It seemed in stark contrast to Sam's usual warmth. He'd just assumed Sam's family would be the same—easygoing and relaxed.

"Mrs. Ryan," Aiden said, stepping forward and offering her his hand, "I'm Aiden Lind. Very pleased to meet you."

Claudia Ryan's handshake was as measured as her expression. Not unfriendly exactly, but hardly the warmest greeting Aiden had ever received. He reminded himself that he'd felt the same way the first time he'd met David Somers—awkward and self-conscious—and he figured he shouldn't make too much of it. David had become one of his closest friends, after all.

"We're happy you're joining us, Aiden." She motioned them both inside. Even her slight Southern drawl was polished and understated. Sophisticated.

Aiden had expected the interior of the house to be impressive, given what he'd seen outside. He wasn't disappointed. The front hallway had a vaulted ceiling with a modern chandelier suspended from the highest point, marble tile on the floor, and several understated watercolors hung on the walls.

From this vantage point, Aiden could better see the living room he'd glimpsed through the window. A fire roared in the fireplace. White pile carpet blanketed the floor. The furniture was typically Southern with Queen Anne influences, the porcelain knickknacks perfectly placed. The only similarity to the apartment Aiden shared with Sam was the extraordinary neatness. No. "Neat" didn't cover it—fastidious, maybe. Meticulous. Aiden made a mental note not to leave his shoes in the vestibule overnight.

"Please," Mrs. Ryan said, "have a seat. I'll bring you both some sweet tea."

"Thank you," they chorused in reply. Aiden thought a good shot of bourbon might be a better option. He hadn't been this nervous since his first audition after college.

"You doing okay?" Sam asked as Claudia left them alone.

"I'm fine." Aiden sat down on the overstuffed couch, felt the down filling deflate beneath his ass, and tried not to laugh. He wondered if it'd leave an indentation after he got up. He thought briefly about the plastic covers his grandmother used to put on the sofa and love seat when he and his sister came to visit.

Stop it! He bit his lip and repressed a snort.

Sam must have noticed his odd behavior, because he took Aiden's hand and squeezed. "I know she's a bit intimidating when you first meet her," he said in a low voice, "but she warms up with time."

IT WAS not, Aiden thought in retrospect, a bad first meeting as first meetings go. Sam's mother returned with sweet tea garnished with fresh mint and tiny cucumber sandwiches with the edges cut off. She then proceeded to engage both of them in polite conversation ranging from the warm Memphis weather to the Memphis Symphony's recent concert season.

"You should sing with them, Aiden," she murmured. "They're a fine orchestra."

He smiled in return and thanked her for the suggestion.

Aiden's own mother would have been impressed with Claudia Ryan's grace under pressure. Aiden didn't doubt the woman was on her best behavior with him. She clearly adored Sam—worshipped him, from what Aiden could tell—and she just as clearly wanted to like *him*.

Later he and Sam went out to the car to fetch their suitcases, as Claudia put it, then took a few minutes to relax in the guest bedroom. Aiden had to smile at the twin beds.

"It's no reflection on you." Sam locked the door behind them and stole a very relieved kiss. "My folks sleep in separate beds." He nuzzled Aiden's neck, then added in a throaty growl, "The good news is that their bedroom's on the other side of the house. If you're good—" He nibbled Aiden's ear. "—you can come over and play." He patted the bed suggestively.

For the first time that day, Aiden relaxed, melding his body against Sam's and holding him. "I want them to like me." He had a hard time admitting it. He felt so vulnerable, so unsure of himself here, knowing Sam's family was watching his every move. "I know how important it is to you."

Sam sat down on the bed, and Aiden tumbled on top of him. "I want them to like you. But it wouldn't matter if they hated you. I love you, Aiden. That's what's important."

Aiden wanted to protest, to tell Sam that it *would* matter if his family detested him, but Sam rolled him over and began to unbutton his jeans. The next thing he knew, Sam had taken him into his mouth, and Aiden was struggling not to cry out.

"You're evil, Samuel Ryan," he hissed, keenly aware that Sam's mother was only a few rooms away working on dinner and that Sam's father would be coming home any minute now.

Sam released Aiden for a moment. "I love it when you moan."

Aiden bit his cheek so hard, he could taste a hint of copper on his tongue. He pulled a pink frou-frou monstrosity off the pile of ruffled floral and lace throw-pillows on the bed and put it over his mouth to stifle the low growl that slipped from his lips. This was one time he cursed his resonant voice.

"I want to fuck you," Sam said as he came up for breath.

Aiden only had sex in his parents' house once, and it was one of the hottest memories he had of high school. They'd nearly gotten caught, too, he and Joey Stanhope. If it hadn't been for the barking dog next door.... "God, yes," he said, trying to focus as Sam nipped at his crown and cupped his balls. "Fuck me, Sammy."

Sam released his cock long enough to say, "Not before I make you come."

"Works for me." Aiden gasped as Sam took his cock deep in his mouth and sucked hard. He wasn't sure where Sam had gotten the lube from—had he thought so far ahead that he'd stashed it in his pants pocket?—but then Sam slid slippery fingers over his hole, breaching him a tiny bit, then pushing harder inside and brushing his gland.

It was just too much, the anxiety of coming here, meeting Sam's family, knowing they were doing this in the same house as Sam's parents—Aiden came far faster than he'd planned, into Sam's hot mouth. He pulled Sam up and kissed him hard, partly to muffle his own moans and partly because he wanted—*needed*—to taste Sam. Tasting himself on Sam's lips made it that much better.

A minute later, he was facedown, pressed into the pile of pillows, with Sam's gorgeous cock up his ass. He couldn't help but chuckle to wonder what Claudia Ryan would think if she knew what they were doing, and he thanked God Sam wasn't as uptight as his mother seemed.

"Christ, Aiden, you feel so good." Sam's fingers dug into Aiden's hips, the sting only serving to intensify the disembodied feeling Aiden had happily settled into. Like this, he could forget about trying to be someone he wasn't. With Sam, he could be himself.

Sam slipped a hand under Aiden and took a nipple between thumb and forefinger and pinched it hard, the way Aiden liked it. Sam liked to joke it was an On switch for Aiden's cock. Today was no exception. The sting made his cock reawaken with a twitch. Aiden shifted his weight onto his left arm and took his cock in his right fist. "You're going to make me come again this way," he warned playfully.

"Just try to avoid shooting into the chintz mountain." Sam said, laughing outright. "Might be hard to explain why my mother's pillows are crunchy."

"I'll do my best—"

Sam pulled out and shoved back hard, then grabbed Aiden's ass.

Aiden whimpered. Whatever their issues, whatever the distance between them, sex between them was always great.

"I've got a special Christmas gift for you." Sam teased Aiden with long, slow strokes. He bent down near Aiden's ear, his chest against Aiden's back. "So I can pinch your nipples and squeeze your ass at the same time."

"Oh, shit. Sammy… stop it. I'm having a hard enough time not… ahhh… yelling… here." Sam had been threatening to buy him a set of nipple clamps for the past few months. In no time Aiden was hard just from thinking about Sam putting the clamps on him, maybe twisting them or pulling on them.

He loved that Sam was willing to try almost anything. They hadn't spoken about it, but he'd guessed that Sam had always wanted to try a little kink and maybe Nick hadn't been the type. He'd sensed it the first time they'd slept together, six years before. He decided he'd get Sam a Christmas present he'd remember too.

"Thinking about… my… present?" With each word, Sam thrust a bit harder.

Aiden knew he was grinning like an idiot now. He tightened his muscles around Sam and heard Sam's stuttered breath in response.

"You are *so* going to pay for that." Sam ratcheted up the pace.

"Oh, fuck!" This time Aiden shoved his hand in his mouth, whimpering again and panting, hoping he wasn't making as much noise as he thought he was.

They were both coming a minute later—Sam first, followed by Aiden, who hoped it was only his hand covered in spunk and not the bedding. As Sam hopped off the bed to retrieve a towel he'd apparently hidden under the pillows, Aiden rolled onto his back and shook his head. "You're evil, Ryan. I'm sure your mother could hear us."

Sam wiped himself and Aiden before climbing back onto the bed, his ass coming to rest over the edge. "Nah." Sam shot Aiden a look of smug satisfaction. "If she's in the kitchen cooking, she'll have NPR cranked up loud enough she wouldn't hear you if you yelled. Her hearing's terrible."

"Why you little…!" Aiden pulled Sam closer and pretended to hit him on the head.

"Yeah. I know. But it was twice as hot thinking we'd get caught, wasn't it?"

Aiden let out an audible breath.

"SO, AIDEN," Samuel Stetson Ryan III said as they sat down to dinner a few hours later, "my son tells me you're quite the singer."

Aiden smiled and smoothed the cloth napkin on his lap, then nearly jumped as he felt Sam's leg press against his thigh. "Thank you, sir," he answered, supremely uncomfortable once more. To be fair, he was usually uncomfortable with that sort of praise, but it was far worse coming from his partner's father.

There was a moment of awkward silence before Sam chimed in, "Aiden's making his Metropolitan Opera debut next fall."

"Isn't that lovely," Claudia said. If anything, Aiden decided, Claudia seemed bored by the topic. "Sam used to live in New York, of course. Before Nicholas died. Lovely loft in Brooklyn Heights."

Aiden smiled and hoped it looked convincing. The butterflies in his gut had morphed into a swarm of bees at the mention of Nick's name.

"Aiden and I met in New York years ago, mother. I told you that." Sam looked nearly as uncomfortable as Aiden felt. Irritated too, which made Aiden feel surprisingly good.

"Oh, that's right. Did you know our Nicholas?"

Deep breath. Just breathe. This time Aiden felt Sam's hand on his thigh, squeezing. Thank God for Sam.

"No, ma'am." Aiden thanked the heavens that the Ryans were not Southern Baptists and lifted his glass of wine. He took a quick swallow and added, "We first met about a year after Nick died."

"Oh. I see." Claudia went back to delicately cutting her food. From the look on her face, Aiden guessed she'd realized her mistake in bringing up Nick but wasn't sure what to do about it.

"I wish I could have met him." It was the truth. He looked at Sam as if to reassure him that it *was* true, and saw something flicker in his lover's eyes. Respect, perhaps? Aiden wasn't sure.

They still hadn't spoken about Nick, he and Sam. Aiden blamed himself for that. He was afraid of what he might learn. Of what he might not live up to.

"So, Dad," Sam said, "how's the firm running these days?"

Sam's father brightened visibly at the familiar territory. "You know what they say. 'Bad economy, good for business.'" He speared a piece of meat and looked pointedly at his son. "Could use another pair of hands. Someone to take my share when I retire."

Aiden knew how much Sam dreaded the topic of his father's firm, so he was surprised when Sam answered simply, "I'm happy where I am, Dad. But I appreciate the offer. Maybe someday I'll take you up on it."

Claudia's face softened. "Samuel"—she shot a look of reproach at her husband—"you know how well your son is doing. I showed you the article in the bar journal. You should be proud of him."

Sam's father looked momentarily irritated, then moved on to another topic of conversation without acknowledging his wife or his son. Sam's face softened with his mother's defense of him, the tiny wrinkles at the corners of his eyes now more pronounced. Aiden decided he liked Claudia.

Later, as he and Sam helped clear the dishes over Claudia's protests, Aiden overheard her tell Sam once again how proud she was of him. Then, before shooing them both out of the kitchen, she said, "Savannah and Tom should be here by eleven tomorrow. Rebecca will be here after breakfast to help me finish the cooking. Ceci says she and Beau will call after dinner." She smiled at Aiden. "Cecilia's pregnant with her third child. She's due any day now. It was too much for her to make the trip up from Texas this year."

"Thanks, Mom." Sam leaned over and kissed her cheek. "For everything."

Back in their room later, Aiden lay on his bed, hands propped under his head. "Your mom's a good cook."

"Yeah." Sam's voice was subdued, as if he were considering something. After a moment, he added, "Look, Aiden. I'm sorry about tonight. I don't think my mother realized—"

"Nothing to apologize for. She obviously loved Nick." *And so did you.* "Besides, I like her. I like how she stood up for you to your father."

Sam got out of his bed. "Got room for me?"

"Always."

There wasn't enough room for two people, let alone two people their size, but Aiden wasn't complaining. He lay on his side so that their chests touched. Sam laced his arms through Aiden's, their faces nearly touching on the pillow.

"She'll love you too," Sam said as their eyes met.

Aiden wished he could be so sure.

CHAPTER *21*

SAM woke before Aiden. At some point during the night, he had gone back to his own small bed. He hadn't slept much. He guessed Aiden hadn't slept much either, judging by all the tossing and turning he'd done while Sam had been awake watching him. In spite of himself, Sam felt guilty for dragging Aiden along. He should have just told his parents he couldn't come this year, given Aiden time before he forced him to meet the "in-laws."

He trudged downstairs in pajama pants and a T-shirt, squinting at the bright light in the kitchen. He'd barely managed to scoop some coffee into the coffeemaker when he heard the back door open.

"Sammy!"

"Hey, Becca." Sam smiled as she wrapped her arms around him and pressed her face against his back.

"Why aren't you still in bed snuggling with your new man?"

"Hard to snuggle in a twin bed." Sam poured the water into the coffee machine and watched the liquid begin to drip down into the pot.

"Ouch. Nice to see you too, Sammy."

"Sorry. I didn't sleep enough last night." He hoped the explanation would satisfy her curiosity, although he doubted it. Becca was hardly shy when it came to asking about anything.

"Dinner that bad?"

Sam shrugged.

"Let me guess. Parental units got you down?" She put her hand to her chin and frowned in an uncanny imitation of their father.

"Don't go there." He pulled a mug out of a cabinet, swapped the cup for the carafe until it filled, then replaced the carafe without spilling a drop.

"Impressive. Learned a new skill?"

"I'm not in the mood, Beck." He took the cup and walked out of the kitchen, sat down on the couch in the family room, and put his bare feet on the coffee table. She smirked. He'd never have put his feet up if his parents had been around, and she knew it.

She followed and sat down beside him. "So tell me about him. Arden?"

"Aiden." She knew *damn* well what Aiden's name was; she was working him. He tried to keep his cool. Snark at six in the morning wasn't his strong suit.

"Tell me about Aiden."

"How's school?" he countered.

"Fine." She kicked off her shoes and socks and wiggled her toes. "Same old, same old. One more semester and I'm out of this town."

"Good for you."

"Don't patronize me."

He sighed and drank some more of the coffee.

"Tell me about Aiden," she repeated, tucking her legs underneath her and frowning, her blue eyes narrowed.

"I'm really not in the mood."

"You love him?"

"Yes."

"He love you?"

"He says he does."

She snickered. "Trouble in paradise, then?"

"No."

"Mom and Dad give him grief?"

He stood up and retrieved his now empty cup from the table. "I don't want to talk about this right now."

"Why not?"

Damn good question.

He walked back into the kitchen without answering her and leaned against the counter. He closed his eyes and exhaled slowly. The image of a man flashed through his mind. But it wasn't Aiden. It was Nick.

"One of these years, we need to swap holidays," Sam could hear Nick say. "Thanksgiving in Rockland County. Christmas in Memphis so I can hear your dad play those cheesy Elvis Christmas songs." He wore an impish smile.

"You just want to see my dad get all teared up."

Nick grinned. "Yeah." He leaned over and kissed Sam. "What gets you all teary eyed, Sammy?"

If you only knew, Nick.

"You okay?" His sister's hand on his shoulder brought him back to the present.

His eyes burned and he clenched his jaw to fight back the wave of pain that slammed into him. He'd been back home how many times since Nick had died? And yet this visit was different. "I'm fine." He didn't mean to snap at her. God knew she was only trying to be kind.

"Sorry, Beck. I guess I'm tired." This visit had been a mistake. He was sure of it.

He plodded back to the bedroom without meeting her eyes, afraid that her sympathy might push him over the edge. Aiden rolled over at the sound of the closing door, but he didn't wake up. In spite of the coffee, Sam was asleep a few minutes later.

"MORNIN', sunshine." Aiden stood in the doorway to the bathroom as Sam rubbed his eyes. He was toweling off his hair and smiling at Sam.

The smell of turkey hung in the air, the sound of clinking dishes resonated from the other side of the house, and the sun was already high in the sky, streaming in through the wooden blinds. "What time is it?"

"Eleven."

"Shit. Mother will be wondering—"

"It's been taken care of." Aiden was grinning now. "I helped her scrub the sweet potatoes, helped Rebecca polish the silver, and got the crystal wineglasses down from the top cabinet."

"You're good."

"I try. Your mom seems to have warmed up to me a bit. Called me 'Nick' a few times." He laughed, but Sam heard a bit of an edge in Aiden's usually warm voice. "Not so sure about your sister, though. She gave me one of those looks, then grilled me on our relationship." Aiden made a face, and Sam snorted.

"That's Beck. Baby of the family. Smart as hell and smart mouth too." He didn't mention that she'd adored Nick like a brother and would probably compare Aiden's every move to Nick's. "What did you tell her?"

"Very little. Besides, your mother was right there."

"Sorry about that. Beck means well, she's just a bit overprotective. And she knows that my parents are still a little uncomfortable about my sexuality, even after all these years. At least she didn't ask you what flavor lube you prefer."

"She did ask if we were using a French letter."

"Fuck. In front of my mother?" Sam blanched.

"Honestly, I had to look it up on my phone. It's not exactly what we called condoms back in Fenton. Don't worry, I don't think your mother heard. She was too busy straightening the silverware and listening to some recipe for hot-pink cranberry sauce on NPR."

"This was a mistake." Sam realized that Aiden might take this the wrong way and quickly added, "It wasn't fair of me to subject you to this."

"I'm glad you did." Aiden pulled Sam up off the bed and pressed his slightly damp skin against Sam's neck. "Besides, your family's a hell of a lot easier to deal with than mine. Becca's trying to see what I'm made of, and your parents are only looking out for you."

The loud knock on the door made them both jump. "What do you want, Becca?" Sam growled. There was only one person who knocked like that.

"Just making sure you weren't going to spend all day f—"

Sam opened the door, cutting her off. "Please come in," he said in his calmest, most lawyerly voice. "Let's talk."

"I'll go help your mother." Aiden gave Sam a knowing smile. "See ya later, Becca."

The minute the door closed, Becca sat down on one of the beds, crossed her arms over her chest, and said, "He's okay. I guess."

Sam reminded himself, as he took a moment to master the urge to give in to his rekindled anger, that she was only twenty. It was easy to forget how young she was—she'd gone to college at seventeen. In his last year of college, he'd spent nights hanging with his friends at bars, picking up men, and barely managing to pass his classes at NYU. Until he'd met Nick. Becca had done her best to push all their parents' buttons, but she'd still managed to stay at the top of her class. Lord knew, Sam probably would have driven his parents insane if he'd stayed in Memphis for college.

"I'm so glad you approve." Well, he might be more than ten years older, but he wasn't dead, either. She'd learned about attitude from the best, after all.

She glared at him. "Don't treat me like a kid, Sam."

"Then don't act like one."

"Fine," she said. "So what did you want to talk about?"

"Why you're so hard on Aiden."

"I'm not—"

"Like hell. Bringing up condoms with Mom around—that was supposed to make it easier for him?"

"I didn't say 'condom'. I said 'French letter'."

"Right."

"Mom wouldn't have had a clue."

Sam said nothing but sat down on the opposite bed, facing her.

"All right, all right. I shouldn't have said it. I don't know why I did. It was stupid of me."

"You're right. It was stupid."

She glared back at him for a moment. Then her expression softened. "You miss him, don't you?"

"Who? Nicky?" The thought had crossed his mind—that there was more to his shitty mood than just lack of sleep and his parents calling Aiden "Nick"—but he'd brushed it off.

She nodded.

"Yes. I miss him." Why lie to her? It was bad enough he'd been lying to himself. "You do too, don't you?"

"Of course I do. But that doesn't have anything to do with Aiden."

For the first time this morning, he smiled. Suddenly everything seemed clear to him. "But it has *everything* to do with Aiden, doesn't it?"

She scowled at him.

"Come on. You know I'm right."

"Aiden's so… I don't know… uptight. He tries too hard." She looked everywhere but at him.

"He's nervous, Beck. Hell, so am I, and you're my family."

"There's nothing to be nervous about." She straightened up a bit and finally met his gaze. "It's not like you'd dump him if Mom and Dad didn't approve."

"Of course I wouldn't. But put yourself in his shoes. You'd probably be shitting bricks right about now."

"Maybe." She nibbled on a fingernail and looked away from him, then laughed. "Mom and Dad are a trip, aren't they?"

"Sometimes. But they mean well."

"You only say that because you aren't looking at yet another entire summer spent with them." She was chewing on her finger again.

Sam got up from the bed and sat down next to her, his shoulder pressed against hers. "It gets better. You're looking to go out of town for grad school, right?" She nodded. "Then it's another summer and you'll be out of here."

"I'm not sure I can even handle that. Did you know I wore eyeliner last week and Mom just about freaked?" She snorted and shook her head. "I'm fucking twenty years old, Sammy."

"It's only a few more months."

"Yeah."

He put his arm around her shoulders and pulled her close. "I miss him too. Nicky."

Tears welled up in her eyes. "I know it's been a long time since he… since he died. I was just your bratty sister back then."

"Still are." Sam smiled reassuringly at her.

She elbowed him. "You know what I mean."

"Yeah. I do."

"He was so cool. He let me try out his paints. He even snuck me this book with all these cool tattoo designs in—"

"He... *what*?"

She laughed. "He made me promise I wouldn't get one until I was twenty-one."

Sam rubbed his forehead and sighed theatrically. "Sounds like Nick."

"You know, I always wondered if he had a tat." She eyed Sam with a bit of mischief in her expression. "I never saw one."

Sam chuckled and rubbed the back of his neck. Nick had gotten a tattoo on his ass about a year after they'd gotten together. Sam's name with flames rising from each letter. Nick had designed it himself. It had been a bit of a dare. Sam hadn't thought he'd actually do it, but when Nick came home one night and dropped his pants, Sam decided it was about the hottest thing he could think of.

"You're blushing," Becca pointed out triumphantly. "So he *did* have a tattoo!"

"Don't change the subject."

"I wasn't. We were talking about Nicky."

"Look, Beck," he said, doing his best to steer the conversation back on track, "I loved him. We all did. But Aiden's a great guy too. You need to cut him a break."

"Okay. I'll try."

"Thanks." He hugged her tight.

"He is kind of cute," she said as she got up from the bed a moment later. "I looked him up online. He's bisexual, right?"

Sam laughed and shook his head again. "Becca...."

"Just sayin'." She grinned at him and added, "If he ever gets tired of you, I'd definitely be interested."

He got up off the bed and made as if he were going to strangle her. She waved and walked out, closing the door behind her. For a minute or two, he stood there and let the pain settle back into his gut. He was used to it. He'd get past it. He had to.

I loved you, Nicky. But I love him too.

BY THE time Sam showered and dressed an hour later, Savannah and Tom had arrived and were chatting with Aiden, who appeared to be holding his own. As usual, Sam's father said very little, instead sitting by the fireplace smoking a pipe over Becca's vocal protests and feigned coughing. Claudia flitted between kitchen and dining room until Savannah announced that she and Tom were expecting, after which Claudia's flitting became a frenzied and overjoyed buzzing as she hovered happily over her daughter. Claudia then lectured her husband until he put out the pipe with a look of long-suffering patience. Sam was just relieved that he and Aiden were no longer the center of his parents' attention. Aiden, too, seemed to appreciate sitting back and listening to Savannah's plans for the baby's room and the upcoming ultrasound, during which they hoped to learn if it was a boy or a girl. This led to a lively discussion of potential names.

Two hours later, after they'd finished dessert—Aiden gushing over Claudia's chess pie, and rightly so—Sam and Aiden finally convinced Claudia to let them do the dishes.

"Thanks." Sam took a large platter from Aiden's hands and began to dry it.

"For what?"

"For being patient."

"It wasn't difficult. They're good people."

"I wish she'd stop calling you Nick."

Aiden shrugged. "It's a compliment. Don't sweat it."

Sam said nothing.

"How were they with him? Nick, I mean."

Different. Warmer. "I don't know," Sam lied. "I never really thought about it." That much was true. Not until this trip. But would it help to tell Aiden the truth? This trip had been hard enough for Aiden, and he'd be leaving directly from Memphis to London on Sunday evening. "But I can tell they like you." That part was also true, to Sam's great relief.

"You sure?"

"I'm sure."

Better to talk about it later, when we're home. He knew enough from his own experience as a lawyer that things were always easier to handle on your home turf.

Sam's response seemed to placate Aiden, who wore a pleasant, relaxed expression. Sam had begun to wonder if it was all an act. Aiden was a good actor, after all. "I'm glad." He handed Sam the gravy bowl. "I know it's important to you."

Sam was about to protest when Becca came into the kitchen and announced, "The parental units told me you can finish the dishes later. They want you to sing for them, Aiden."

THERE were few things Aiden hated more than singing at parties and informal gatherings, and yet he was asked to do it all the time. He complained to his best friend, Cary Redding, about it once. After joking that playing the cello was a distinct advantage when it came to avoiding impromptu performances, Cary had been more than understanding.

"You wouldn't ask a dentist to look at your tooth, would you?" Cary asked as he waved the tequila bottle around, then handed it to Aiden.

"I wouldn't ask a dermatologist to check out my mole, either," Aiden countered.

"Let me see... 'Things not to ask at a cocktail party'... You wouldn't ask a vet to neuter your dog."

"Ouch!" Aiden made a face, then added, "You wouldn't ask a computer programmer to fix your Internet connection."

"You wouldn't ask a beautician to wax your crack." Cary's smile was pure evil. Aiden snorted, sending some tequila up his nose, which made him cough.

This had rapidly deteriorated until Cary ended with, "You wouldn't ask a proctologist to stick his finger up your ass."

"Not without buying me dinner first," Aiden deadpanned. Both of them laughed until they cried. It had meant so much that Cary had understood. But now....

"Sure. I'll be there in a minute, Becca." Aiden knew that this time, there wasn't a choice. Not really.

"I don't think—" Sam began, but Becca was gone before he could finish. "This okay with you?" He looked at Aiden with concern.

"It's fine. Happens all the time." The truth, although not the complete truth.

"You seem uncomfortable with it."

"It's fine, Sam. I sang at David's birthday, remember?" Aiden knew that had been different: he had *chosen* to sing for David, knowing how much it meant to him.

"You sure? Because—"

"I said it's fine." Aiden heard the tension in his own voice. He took a deep breath and tried to recollect himself, regain his control.

Sam touched his shoulder.

"Sorry. I guess I'm just a little tired." He hugged Sam and made a point of smiling reassuringly. He was good at that, smiling like he meant it.

Sam didn't look convinced, but he let the subject drop. When Becca poked her head back in the kitchen to see what was taking them so long, Sam and Aiden followed silently.

It wasn't all that bad, Aiden tried to convince himself later as he lay awake in bed early the next morning. Sam's family seemed to genuinely enjoy his renditions of "He Touched Me" and "Amazing Grace," both of which he'd learned listening to an old Elvis album. Sam's father, it turned out, was a bit of a closet Elvis fan and had opened up a bit about Memphis and Graceland when Aiden told him he'd always loved Elvis's voice.

Still, Aiden was sure Sam's family thought of him as a novelty, not as their son's boyfriend, let alone his partner. The feeling persisted throughout the weekend. By the time he and Sam said their good-byes at the Memphis airport, Aiden was looking forward to getting back to Europe.

CHAPTER *22*

Philadelphia
January

THE courtroom emptied quickly, and Sam gathered up his papers and slid them into his briefcase. He glanced over at the table where the other attorney was also packing up and smiled. The man ignored him.

"Something crawl up his ass and die?" his colleague, Yvette, whispered in his ear. "You'd think he'd be happy with this jury. Judge was riding you pretty hard."

"No idea. Probably tired. It's been a long day."

She raised an eyebrow at him and shook her head.

An hour later, he was back in his office checking e-mail when Yvette came in waving what looked like a newspaper in her right hand. "What is it?" Sam was tired and unwilling to engage her again on the subject of the judge.

"Take a look."

He took the paper from her and opened it. It was a tabloid—the kind of thing you'd read at a supermarket checkout counter, then surreptitiously put back before the person in front of you finished paying for their groceries. There was a large color photo on the front: two men kissing. A passionate kiss. It was a photograph of him and Aiden. The caption read *Heartbroken Opera Singer Finds Romance at Last.*

"And what do you want me to do about this?" He inhaled and slowly released the air between his lips. "It's not a big surprise. I've been out for years."

"But the judge—"

"Already knows I'm gay," he interrupted. "What's he going to do? Call me out on it?"

"Motion to disqualify?"

Sam snorted. "Not likely. What evidence do you have that he's treating me differently because of the article? He won't recuse himself. You know it takes a hell of a lot more than disliking someone to make a judge reassign the case."

"But—"

"Yvette," he warned, "let it go."

"But he's a federal judge."

"And he's not going to do anything to screw that whole 'lifetime appointment' thing up. Trust me."

She huffed softly, then said, "You're the boss."

"If it becomes a real problem, I'll ask Stacey to take over the case. But it won't come to that." He smiled reassuringly at her. "Trust me. I've been at this a few more years than you. Sometimes you have to take the shit."

At the time, he'd meant it. But when he checked his messages back at the office an hour later, he found that his mother had called. She hadn't directly mentioned the tabloid story, but she told him she loved him "no matter what." And she hadn't mentioned Sam's father, either. That was never a good sign. The old man was undoubtedly pissed; he didn't enjoy being thrust into the spotlight. Bad for business.

His mother's message was followed by another from Becca, who told him she wanted "all the juicy details," and would "keep calling until you call me back." He figured he had about two hours before she called again. *Better sooner than later,* he thought as he dialed his parents' number. He'd get back to Becca when he'd had a drink at home. At this rate, he'd need at least a few.

THAT evening Sam stood on the balcony of his apartment, a double shot of whiskey in one hand—his third that night. He'd downed the first after the phone call to his mother, the second after the call to his sister. The liquor burned his throat, and for the first time that evening, he felt relaxed. His phone vibrated in his pocket, and he took a deep breath.

"Hey, Aiden."

"Thank God." Aiden's voice had a slightly heady quality to it, and Sam guessed the performance had just ended. "I thought I'd miss you."

"It's good to hear your voice."

"Sammy," Aiden said, uncharacteristically clearing his throat, "there's something I need to tell you. Something I—"

"I know about the photo."

There was a moment of silence on the other end of the phone before Aiden said, "You... you know? But how?"

"Don't sweat it. I never intended to hide my relationship with you."

"But you never expected it to be plastered all over the papers, either. God, Sam. I'm so sorry. Ever since Cam, I've been their little pet project. I never wanted any of this publicity."

"Not your fault. I guess my little stint as Beau caught their attention. Besides, I was the one who kissed *you* out in the open, remember?"

"Yes, but—"

"I won't make excuses, Aiden. And I sure as hell don't want you to act any differently around me because some nosy reporter wants to know who you're living with."

Sam heard Aiden's released breath through the speaker. "Thanks."

"Listen, Aiden, I'm beat. Can I call you tomorrow afternoon? It's been a long day."

"Okay. Sure." Sam thought he heard a hint of disappointment in Aiden's voice, but he was too tired to deal with it. He'd call Aiden when his head was clearer. "Miss you," Aiden added. It sounded like an afterthought.

"I miss you too."

He missed Aiden. How long had he been gone now? More than a month? Sam didn't give a shit about the photo. Sure, it'd make his job harder in court, but he hadn't been lying to Yvette when he'd said he could handle things.

You could have talked to Aiden. He'd have listened.

But he didn't want to talk over the phone. He wanted Aiden here. Face-to-face. Maybe they'd talk a little; then Aiden would hold him and run his fingers through his hair. Maybe they'd make love or just fuck. Or maybe they'd watch a movie.

Sam refilled his drink and settled back into the chair. The stars were out and even the lights of the city didn't seem to interfere with their bright light.

No moon. A night for reflection.

Sam vaguely remembered Nick saying that a moonless night was the universe's way of telling him *not* to think for a change. "Light sometimes obscures things," Nicky had told him. "It shows you the colors, but it doesn't give you a chance to *feel* them."

At the time Sam had been at a loss to understand. But now.... Did it help him to see his relationship with Aiden in the bright light of reality? Was the gossip shit reality, anyhow? What they had was something special—the comfortable rapport, the long conversations, the way Sam felt in Aiden's arms or making love. That was love, wasn't it? To know that another person made you feel safe? To want them with you all the time?

"I love you, Sammy," Nick told him as they held hands and walked across the Brooklyn Bridge. They had spent the evening at South Street Seaport in lower Manhattan, having dinner with Nick's older sister and her husband. It wasn't the first time Nick had expressed those feelings to Sam, but something about the warm summer night, the sound of their feet against the wooden boards of the pedestrian walk that spanned the East River, just made it feel different.

"I love you too, Nicky." It felt so right, so simple. It infused Sam with confidence, leaving no room for doubt, only the welcome and warm knowledge that this man was the only man for him.

"Why do you think people need to say 'I love you too'?" Sam asked a moment later.

"It's like breathing. Like fucking." Nick laughed like a little kid. "It's something we crave. We imagine love; sometimes we even make it up. But it's always there, the need to be loved. If you overthink it, you can make yourself nuts."

Funny, how the lawyer with all the big words couldn't express things as clearly as the painter whose world was purely visual. But that's one of the things he loved about Nick: he didn't worry if what he said sounded intelligent. It was much like the beauty in his canvases. You couldn't explain it, not easily, but the beauty was there nonetheless.

"I want to spend the rest of my life with you, Nicky," Sam said as he gathered Nick into his arms right there in the middle of the bridge.

"Sounds like a plan." They kissed. "But you didn't have to say it. You can feel it, can't you? We're already there, Sammy. You sound like you're waiting for something, but you're not, really."

Sam sighed and brushed his lips over Nick's. "Yeah. You're right. I'm already there. Here."

Sam's eyes filled with tears at the memory, and he realized he felt guilty, thinking about Nick. He stood up and walked back into the apartment. He'd take a shower and get some rest; then he'd call Aiden in the morning. He'd make the time to talk, even if it meant rearranging his appointments for the day. Some things were simply too important to wait.

"FUCK." Aiden set down his phone and leaned back on the bed. He imagined what Sam smelled like, tried to recreate the crisp scent of his aftershave, but all he could smell was the stale hotel room.

Two more weeks and he'd see Sam again. *If* Sam wanted to see him after this. Aiden couldn't help but notice the distance in Sam's voice. As much as he wanted to rationalize it away as another lousy overseas connection, he knew he'd heard it: the hesitation, the pain.

He needs time. Pushing him is the one thing that'll drive him away for sure.

CHAPTER 23

Philadelphia
February

"SAM RYAN." Sam stifled a yawn and leaned back in his chair. He'd been about to head home—Aiden would be arriving in about an hour—but he knew Peggy had already left, so he'd picked up the call.

"Sam, this is Jacob Altman."

"How are you, Your Honor?" Sam sat straighter in his chair. It was unusual to receive a call from a judge, and Judge Altman was one of the most highly respected federal judges around.

"Please, call me Jacob," the other man said. "This call isn't about a case, and there's no need for formality."

"Of course. What can I do for you, Jacob?"

"FEDERAL magistrate?" Aiden put his wine down and leaned across the table. "Is that like a judge?"

Sam nodded. "They're a lot like federal judges in what they do. It's not a lifetime appointment, though. Just for an eight-year term."

"Shit, Sam, that's great. You've always wanted to be a judge."

"It's only an interview." Sam had said the same thing to Stacey an hour before. "And even if that goes well, all the district judges need to vote on me."

"But to even be considered for the position is wonderful."

"Yeah. And they often look to magistrates when they're floating names to Congress for vacant judgeships. But I wouldn't read too much into it. I'll still have to make it past all the interviews and win enough votes from the other judges." Sam took a sip of his wine, more to steady himself than anything else. He knew he couldn't let himself get too excited about his prospects. The chances of an openly gay man getting the job were pretty slim, not to mention the fact that Sam was relatively young for the position.

"You're selling yourself short." Aiden brushed his hand over Sam's, and he smiled broadly. "You're really good, and you know it. You'd make a terrific judge. It'd probably mean better hours for you than at the firm." This was true, Sam knew. "How about the pay?"

"Federal jobs pay well," Sam said, "although it wouldn't be near as much as my share of the firm's profits. But it's not like I need the money at this point, either. I've got plenty stashed away, and the apartment's paid for."

"So what's the downside?"

"I don't know." Sam took another drink of his wine and felt the tension in his shoulders and neck ease a bit. "Less flexibility in my schedule, maybe?"

"We'll be fine, Sammy. You'd still get vacations, wouldn't you?"

"Yes, but—"

"You have to pursue this, and you know it. We can work things out. I'll work my schedule around yours. This is too good to pass up."

Sam took a deep breath and forced a smile. Maybe Aiden was right—it was something Sam had always wanted. Something he'd hoped for since he'd started practicing law. They'd be able to coordinate their time off.

Aiden stood up and put Sam's empty plate atop his own. Sam began to protest, but Aiden said, "Nope. My turn. You cooked, remember?"

"Thanks." Sam watched as Aiden took the dishes into the kitchen. A few moments later, he heard the water running in the sink. He took another deep breath and refilled his glass of wine.

He's right. It'll be fine.

So why was his gut so tense? And why did he feel as though this was a huge mistake? He got up and went into the kitchen. He wrapped his arms around Aiden's waist and kissed him on the cheek.

"Hey, you," Aiden said as he scrubbed one of the pots.

"Hey. It's good to have you home." He put his head on Aiden's shoulder and sighed audibly.

For a moment Aiden was silent, though Sam noticed that he had stopped scrubbing and seemed to be staring down at the soapy water. Sam waited for Aiden to speak. When he did, Aiden's usually confident voice sounded tentative.

"Sammy?"

"Hmm?"

"Are you okay with this?"

"Okay with what?"

"With me traveling so much."

What other choice is there? It'd be selfish of him to force Aiden to turn down work, and the last thing he wanted was for Aiden to resent him for interfering in his career. "Of course I'm okay with it."

"I was thinking that maybe I'd ask Chuckie to free up a few more weeks… you know… so that I'd be home for longer in between gigs. Maybe skip some of the master class stuff I've used to fill in the empty slots in my schedule."

"But that wouldn't be fair to you." *It's not like you assign more cases to other attorneys so your schedule is free when he's home.* He was surprised that he hadn't even considered it. He made a mental note to talk to Stacey about cutting back a little. They had plenty of associates who could cover for him.

"I worry sometimes. That's all." Sam felt Aiden's body tense with these words.

"I love you, Aiden." Sam nuzzled Aiden's cheek. "Of course I want you around more. But I knew what I was getting into when I asked you to move in." Sam hoped he sounded more convinced than he was.

Aiden turned around and, clearly forgetting he'd been doing the dishes, took Sam's face in his wet, soapy hands. "I love you, Sam," he said. "I just don't want you to regret this."

"I don't." It was the truth. At least in that moment, it was the truth.

"SO WHEN do they make the decision?" Stacey asked Sam five days later as they went over the billing reports in Sam's office. Sam hated this part of the job, but the accountant couldn't make the decisions about bonuses and case assignments.

"Sometime in the next few months. I have to make the rounds. Talk to the judges who want to interview me. Then they'll vote." He swirled his coffee around in his mug and stared absentmindedly at the paper in his hand.

"So how's Aiden?" she asked.

"He's good. Left yesterday for London."

She raised an eyebrow.

"What's that look for?" He didn't have the patience for this, not first thing in the morning. Not after Aiden had left again and he'd spent the night tossing and turning, alone in their bed.

"Just that I asked how Aiden was, and the first thing you tell me is that he's gone again."

"He's an opera singer, Stace. That's what he does. Travels around and sings."

"And you stay home."

"Right."

"Sammy," she said, putting her feet up on his desk and sighing theatrically, "you look miserable."

"I'm not—"

"I know you too well, Sammy. Don't bullshit me."

"Relationships are difficult," he replied with keen irritation.

"Yeah. They are. So what are you doing about making it *less* difficult?"

"The usual. Spending time together, that sort of thing. The things you do when you live together."

"What about when he's away?"

"What about it?" He shrugged. "We talk on the phone. Skype sometimes. E-mail. The usual."

"Why not visit him?"

"You mean in Europe?" Sam frowned when she nodded. "He's working. I'd be in the way."

"Have you asked him if you'd be in the way?"

Sam stood up. "Look, I know you want to help. We'll be fine. It's always a little rocky at the beginning. It was with Nicky too."

She raised an eyebrow. "I don't remember it that way. You and Nick fit perfectly, right from the start. At least that's what you always told me."

"Are you saying that since Aiden and I have..." He hesitated, trying to find the right word. "... challenges, that this relationship is a mistake?"

"Are you serious?" She glared at him. "Look, Sammy, I like Aiden. And you obviously love each other. Don't play dumb."

Sam said nothing.

"Sam," she said, tapping her pen against a piece of paper, "I know I'm hardly the relationship guru here. Hell knows my track record with men isn't great. But I know that if you don't talk about things, they just get worse."

Sam knew she was right. When had he and Aiden talked about their relationship? If he felt like things between them could be better, Aiden probably felt the same.

"Maybe you're right."

She laughed and shook her head.

"Okay, okay. You're always right. It's why I haven't strangled you yet even though you've made me look like an idiot." He stood up and refilled his cup of coffee. "I was thinking maybe I'd ease up a bit on my caseload so I can spend more time with Aiden when he's in town. Maybe assign some of the bigger cases to Yvette. She's been chomping at the bit for more responsibility, and she was great on the Harvest case last month."

"Works for me. Do it. Don't just talk about it. But talk to him, Sammy. Before things get too difficult. Tell him you're having problems with the way things are. He'll understand. You can work it out. I know you can."

He headed for the door and waved dismissively. "Okay, okay. I'll talk to him. Promise."

"And if you ever want some real time off, you know it's fine," she called after him as he walked out of the room.

CHAPTER 24

London
April

"HEY, Chuckie."

Aiden pressed his cell phone between his chin and his shoulder, sat down on one of the kitchen chairs, and poured himself some coffee. He'd been in London for only a few days after the stopover in Philadelphia with Sam. It had been too short a visit with Sam, as always, but it had been a great one. They'd spent most of their free time in bed. No cooking, strictly takeout. After the conversation in the kitchen, the visit had gone a long way to reassuring Aiden that Sam wouldn't be scared off so easily.

I have to believe him when he says it's okay.

He hadn't planned on stopping in London before he flew to Rome, but David had offered to help coach him on the role of Scarpia in Puccini's *Tosca*. It was an offer Aiden couldn't refuse. A few days wouldn't matter as much this time, since after Rome he'd be headed back to Philly for a full three weeks. He was already thinking of the things he and Sam could do with that much time together.

Museums, long walks, fucking....

"Don't call me Chuckie," Aiden's agent chastised. "So tell me about the Paris gig. Did you make me proud?"

Aiden snorted. "If you mean will they hire me again, I think it's an unequivocal yes. They'll probably be calling you about a *Manon* soon."

"Massenet?"

"Do you really see a Parisian opera house performing the Italian version? No. *Manon.* En français."

"I'm glad to see you're getting cast in more of the villain roles. Means they're seeing your flexibility as an actor."

"They're not bad guys. They're misunderstood."

"Right." Charles laughed. "That's what they all say."

"To tell you the truth, I'm looking forward to that *Falstaff* you were talking about. At least he's a funny villain and he doesn't get stabbed to death by the soprano. Where's the contract?"

"That's part of why I called."

"Need my okay?"

"No." Chuck Ritter drew an audible breath. "Seems like we've run into a little problem with the Scotland gig."

"What kind of problem? Don't tell me the company went bankrupt. I've been hearing about too many—"

"Not bankrupt. I got a call today from the artistic director of the company telling me they aren't interested in you."

"What?"

"You heard me right. They said they aren't interested."

"But *they* were the ones who contacted *you* about having me sing the role." Aiden put down his coffee and frowned. It would have been his first opportunity to perform the opera, and he'd been looking forward to it.

"Yep."

"What's going on, Chuck? This is the third time you've told me about something and it didn't pan out."

Aiden stood up and walked over to the window, looking out at the clouds that had begun to descend over the city. It would rain soon—the cold, damp rain Aiden hated. Italy couldn't come soon enough.

"I was hoping you could tell *me*."

"Me?"

"Have you pissed anyone off?"

"No. I told you, I've learned my lesson. No more Hollywood starlets or Italian pop divas." He hadn't meant to sound so defensive, but it still irked him that he had fucked up so royally with Alexandria.

"Married women?"

Aiden's jaw clenched. "No. I told you. It was a huge fucking mistake, and not one I'm likely to repeat." *Not to mention the fact that I didn't do anything with her.*

"Sorry, Aiden, you know I had to ask."

"I know." He wasn't angry with Chuck, he was angry with himself. He'd been stupid. Taken chances. Between the confrontation with Cam in Paris and the photo with Alexandria....

Fucking Cam! Of course he was behind this. He had to be.

"Look," Chuck said, "it's probably nothing. Just a fluke. Maybe they found someone cheaper, or maybe some benefactor had a nephew she wanted to see in the role. You never know. And the others—Aiden, you know this stuff always happens. People change their minds, productions don't happen."

"Yeah." *Only not this often.*

"So how's the *Tosca* coming?"

"Great." Aiden rubbed his neck and tapped his foot against the ancient radiator under the window. "Listen, Chuck, I gotta run. Can I call you back tomorrow? There's something I need to do."

"I... ah... sure. No worries." Aiden ignored the hesitation in the other man's voice. "Take care of yourself, okay?"

"You too, Chuckie."

"Don't call me—"

Aiden disconnected the call, went to the table, and opened his laptop. He googled "Cameron Sherrington" and the name of the Scottish company. There was nothing he could find to connect the two. Sherrington Holdings hadn't given the company any money that he could tell, and there were no mentions of Cam in Edinburgh. It didn't look as though Cam had ever been to the city.

Fucking hell.... He leaned back against the sofa and was about to close his eyes when his cell rang again.

"Look, Chuckie," he said. "You don't have to worry about me. I'm—"

"Aiden?"

Aiden nearly dropped the phone. "Sam? Shit, I thought you were Chuck."

"If this is a bad time," Sam began, "I can call back."

"Do you mind? I'll give you a call later, after dinner."

"Sure." Aiden thought he heard disappointment in Sam's voice, then dismissed it as being his overactive guilt at work. He needed to do a little research—to figure out what Cam was up to. Then he'd call Sam back.

"Great. Thanks, Sam. Talk to you later, then?"

"Yep. Later." Sam disconnected the call before Aiden could say, *I love you.*

Aiden took a deep breath, then went back to the computer search he'd been working on. *Dammit, Cam. What the fuck are you doing?*

AIDEN spent half the afternoon tracking Cam down. The rain had begun to fall in earnest. Aiden flipped up the collar of his leather jacket and shivered.

"You're a weather wuss," Sam had said after he and Aiden went to the open-air market in the middle of a snowstorm.

"There's a reason why all the smart people live in the South," Aiden shot back. They'd warmed themselves by the fire later that morning, drinking coffee laced with Jack Daniel's and making love on the carpet in front of the fireplace. Aiden figured it was a fair trade.

Aiden had first stopped by the house he used to share with Cam. It was stupid. He had Cam's number. He was relieved the place had been empty, but he'd wanted to go there, anyhow. Seeing it again, he knew he couldn't have handled going inside; he missed the place too much. He stood in front of the beautiful Edwardian as the rain made soft noises on his umbrella. He finally tapped his phone when he couldn't stand it anymore. He needed to get this over with.

"Hello?"

Aiden took a deep breath. "Cam, we need to talk."

"Aiden? Is that you?" There was a certain breathless quality in Cam's voice.

Of course he's happy to hear from me. It's what he's wanted. It's why he's doing this. "Surprised?" Aiden asked.

"I... well, honestly yes. I hadn't expect—"

"Cut the bullshit, Cam. Where can we meet?"

"Meet? You're in London?" Cam had always been a consummate actor.

"Just tell me where to meet you."

"How about Z?"

"The hotel?" Aiden had heard of it. Everyone had. It hadn't existed when Aiden and Cam were together, but Aiden had heard David mention it. It wouldn't have been Aiden's choice—too trendy and far too expensive.

I'm only going to talk to him. Tell him to fuck off and be done with it.

"Fine. Nine o'clock." He'd go back to the apartment, dry himself off, and change into something better than sweats. Maybe he'd get there a little on the early side and have a drink first. It'd be easier that way.

"I'm so glad you're going to give me a—"

Aiden tapped the phone and shoved it into his pocket. His jaw hurt, he'd been clenching it so tightly.

CHAPTER 25

THE bar at the Z was a study in modern design. Zyng, as the bar was aptly named, was far larger than Aiden had expected and took up nearly the entire sixth floor of the hotel. Textured glass dividers wove in and around mirrors and modern seating in shades of red, silver, and gold. It was still relatively early, right before nine o'clock, but the bar was already filling up with men and women, mostly young, well-dressed, and obviously affluent. Dolce & Gabbana, Missoni, Prada.

The place already vibrated with a steady techno beat. Aiden hated places like this, but he'd tolerated them for Cam's sake. He knew his dark jeans and simple cotton shirt were stylish, trendy, even if they hadn't cost him an entire gig's pay. He'd gotten good at pretending he was something other than the backwoods kid from Buttfuck, Mississippi. David had given him the confidence to mingle with the rich and famous. Cam had shown him a lifestyle he hadn't even understood existed. But underneath it all, he knew he'd never belong here.

He left his jacket and umbrella at the coat check and walked directly to the bar. "Bourbon. Straight up," he told the bartender, an outrageously attractive brunette. He'd fantasized about women like her, growing up. Until he realized he'd never have a chance in hell with one. He dated a few women like that after he'd left Cam. He'd worn his bisexuality like an expensive suit, and he'd been the talk at parties: the rising American singer who'd dumped his billionaire boyfriend on the front page of the tabloids. Ironic, that he rarely slept with any of the men or women he'd made sure to be seen with. He'd only wanted to hurt Cam, but he'd ended up hurting himself.

Aiden regretted not telling Cam where they'd meet, but letting Cam take the lead had always been easier. He'd fallen into old habits far too easily, he told himself, and he made a promise not to let it happen again. *He'd* control this conversation.

The bartender put his drink on the counter and Aiden deposited a bill in return, nodding his thanks and leaving before she could get him his change. He didn't know the place, but he knew Cam. He'd have found the perfect spot: isolated enough for them to talk, but where he'd still be visible. Aiden scanned the club as he drank deeply, ignoring the burn. A few more seconds and his chest warmed. His shoulders relaxed. From the bar, there were three separate seating areas and a dance floor that ran like the spokes of a wheel, each decorated in a slightly different scheme.

He ignored the first, with the long black benches running along its length. Too open. Too few places to sit and no privacy at all. The second was even longer than the first, with a series of S-shaped settees and small cylindrical tables that echoed the colors of the glass. *Not here.* He turned around, bypassing the dance floor for the last seating area, which was peppered with smaller groupings of upholstered chairs. Some were round, others square. Solid colors. Each grouping sat no more than four.

Bingo.

He spotted Cam toward the center of the room, standing and facing the window that looked down onto the street. Taking one more swallow, he walked toward Cam, then paused before drawing closer. Cam was exactly as he remembered him, with his slightly effeminate beauty and almost boyish stance. He wore a pale sweater—cashmere, no doubt—in the perfect shade of green to set off his hazel eyes. His jeans were fitted just enough to emphasize his pert little ass. He wore a single diamond stud in one ear. Aiden almost smiled—Cam only wore the earring when he was out to impress someone. It surprised Aiden to realize that someone was *him*.

Aiden walked past a group of women who were laughing as they passed an iPhone around, sharing photos of God knows what. One of them looked up and smiled at him. Aiden returned the smile mechanically.

"Cam."

Cam turned around and smiled. "Aiden. So good to see you." He moved to embrace Aiden, but Aiden stepped back. The result was an awkward peck on Aiden's cheek, although Cam handled the rebuff like a pro, expertly maneuvering to Aiden's side and guiding him to one of the chairs. Cam had clearly anticipated Aiden's cool response. "You look fabulous. I like your hair a bit longer. I'm glad you finally took my advice. It's really quite—"

"I'm not here to chat, Cam."

Cam looked genuinely disappointed, and for an instant, Aiden hesitated. He was angry, angrier than he'd been when he'd walked in on Cam and Jarrod more than two years before. But he was also tired. Tired of the games, tired of worrying about things between him and Sam, tired of being angry. He'd loved Cam, enough that he'd thought they'd spend their lives together, and now....

"Please, Aiden"—Cam fiddled with the ear stud, obviously uncomfortable—"have a seat."

"Thanks." Aiden tried to gather his thoughts.

"So what can I do for you?" It was an odd thing to say, and Aiden wondered vaguely if he'd been wrong about Cam. Not that the man would gloat to his face, but still, if he'd been trying to sabotage Aiden's career, would he look so... contrite?

This is Cam, remember? The man who cheated on me, then came home and made love to me without even batting an eye. King of the bullshitters.

"I know what you're doing, Cam. Get a life. Leave mine alone."

"I... I don't know what you mean," Cam answered, frowning. "Other than the flowers, I—"

"Don't mess with me. It's over. *We're* over. A long time ago. Let it be. Move on." Aiden hadn't meant to raise his voice—it was part of the reason he'd agreed to meet Cam in public. Here, he wouldn't be tempted to punch the hell out of the little shit.

"I don't know what you mean."

Aiden stood up abruptly and grabbed for the collar of Cam's shirt, snagging one of the buttons, which popped off and landed unceremoniously on the floor. *Oh, that's great. So much for not making a scene.*

Cam put his hand on Aiden's wrist, meeting his gaze with a look of surprise and... guilt?

No. Not guilt. He's scared I'm going to beat the shit out of him. For an instant, they both stood there. Then Aiden released his grip on Cam and stepped back as though he'd been burned. What the hell had he been ready to do to Cam? His lack of self-control scared the crap out of him. He was exhausted and worried about both his career and his relationship with Sam, but to come so close to hitting Cam? He felt physically ill and disgusted with himself.

"Leave me alone," Aiden said, then turned and walked out of the bar.

AIDEN arrived back at David's place. It was empty. Dark. *Lonely.* David had left the night before to meet Alex in Rio. Aiden wished David were around; he could use an ear right about now. He thought briefly about Sam, but the last thing he wanted was to worry Sam, or worse, to involve him in his bullshit with Cam. *Bad enough that he has to put up with my traveling.*

It was after midnight when he climbed into bed. He left the drapes open so he could look out at the sky. Patches of stars were visible between the lifting clouds. He thought of Sam again and his chest ached with need. He imagined how it felt when Sam held him, the smell of Sam, how it felt to run his fingers through Sam's hair.

What the hell am I doing? Maybe it wasn't such a terrible thing to have a bit more time on his hands. He didn't need the money. It wasn't as if a few fewer gigs each year would have much of an impact on his reputation or his career. He'd talk to Sam. See what he thought about him spending more time at home in Philly.

CHAPTER 26

SAM yawned as he turned over yet another piece of paper in a foot-high stack on the conference table. Yvette rubbed her eyes and played with the remainder of a sandwich she'd picked to bits as they worked. They'd spent the past six hours looking for a single document in a sea of documents. Sam wished he'd had the presence of mind to get Peggy to scan them in. He'd thought it wouldn't take them this long—he could swear he'd seen the document the witness had described in his deposition, and he was pretty damn sure it didn't say what the man had sworn, under oath, that it said.

It also didn't help that he was distracted. He'd expected Aiden to call him in the morning. But he'd checked his cell at least a dozen times, and Peggy said there'd been no calls on his office phone. He knew Aiden was probably preoccupied or that he'd plain forgotten he'd promised to call. But the conversation of the night before had left Sam edgy. Something was going on, and he was pretty sure Aiden didn't want to burden him with it.

You could call him. It wasn't the first time he'd had this thought, but he figured he needed to learn that Aiden not calling didn't signal the end of the world. Sam could handle it. He was a big boy.

His cell phone rang and he started. Becca. She'd been waiting to hear about the fellowship at Temple. Not that their parents couldn't afford to send her to graduate school in Philly, but he knew she wanted a modicum of independence after being so dependent upon them for the past four years.

"I'll be back," he told Yvette as he tapped the phone. He stepped out of the conference room and into the hallway. "Hey Beck. Got some good news?"

"Just checking in. Nothing yet." Her voice sounded a bit strained, and he wondered if she'd had another run-in with their parents about leaving Tennessee. "I should hear by Friday."

"Great." He decided not to ask why she'd called, figuring she'd get to the point soon enough.

"Sammy?"

"Yeah. I'm here."

"Everything okay with Aiden?"

He chuckled. "Everything's fine, sweetie," he answered with a sigh. "He'll be home in about three weeks."

"Oh."

"Something up?"

"Why would you—"

"I know you too well. What's going on?"

He heard her take a long breath. "You know I like Aiden, right?" Not an auspicious way to begin a conversation.

"Sure." *Just not as much as Nicky.*

"Well, I was surfing around. You know, checking out what he's been up to. Mom said she hoped he might perform near Memphis sometime and… I don't know…."

"Beck, just tell me. I don't have time for—"

"Do you know this guy? Cameron something or other? British? Made of money?"

"Cameron Sherrington." Sam hoped he didn't sound as irritated as he thought he did. "Yeah. I know him. He and Aiden lived together a few years back." *Little shit.*

"There was this photo," she blurted out. "I mean, it's probably nothing, but I… I thought you should know."

"What kind of a photo?"

"They were at some fancy club in London. Or at least, that's what the article said. I can send you the link if you want."

Shit. He really didn't want this crap with the press again. "Not interested," he told her.

"Well, I kind of already sent it. You can delete it if you want. I only thought—"

"Thanks, Beck. Next time, don't bother. Aiden gets this kind of thing all of the time. It's better to ignore it."

"Okay. No prob. Sorry. It's only that I worry about you with him gone so much, and—"

"Don't worry. And call me when you hear from Temple, okay?"

"Okay."

"Take care, Beck."

"You too, Sammy. I'll talk to you soon. Keep your fingers crossed!"

"I will. Love you."

"You too."

He heard her hang up the phone and he slid his cell into his pocket. For a moment he considered going to his office and looking at his e-mail. Then he shook his head and let out a long breath. *Stop it. It's all bullshit. They're probably running stories from a year ago and making it look like it happened yesterday.*

By the time Sam got home that night, however, Aiden still hadn't phoned and Sam was having a hard time *not* thinking about Becca's call. It was nearly eleven when he gave in and opened his laptop. He scanned through his e-mail, hoping there would be something from Aiden, but he found nothing. Finally, frustrated and trying to rationalize away his hurt at Aiden's silence, he opened Becca's e-mail and clicked on the link.

Shit. The photo was grainy, taken without a flash and, Sam guessed, on a cell phone. Still, there was no mistaking Aiden and Cam. The caption under the photo was *Lord Sherrington's Patience Rewarded?* In spite of himself, Sam read the short article.

World-renowned operatic sensation Aiden Lind was spotted Thursday night at Zyng. Sources close to Mr. Lind report that his sometime relationship with his handsome American barrister has been strained as of late. Lind reportedly met for a tête-à-tête with former lover and flatmate Lord Cameron Sherrington over drinks. Rumor has it....

Sam shut the laptop so hard the sound echoed in the living room. He tossed it unceremoniously onto the couch and strode over to the glass windows overlooking downtown. The night was clear, and the moon made the windows of a nearby high-rise glitter.

There's nothing to it, and you know it. He pulled a glass out of a nearby cabinet and poured himself a double shot of whiskey. He finished the booze in less than a minute, then set the glass back down with such violence he worried he might shatter it. Not that he gave a shit—he was too rattled to care. He hadn't intended to, but he found himself pouring another double. He drank this one a bit more slowly, and by the time he'd finished, he felt a nice buzz. He hadn't forgotten or stopped worrying about Aiden, but at least he wasn't wound quite as tightly as before.

What time would it be in London right about now? Four in the morning? He could never get the time difference straight. Was it five or six hours for the UK? It didn't really matter. It was too late to call. Or too early.

He got ready for bed, knowing he'd probably not sleep. When he finally closed his eyes, he imagined Aiden, naked, fucking Cam in a four-poster bed along the lines of what he remembered seeing in Versailles. It didn't matter that that was France and Cam was English—the image stuck. Red velvet sheets, carved mahogany, Aiden's skin wet from exertion, his hair stuck to his face.

"Stop it," he said aloud as he punched the pillow on the empty side of the bed. He glanced at the display on the clock radio—11:00 p.m. He forced himself to close his eyes again, but he opened them nearly as quickly. There was no way he was going to sleep. He got out of bed and threw on a pair of jeans and a cotton sweater, then combed his hair and slipped on a pair of shoes. He was out the door minutes later, headed for The Door, the gay bar a few blocks down the street from his apartment.

CHAPTER 27

SAM stumbled back into the apartment at three in the morning, alone.

Thank God for that, he thought as he woke six hours later to the bright late-morning sun. He'd never have forgiven himself if he'd done something as stupid as ending up in bed with someone else. In spite of his anger and hurt—in spite of the thrumming jealousy that he was almost too embarrassed to admit even to himself—he couldn't have cheated on Aiden. Not after everything Aiden had been through. Still, he couldn't help but wonder if Aiden—

Call him. Stop acting like a stupid kid and call him!

He managed to down a cup of black coffee. His stomach protested, but he ignored the nausea. He'd always thought of it as penance of a sort, after he'd been idiotic enough to get drunk. Still no message from Aiden. He checked his e-mail. Nothing. Two days, and still nothing. He tapped the phone and took a deep breath.

"Sam?" Aiden's voice sounded hoarse.

"Hey." Sam tried to sound casual. "Hadn't heard from you in a few days, and I thought I'd check in. You okay?"

"Oh, fuck. I said I'd call you, didn't I?" Sam heard Aiden's muffled cough on the other end of the line. "Shit, Sammy. I'm sorry. I had to take care of something, and I totally forgot."

"No problem." Boy, was *that* bullshit.

Aiden coughed again. "Sorry. I came down with some crud. Ended up having to take the train to Rome—doctor said I couldn't fly. I got here about three hours ago. I should have called you. I'm sorry."

"You going to be able to sing?" Sam's anger was now tempered with guilt. Aiden sounded terrible.

"I'll be fine. I'm taking today off. I can mark tomorrow, if I need to."

"Mark?"

"Sing half voice or down an octave. I do it anyhow when I've got long rehearsals where we're working with the director. I know the role well enough that I can wait to work with the conductor."

"Oh. That's good." Sam refilled his coffee cup. "Listen, Aiden," he began, knowing it wouldn't help anything to keep what he knew to himself, "there's something I wanted to ask you." Better to say something now. There were already enough things they had to deal with—his stupid jealousy was something they didn't need.

"Sure. Of course. Anything."

"The other day, when I called... you seemed, I don't know, distracted."

"Yeah." Aiden's sigh was audible through the speaker. "But it's nothing. Business stuff. A few canceled gigs."

"Canceled gigs?"

There was a slight pause on the other end, and Aiden finally said, "Yeah. Chuckie called right before you did. The folks in Scotland—the gig I told you about, remember, the production of *Falstaff*?"

"I remember. You were really excited about that."

"They canceled. No reason. They said they weren't interested."

"You've had that happen before, right? Not that it's a good thing, but—"

"I've had a bunch of cancellations. More than usual. Ever since Paris."

Paris. Sam's hungover brain kicked into gear at last. "Ever since what happened with Cam."

"Exactly."

"Is that what you were doing with him at the club?"

"I... *what*? How did you know?"

"There was an article about you two. Someone told me about it and—"

"Oh, crap." Aiden coughed again. "What did it say? No, don't answer that. I can just imagine. I went to meet him. I meant to tell him to stay out of my life, to stay out of *our* lives. It was a mistake. Shit,

Sammy. Don't tell me you thought...." When Sam didn't immediately answer, Aiden added, "Sam. Oh, God. I'm so sorry. You have to know I'd never do that to you. You have to believe me."

"I know. And I do believe you." Well, intellectually at least, it was true. He hadn't believed that Aiden would cheat on him. He hoped he sounded convincing, because he wasn't feeling as certain as he'd like.

"Good." Aiden sounded somewhat relieved. "Because I'd never do that to you. I wouldn't do it to anyone, after what I went through, but I sure as hell wouldn't do that to you."

"Damn, Aiden. I miss you. More than you know. I wish I could take care of you. Make you some chicken soup."

"You don't know how much I'd like that. But it won't be that long now. Only a few more weeks and I'll be back for almost a month. Maybe we can get away for a little bit. A B and B in Lancaster County?"

"Deal. I'll look into it." Sam felt his eyes burn and rubbed the bridge of his nose. *Stop feeling sorry for yourself.*

Aiden sneezed, bringing Sam back to himself. "Sorry."

"You should get back in bed. I'll call you later to check on you, okay?"

"Sounds good. Love you, Sammy."

"Love you too, Aiden."

Sam set the phone down on the counter and closed his eyes. When had this whole thing gotten so difficult?

The minute you decided to make this work. He hoped he hadn't made a huge mistake. What if it didn't work? What then? He wasn't sure his heart could handle another blow. And Aiden? He didn't want to let Aiden down. That was the last thing he wanted. And God, he loved Aiden. *But maybe that's not enough.* He pushed the thought from his mind.

CHAPTER 28

Philadelphia

May

AIDEN put the key in the lock and yawned. His flight from Frankfurt had been late arriving in New York, and he'd missed his connection. He'd gotten on another flight to Philly, but it had been delayed because of thunderstorms in Atlanta. He decided it was one of the great mysteries of travel, how in the twenty-first century a thunderstorm nearly a thousand miles away could delay a short flight between two of the largest cities in the US.

Would've been faster if I'd taken the train, he thought as he dragged his bag through the doorway just after eleven o'clock. He was exhausted, having spent more than twenty-four hours in transit from Vienna. He was sure he smelled terrible, his teeth were coated with film, and the back of his hair was flat from leaning against airplane seats. He was thirsty and slightly sick to his stomach from the philly cheesesteak he'd grabbed at the airport.

"Welcome home." Sam stood up as Aiden dragged his luggage inside, and took it from Aiden's hand.

"I can get that—"

Sam had already wheeled the luggage into the bedroom. Aiden had been hoping for a hug, maybe. Something more than skycap service, at least. He rubbed his eyes, kicked off his shoes, and walked into the kitchen. He took a glass down from the shelf and filled it with water, then leaned against the counter and drank it all without pausing.

He wanted to be happy to be home, but right now he was too brain-dead to be happy.

When he headed back into the main hallway, Sam was picking up his shoes and putting them away in the closet. "I'll get those," he began to say, but Sam had already closed the door. "You didn't need to do that, you know."

"I know." Sam offered him a smile.

"Thanks." Aiden bit back the temptation to tell Sam he didn't need a maid. Instead, he made his way to the bathroom. "I don't want to kiss you before I brush my teeth." How the hell was *that* for an excuse to avoid snapping at Sam?

His toothbrush was waiting for him. He smiled. Something about that fact—that there was a toothbrush hanging on the stand, waiting for him to return—made him relax a bit. It *was* good to be home. He ran the water over the brush, watching it for a minute in a state of semiawareness as he struggled to keep his eyes open.

"How was the trip?" Sam's voice from the bedroom brought Aiden back to himself.

"Good." He took the toothpaste with renewed determination before brushing his teeth as quickly as he could. Maybe they'd have time for a quickie before bed—before he fell asleep, that was. He splashed some water on his face and ran a quick brush through his hair, then walked back into the bedroom, pulling his shirt over his head as he moved.

Sam was unpacking his suitcase.

Fucking hell.

"Sammy...." Aiden did his best not to sound like a total ass. "Why don't we leave that for the morning? I can put it away myself, you know. I'm not that big a slob." He wasn't a slob at all, he reminded himself. In fact, the housekeeper at David's London flat complained that he did *too* much of the cleaning himself and that there was nothing for her to do.

"It's not a problem." Sam tossed Aiden's dirty socks and underwear into the rattan hamper. "Force of habit."

Right. As in, Nick was a slob and you had gotten into the habit of picking up after him.

"Stop it, Sam." He hadn't meant for it to come out quite so forcefully.

Sam turned and looked at him, clearly shocked.

"I said I can do it in the morning." Aiden hoped that this time he hadn't sounded so pissed.

"Sure." Sam averted his gaze. He looked uncomfortable. Hurt.

Great. The guy was trying to be nice, and now I've hurt his feelings. Why did it always feel like he was walking on tiptoes when he got home from a trip?

"Listen, Sammy. I'm sorry. I shouldn't have snapped at you. I'm tired."

"It's okay." Sam wore that expression Aiden hated—the one where he showed nothing. God knew what was going on behind those blue eyes of his when he looked like that.

I'm really a shit.

He walked over to Sam and pulled him close. He could sense the hesitation in Sam's body in the way he didn't move to return the embrace immediately. Even this close, Sam felt distant.

"I missed you." Aiden meant the words. He really did.

Sam's mechanical response cut Aiden to the quick. "Missed you too."

"Come to bed?"

"Sure."

They undressed in silence, Aiden slipping between the sheets, naked, and Sam following wearing only his boxers. The sheets felt like heaven, soft and welcoming. Aiden turned and put his hand on Sam's chest, stroking the soft skin there. "I'm sorry. I didn't mean to snap at you. It's just...." He hesitated, unsure of how to broach the subject. "Sometimes I sort of feel like I'm a guest here. That I should be doing more."

"I'll try not to hover." Aiden thought he heard a hint of hurt in the other man's voice. "I want to make it easier for you, that's all. Traveling is so stressful."

"I don't mind it. It's a little like what you told me about trials— they're exhausting, but they're part of your job."

"I like taking care of you, Aiden."

"And I like it when you do. But I also want to help out more around here. You know, helping you clean, doing the grocery shopping when I'm home. I want to help pay some of the bills."

Sam waved a dismissive hand. "You don't need to do that. I've got plenty of money, and Carol comes twice a month to help clean the place. All you need to do is relax when you're home."

Aiden was too tired to press the issue. He understood Sam's need to make him feel like this was his safe harbor. But Aiden knew he needed to share some of the work around the apartment. Since he'd left Cam, he'd felt as though he was a nomad. He needed a place to call home, and that meant more than putting his feet up and having Sam wait on him. Not that he didn't appreciate Sam's attentions. He did. *Let it go. We can talk about it later and I can explain it to him. He'll understand.* He kissed Sam tenderly on the lips. "I love you, Sammy."

"I love you too," Sam said. And for the first time that night, Aiden genuinely believed it.

I love you more than you know, thought Aiden as he began to drift off. They fell asleep a few minutes later, Aiden spooned against Sam's back.

THE next day was Friday, and Aiden knew Sam had to be at the office early, so he slept in late. He figured he could go for a run later, maybe practice if he felt like it. He'd been going nonstop since London. He had three weeks at home, so he wasn't worried. He had no new roles to learn that he hadn't already been working his ass off on, and he figured he could take a couple of days and goof off. He could think of a few ways to do that, with Sam's help.

With this thought, Aiden let his hand slip beneath his briefs to his cock. Sam wouldn't be home soon enough to take care of his morning erection, so he pushed his underwear down, grabbed the lube out of the bedside cabinet, and slicked up his hand. It was easy to imagine Sam sucking him off—he could still smell Sam's lingering scent on the sheets. He brought Sam's pillow to his nose and inhaled.

The man smells so damn good.

It didn't take long before he was coming, moaning his release. He dragged himself out of bed a few minutes later, wiped his belly with a towel, and tossed it into the hamper. He pulled his briefs up from his hips and splashed some cold water on his face, which was still flushed from orgasm, and he grinned back at his reflection.

Damn, it's good to be home.

He walked out of the bedroom toward the kitchen, figuring he'd make some coffee. The last thing he expected was to run into someone—a woman—in the hallway.

"Becca?" He almost didn't recognize Sam's sister. Her hair was a bright candy-apple red. She had an eyebrow piercing he didn't remember from Thanksgiving, and she was wearing kohl eyeliner, a black tank top, faded jeans, and Dr. Martens. Good thing he was surprised, or he'd have probably laughed. He'd known a few kids from high school who'd dressed like that. What was she? Twenty? Twenty-one?

"Oh, hey, Aiden. I forgot you were coming back. Sammy said something about it yesterday, but it slipped my mind."

Aiden tried to wrap his brain around her words. "I didn't know you were visiting." He felt suddenly self-conscious. He was wearing nothing but his boxer briefs. *Shit.*

The smile on her face faded.

"Everything okay?" he asked. He was missing something big here, but he was *so* not up to dealing with anyone before his morning cup of coffee. His brain felt like mush.

"He didn't tell you, did he?"

"Tell me what?"

She bit her lower lip, then said, "I'm going to be living with you guys for a few months. At least until I can get into graduate housing in August."

Aiden did the math. That was more than two months away, at least. *Sam asked her to stay for two* months *and didn't even mention it?* He rubbed his face to cover his deep inhalation, releasing the tension he could already feel building in his jaw. Damn good thing he could act.

"Oh," he said. He schooled his features so that his face appeared calm, controlled, even pleasant. Inside, however, the anger and hurt were slowly building. He needed caffeine, or he'd lose it. *This isn't her fault.*

"You look like you could use some coffee." She smiled. "I made some. Help yourself."

"Thanks." She poured him a cup, and he silently thanked the coffee gods that the coffee was dark. He didn't think he could get through this on an American brew.

"So where are you going to school?" he asked after he'd finished his second cup. He was starting to feel a bit more human now. At least he was fully dressed, having gone back to his room and thrown on some sweats. He knew none of this was Becca's fault. Still, he could feel the anger building toward a crescendo. He needed to keep talking.

"Temple," she said. "I got a fellowship in biomedical engineering. The parental units weren't too thrilled, so Sammy offered to put me up." She leaned over to him and said in a feigned whisper, "I didn't want to stay in Memphis for the summer, and they close the dorms right after finals."

She hadn't wanted to live with her parents for the summer. He understood the feeling. The summer after his first year at Indiana, he'd bounced from couch to couch to avoid going back to Mississippi. By the summer after his sophomore year, he'd gotten an apprenticeship in Central City, Colorado, and been given room and board in exchange for singing.

"How long are you home for?"

"Three weeks. Then I'm back in Europe for almost two months." Not a topic Aiden wanted to think about, only now he wasn't so sure going back to Europe sounded all that bad. *Better than dealing with Sam.*

"Oh," she said. "That must be hard for you guys."

Understatement of the century. Shit, but he didn't want to talk about this, not with her, of all people. He glanced at the clock. "Damn. I didn't realize it was so late. I told a friend I'd meet her for lunch." It was bullshit, but he figured Becca didn't know he was lying. Or that he didn't have any friends in Philly. Or that he was pissed as hell with Sam and feeling like shit.

"No problem. I'm working tonight. But maybe we can all do something together tomorrow afternoon. Do some sightseeing or go to a movie?"

"Sounds great."

He got up from the barstool and retreated to his room. A half an hour later, he waved to her as he left the apartment. He had no idea what he was going to do for the next six hours.

CHAPTER 29

SAM looked at the clock again: 7:00 p.m. He and Aiden had talked about an early dinner and catching some music downtown. He'd tried calling Aiden's cell about a dozen times, but he only got voice mail. "Hey, Aiden. I'm home. Looking forward to dinner at Vinnie's. Stacey said they've got a jazz trio playing at Nighttown starting around nine. She says they're supposed to be really good. Call me." He hoped he didn't sound too worried. It wasn't as though Aiden needed a babysitter.

By eight, Sam was pacing in the living room. He'd called Cary in Milan and David in London, succeeding only in leaving lame messages asking if either of them had heard from Aiden.

The guy lives with you, and the only two people you know to call are in Europe? It was absurd, and he knew it. He was half-tempted to find Aiden's parents online and call them too. Only the realization that he had no idea how to explain that he was looking for Aiden stopped him from looking up the Linds. Then again, if his own parents had seen the tabloid photo, maybe the Linds had, as well. That pretty much decided it for him: he'd wait.

By the time he heard the key in the front lock, it was nearly ten. Sam's relief at seeing Aiden safe and sound turned to anger nearly as quickly. "Where the hell were you?" he demanded.

Aiden's expression was hard. "Out" was all he said as he walked past Sam toward their bedroom.

"What the hell... Aiden, where do you think you're going?"

"I'm tired."

Sam grabbed Aiden's upper arm and turned him around. "Don't just walk away."

"Why the hell not?"

Aiden's response took Sam aback. He saw the raw anger on Aiden's face. For the first time that night, Sam's brain kicked in. "You're angry with me."

"I'm surprised you noticed. I'm beginning to think I'm only window dressing. You know, the boyfriend you can show off to friends but who doesn't ask anything of you."

"What are you talking about, Aiden? I lo—"

"Don't even go there, Sam. This isn't about whether you love me or not. It's about what you think about me. About *us*."

"What's happened?" Sam racked his brain for the reason Aiden was about to bite his head off. "I know last night was a bit rough, but I thought we'd moved past that. Then today—"

"When were you going to tell me? When she'd been living here a *month*?"

"Oh, fuck."

Aiden's laugh was a knife's edge. He shook his head and blew out air from between tense lips. Sam could see the pain glitter in his eyes. "You know, I was hoping I wasn't right—that you actually thought about asking me. Not that I'd have minded her living here. Hell, I like Becca. But I'm not supposed to be a fucking *guest*, Sam. This is my home too."

"Aiden." Sam rubbed a hand over his mouth and jaw. He felt like the biggest asshole on the planet. Worse, he totally deserved to feel like that. He *was* that big an asshole. "I'm so sorry. I can't believe… you're right, of course. I fucked up. Big-time." It stung to see that look on Aiden's face. Aiden, who'd done nothing but try to make this relationship work. Who was willing to work less so he could be home more often.

"It's okay."

The words were a blow to Sam's gut. Of course it wasn't okay. But what could he say to that? *I'm really sorry* was all he could think of.

"Look, Sam," Aiden said. "I'm beat. Can we talk about this in the morning? I should get some sleep."

"Sure. Of course. You're probably jet-lagged and—"

"Good night, Sam." Aiden walked down the hallway, and a moment later Sam heard the bedroom door close.

Sam stood there for a good five minutes, unsure of what to do. Waiting—hoping—for Aiden to come back. To tell him he forgave him for being such an inconsiderate shit. But Aiden didn't come back out, and Sam finally decided to get a beer from the fridge.

When he climbed into bed after midnight, he hoped Aiden might wake up, that maybe they'd sleep like they usually did, spooned against each other. But if Aiden did wake up, he made no move to touch Sam. The bed felt far too big, bigger even than when Aiden was traveling.

CHAPTER *30*

AIDEN woke up before sunrise, jet-lagged. What time would it be in Europe now? Almost lunchtime? He hadn't slept well. *No surprise there.* He'd spent most of the night arguing with himself about whether he should have apologized to Sam when he'd come to bed. Instead, he'd pretended to be asleep. *So much for maturity.*

Yeah, he was still angry with Sam. But Sam had done what he'd hoped Sam would do: he'd apologized. He hadn't made excuses. Aiden knew Sam had been miserable to realize his mistake, and Aiden had been too tired to talk about things. He hadn't been lying when he said he was happy to have Becca stay with them, either. So why did he still feel like shit this morning?

He slipped out of bed and headed for the kitchen.

AIDEN wasn't in bed when Sam woke up. He glanced over at the clock. It was nearly ten. *Shit.* Too late for the open-air market; it'd be a zoo by now. He dragged himself out of bed and threw on a robe, then made his way to the kitchen.

"Morning, sunshine." Becca and Aiden were seated at the counter, drinking coffee. "Mr. Wonderful here made pecan pancakes. There's a few left in the oven."

"Thanks."

"Coffee's still hot."

Sam met Aiden's gaze but saw nothing there. It was worse this way, Sam decided. At least if Aiden was angry, he might be able to talk to him. But acting as if nothing had happened? *He wouldn't bring it up in front of Becca, anyhow. He wouldn't want to involve her in this.*

"Great." He filled a coffee cup, pulled a few pancakes from the oven, and plopped them onto a plate.

Becca smiled and passed him the maple syrup. "Gotta run, boys. I've got the night off if you want to have dinner." She made the sign of a phone with her hand then left them alone.

"Aiden, I'm so—" His words were cut short by Aiden's lips.

"I know." Aiden wrapped his arms around Sam and drew him close. Sam nearly sighed with relief. "But you knew we were going to end up fighting sooner or later. Every couple fights sometimes, right?"

Sam didn't know what to say.

Aiden frowned and stepped back toward the counter, then leaned against it. "Sam? Didn't you and Nick ever fight?"

Had they? Sam struggled to remember. "I guess so. It was a long time ago. But it doesn't matter," he added quickly. "The point is that I fucked up."

You're doing great here. Open mouth, insert foot.

"Right." Aiden smiled. Sam was beginning to recognize that particular smile, and it made him nervous. It was like a mask, something Sam imagined Aiden might use when greeting his public after a performance. He hated that smile.

IN THE end they spent the afternoon at the Philadelphia Museum of Art. Sam had only been a few times since he'd moved to Philly, and Aiden had expressed an interest in seeing some of the new acquisitions in the museum's collection of European paintings. Sam figured it would be a good distraction from the tension at home, although Becca had had the good sense to stay away. He would thank her later—after he'd apologized to Aiden a few dozen more times.

The next week was uneventful. Sam took nearly every afternoon off from work, and Aiden practiced while Sam was gone. By the time the week was over, they'd settled into a bit of a routine, and Sam began to relax. Aiden, too, seemed more comfortable than he'd been on previous visits.

Sunday came far too soon. Sam would be prepping for trial starting the next morning, so they decided on takeout and a movie. It was a wonderful evening. He sat with Aiden's head in his lap, Aiden curled up like an oversized cat on the couch, wearing only a pair of sweats. Sam stroked Aiden's bare skin throughout the movie. By the end, he realized he'd barely been aware of the movie at all. All he could think of was fucking Aiden into the sheets.

Aiden rolled onto his back as the credits rolled. He gazed up at Sam with an evil grin. "Bed?"

"God, I thought you'd never ask," Sam told him.

"You have no idea how the movie ended, do you?"

"Nah. I've been fantasizing about what I'd do to you since they all died in the storm."

"You're a callous bastard, Samuel Ryan."

"No, just horny as hell. I'm not used to having you home. It's a little like Christmas every day," Sam admitted.

"Then you'll have to unwrap me."

Sam rolled his eyes. "I think you said something about bed?"

Aiden grabbed Sam's arm in response and began to pull him toward the bedroom. Not that Sam needed much encouragement. Five minutes later they were both naked and Sam was sucking happily on Aiden's hard cock and stretching him with lubed fingers.

"Shit, Sammy," Aiden groaned as Sam increased the suction. "You're merciless. Oh... fuck! I'm gonna come if you keep doing that."

"Good," Sam said as he came up for air. "Then I'll have to make you come again with me inside of you." He liked that idea a lot. It was only about nine, so he figured they had plenty of time.

The suggestion was, apparently, all the encouragement Aiden needed. He spilled into Sam's mouth and hung on to Sam for dear life. Yes, he could definitely get used to this. He thought vaguely about Stacey's suggestion that he travel with Aiden. Maybe she was right. What harm could it do to ask? Even a few more weeks together each year would be great. *I'll ask him tomorrow.*

He thought of Nick and how they'd spent nearly every night together, occasionally watching TV, mostly reading books or playing

Scrabble. Sometimes they ended up having sex, but more often they ended up in bed together just spooning and talking about everything and nothing at all.

Sam realized this was what he'd been missing with Aiden gone so often: spending time hanging out. No plans, no rushing, no thinking about the fact that Aiden would be leaving soon. Not that the sex wasn't something he missed—he'd spent more than a few nights jacking off, trying to imagine Aiden's hand on his cock—but it was only part of the mix. In spite of the rocky start to the visit, he'd noticed how Aiden relaxed as the week went on. Things were easier between them. Natural. It was, Sam realized, the way he'd felt with Nick when they'd been together. Comfortable. Reassuring. Warm.

Before long, Sam thrust into Aiden from behind, his body slapping against Aiden's ass while Aiden stroked himself. It was a heady feeling, having sex like this. The unrestrained, physical sex where Sam let himself go—let himself feel without thinking about it.

"Oh fuck. Nick!" Sam cried out as he came, digging his fingers into Aiden's hips so he wouldn't fall over. The words were out of his mouth before he realized what he'd said. Ice crept through his body, starting at his hands and working its way to his chest, where it settled in and clawed at him. In the instant it took him to recover, he felt Aiden tense beneath him.

"Christ. Aiden. I didn't mean…. I didn't realize what I—"

"I'm going to take a shower."

"Aiden. No. Wait!" But Aiden was gone, and when Sam went after him, he found the bathroom door locked.

AIDEN sat on the hard tile floor of the shower, letting the water fall on him, knees pulled against his chest. He wasn't crying. He was numb. For a moment he'd wondered if he'd imagined that Sam had called him Nick. At least until Sam confirmed it for him.

Fucking hell.

He'd thought things were going better between them since the blowup over Becca. They'd been talking—really talking—about the things that were important to them. Sam's pride in the firm he and Stacey had built. Sam's love for his family, about overcoming his fears and coming out to them, knowing he might lose them in the admission. Aiden's last visit home and the confrontation with his father. The sense of loss he still felt knowing he couldn't ever go home again. His love of performing and how it made him feel when he was on stage, lost in the music and the role. Had it all been bullshit?

He didn't mean to say it. In spite of the rational side of him that believed this, he felt dirty. *Shit.* Sex had been the one thing that had always been good between them, and now…. He'd scrubbed himself three times and he still felt dirty.

"You're worthless. You disgust me," his father had told him when he'd done nothing to deny the rumors of his bisexuality that had made their way to Fenton. *"I always knew you'd let your mother down. You're lucky I'll never tell her about this. It would kill her."*

In spite of everything, he'd never once felt any of the guilt his father had wished upon him. He'd never felt anything but confident in his sexuality. Until now. He knew this had nothing to do with his father, but he couldn't push the thought out of his brain: that there was no real love to be found in his attraction to men, that it was the perversion he'd been taught it was since he was a kid. He'd fallen in love only twice, and each time, he'd only gotten himself hurt.

He heard the knock on the door but he ignored it. He didn't want to talk to Sam. The wound was far too fresh coming on the heels of what had happened with Becca. *Maybe tomorrow.* He stood up and washed himself one more time, then shut off the water and toweled off.

When Aiden walked back into the bedroom, Sam was sitting up in bed, waiting. "Aiden, I can't tell you how sorry—"

"Don't sweat it, Sammy," he said nonchalantly. "Shit happens. We can talk about it tomorrow."

"But—"

"I'm tired. We'll talk about it tomorrow." That these were nearly the same words he'd said a little over a week before was not lost on him. Still, it was the truth—he *was* tired. He needed to think about things with a clear head.

CHAPTER *31*

SAM awoke with a headache, having slept right through his alarm. It was nine o'clock and he had a meeting with a client at ten. Aiden was still asleep, no doubt having slept as badly as he had. Sam was in and out of the shower in five minutes. He shaved so quickly he nicked himself several times. Ten minutes later, he was out the door and hailing a cab at the corner—there was no time to walk to the office this morning.

He went about his work in a daze, but not because of lack of sleep. He felt terrible, and he couldn't figure out what to do to make the situation with Aiden any better. *What can you possibly say to take it back?* The question dogged him all day, and he still had no idea how to answer it.

Late afternoon he caught himself staring at the computer monitor and the photograph he'd saved as wallpaper. A photograph of Aiden at the coast, dressed in a wetsuit, his hair sopping wet. Their trip to the coast felt like an eternity ago.

The intercom buzzed, bringing him back to reality with a start. "Mr. Ryan?"

"What's up, Peggy?"

"Call for you. Line six. Judge Altman."

Great. The last thing he needed now was the bad news about the magistrate job. "Thanks, Peggy." He picked up the receiver. "Your Honor, always a pleasure."

"It's Jacob. But I'll let it slide, Sam, seeing as I'm calling during business hours." Sam could hear the smile in the judge's words. "But since I know you're busy, I'll keep it brief. The judges have met to discuss your candidacy for the magistrate position. The decision was nearly unanimous. We'd like to offer you the position."

Sam took a deep breath to steady himself. "I'm honored."

"I realize you may need some time to think this over. How long do you think you might need? Two, maybe three weeks?"

"Two weeks would be fine, sir." Aiden would be going back to Europe in less than two weeks, so Sam would need to make a decision by then, anyhow. "And thank you. I'm honored you'd—"

"You're the best man for the job, Sam. We'd be lucky to have you."

"Thank you. I'll be back in touch as soon as I can."

"I look forward to it," Judge Altman said. "And if there's anything I can do to help you make your decision, please give me a call."

"Thank you, Your Honor."

"Jacob."

"Jacob," Sam repeated. "Thank you." Stunned, he leaned back in his chair. He was thrilled, of course. And yet he had no idea what to do. He hadn't expected it. He'd pushed the whole thing out of his mind; he'd assumed he wouldn't be offered the job. And Aiden.... *How do you talk to Aiden about this when you're barely speaking to each other?*

HE LEFT the office around seven. He'd finished what he'd needed to get done, he just hadn't wanted to go home at six. He was still clueless as to what to say to Aiden. *I'm sorry* didn't seem to cut it. *I was a complete asshole* might be a start. By the time he got home, it was nearly eight. He'd stopped by a corner deli on the walk home and picked up a bouquet of flowers. Better than walking in empty-handed. Maybe Aiden would take pity on him and they could move on. Maybe.

Aiden was sitting in the living room listening to music. Not the usual jazz or rock, but a string quartet. Mozart, perhaps? Sam was getting better at the "guess the composer" game, but he still needed a lot of practice. "Sorry I'm late."

"No problem. I'm sure things were busy today."

"A little." A lie, really, but Sam figured it was easier than telling Aiden the truth—that he'd been a complete mess at work. He'd wait until later to tell Aiden about the job. "Becca around?"

"She left about an hour ago. She's got a date. Some guy from work."

"Seriously?" Sam wasn't sure how he felt about that. "I guess it's natural that she'd date."

"I guess." Aiden's voice sounded flat. Defeated.

"These are for you." Sam handed Aiden the flowers.

"They're lovely. Thanks, Sam." That smile again. The unreadable one. Sam wondered what was going on behind the placid expression. Was Aiden angry? *Of course he is. Wouldn't you be pissed to hell?*

"Look," Sam said, keenly uncomfortable now, "I'm going to change out of my suit. Back in a few minutes, okay?"

"Sure."

Sam hesitated, then walked down the hallway to the bedroom. He pulled off his jacket and hung it on the back of the chair by the door. That's when he noticed the suitcases against the wall. For a brief instant, he wondered if Aiden had taken them out of the closet to get to something behind them. But when he lifted the closest one, he realized they were full. Packed. Overcome with fear, he strode back out into the living room and asked, "What's up with the suitcases?"

"Oh, right," Aiden said. "I got a call from Chuckie. He told me the rehearsals for *Il Trovatore* are starting a week early. Seems the conductor has a conflict, and they had to shuffle the schedule around. I've got a flight around lunchtime tomorrow."

Sam wasn't sure why he didn't feel relieved to hear this. *At least he didn't say, "I'm moving out."* "That's terrible. I was enjoying having you around."

Aiden stood up and put his arms around Sam, then kissed him lightly on the lips. "I know. I was enjoying it too. My flight leaves first thing in the morning. I was thinking maybe we could go out to dinner tonight. Maybe the Korean place over near Front Street?"

"Aiden, I—"

"Shh, Sammy. No worries. We all do stupid shit sometimes. It was an honest mistake. You were with him a long time."

Sam couldn't believe what he was hearing. "You're not angry with me?"

"I'm a little hurt," Aiden admitted, "but I'm okay."

"All right. If you're sure…."

"I'm sure. Now why don't you get out of that suit, and we can get some food."

AIDEN sat on the airplane the next day, staring out at the thick bank of clouds that blocked the view of the water below. He'd left for the airport far earlier than he needed. He hadn't wanted to draw out his good-byes with Sam. It was easy to rationalize the entire thing and even easier to rationalize having lied. He'd lied about the change in his rehearsal schedule. He'd lied about being fine with Sam calling him Nick. He hadn't really lied about understanding how Sam might call him that, though. He knew why Sam had done it.

Because he loved Nick. Because he still *loves Nick, and there's no way in fucking hell I'll ever be able to replace him. I can't even come close.*

There was no denying that he was running away. Then again, he was tired of trying to make things work. It was better to take some time off from the relationship. He'd be back again in less than two months. By then he'd figure out what to do about things. Or maybe Sam would make it easy for him and tell him to move out. He still kept some things at David's place in London. It wouldn't be too painful.

Yeah, right.

"Would you like a drink, Mr. Lind?" the flight attendant asked. "We'll be serving dinner shortly."

"Bourbon."

"On the rocks?"

"Straight up. And make it a double."

"Of course, sir."

CHAPTER 32

Milan
July

"AIDEN."

"Hey, Chuckie. Long time no hear. How's New York?" Aiden balanced the phone between his shoulder and his cheek as he finished up an e-mail to his mother.

"Aiden, we need to talk."

Aiden frowned. He'd never known his agent not to take the bait. Something was wrong. It wasn't as if the reviews of *Tosca* had been disappointing. In fact, they raved about Aiden's performance. Then what?

"I'm listening. Shoot."

Chuck took a long breath. "There've been two more cancellations."

"What the fuck?" He shot up off the couch and, in his anger, nearly dropped his laptop on the tile floor.

He'd been staying outside the city at David's villa during the two-week run of the opera, and he'd been enjoying the downtime between weekend performances. The light rain of the night before had left a soft shimmer over the Italian countryside, but when he looked outside, he saw none of it through his anger.

"Calm down, Aiden. You've got plenty of other—"

"Which gigs?" he demanded.

"The one in Wales and the one in Antwerp."

"What did they say?"

"Nothing. At least, not at first. I've got a friend who works in the front office of the Wales company. I gave her a call when I didn't get a straight answer from management. She only told me that someone put pressure on the board not to sign the contract.

"I made a pest of myself with the Belgian guys. They finally admitted that they'd been offered a large donation to use some other singer."

"Who?"

"The singer?"

"Yeah, the singer. Who'd they offer the role to?"

"Jorgen Johannsen."

"Johannsen?" Aiden scowled. "He doesn't even like singing Verdi. When I was at Covent Garden, he was rehearsing a Mozart opera. Swore up and down he'd never take another gig singing the heavy stuff."

Covent Garden. It was all the evidence Aiden needed. He was sure none of this was a coincidence.

"Aiden?"

"Yeah, Chuck, I'm still here. Sorry."

"So what are you thinking?"

"Do me a favor. Talk to the Wales woman again. See if you can find out anything about this big donor she mentioned."

"You thinking you might know Mr. Moneybags?"

"I'll let you know. When you find something out, call me. Leave me a message if I don't answer. Okay?"

"Sure." There was a pause on the other end; then Chuck added, "You're not going to do anything stupid, are you? Because I don't think—"

"I won't do anything stupid. I promise."

"Okay."

"Call me as soon as you know anything."

"Will do."

Aiden tapped the phone and tossed it onto the couch, then sat back down and opened the laptop. It only took him about five minutes to book himself on the next flight to London.

"TELL Lord Sherrington that Aiden Lind is here to see him."

"Mr. Lind, let me check his sched—"

Aiden walked past the secretary's desk, through a set of double doors, and into a spacious office with a wall of glass that looked out over London. Aiden had never been to Cam's new offices at Canary Wharf. Even as angry as he was, it was hard not to be impressed. Forty floors up, Aiden could see the Thames below and, beyond it, Stave Hill Ecological Park with its lush trees and grass. Clearly, business was good.

Cam was seated behind a sleek glass desk—Italian design, knowing Cam—leaning back in his chair, and speaking to a man Aiden didn't recognize. When he saw Aiden, he stood. "We'll finish this later, John." The man looked surprised but did not protest, exiting the office a moment later.

"Aiden," Cam said, walking over toward him, "it's so good to see—"

"What the hell are you doing?" Aiden demanded, coming back to himself. He was so angry he could barely think straight. He only knew he needed Cameron to hear this, to make it clear to him that regardless of his money, Cam couldn't push him around.

Cam's brow furrowed. "What on earth has gotten into you, Aiden? I don't understand what you're talking—"

Aiden slapped Cam across the face. He hadn't meant to do it, but the urge came upon him with such ferocity that he couldn't help himself.

Cam blinked, looking both confused and hurt, touching the place on his cheek where Aiden had made contact, an unspoken question on his lips.

"I've had enough, Cam. Enough of the bullshit. Enough of you denying that you had anything to do with it. I thought I'd made it clear, months ago, that I'm tired of you stabbing me in the back and then pretending you're sorry for fucking me over."

Cam said nothing. Was he trying to understand where Aiden's anger was coming from? This thought infuriated Aiden all the more—how the hell could the man *not* understand?

"You know," Aiden said with a bitter laugh that echoed about the large office, "I loved you once. I thought I'd spend the rest of my life with you. And even after I left you, I doubted myself. My decisions." He swallowed hard and continued, "But now, after what you've done to my life and my career…. Does it make you feel better to know that my life's a mess because of you? Is that what you wanted?"

"I haven't—"

"That's what you said the last time. You said you hadn't done anything. It was all bullshit."

"I know I shouldn't have talked to the reporter after you left. I admit that I'd hoped she'd get through to you where I couldn't have. I didn't realize she'd go after you in the States. But I haven't done anything since. I had nothing to do with the photograph at the club. Truly I didn't." Cam appeared genuinely contrite, but then again, he'd always been well practiced in the art of contrition.

"You should be happy." Aiden's jaw tensed, and he nearly spat the words. "Thanks to you, Sam and I are barely speaking to each other." He knew that Cam's little scheme hadn't been the problem at home, but in that moment he didn't care.

"I… I'm sorry."

"Like hell you are."

"Please believe me, Aiden, I hadn't intended—"

"You're really good, Cam. You should be proud of your handiwork. I've lost nearly eight jobs now thanks to you. Congratulations." He bowed theatrically. "What did you figure? That if you took away both my music and the man I love, that I'd come crawling back?"

"No, I—"

"Don't even answer." Aiden took a deep breath. "There's nothing you can say that will make it better. I don't even know why I bothered to come here. What can I do, anyhow? You've made good on your threats. Bravo! Now stay the fuck out of my life." Aiden stormed out of the office, heading straight for the elevator and watching the doors close right as Cameron came down the hallway.

Two minutes later, he headed out of the building into the steady rain that had begun to fall. Funny how the London rain used to make this place feel more like home. Now he hated it. The traffic on the street whizzed by, but he ignored it. He'd normally have hailed a cab to take him back to David's apartment, but he needed to walk. He needed to think. He was still too angry, not only with Cam, but with himself.

He pulled his phone out of his pocket. Sam had called again. That made three calls Aiden hadn't returned. He wanted to talk to Sam, but he was afraid if Sam asked him why he wasn't coming back to Philly next week, as they'd originally planned, he'd say something stupid.

Like *Maybe this entire relationship thing was a mistake.* He was tired of trying to live up to Nick's memory. Tired of being second best. *Fucking Saint Nick.* He knew he wasn't being completely fair to Sam, either, but it was easier to be angry with Sam than with himself.

He walked to the corner to cross onto West India Avenue.

"Aiden!" he heard a voice behind him call. He turned around to see Cam running down the street after him.

Fucking hell. Would the man not simply disappear?

"Aiden, please," Cam yelled, "give me a chance to explain!"

As if!

Aiden turned back to the street and stepped over the curb. He didn't see the taxi on the roundabout until it was barely a foot away from him. The last thing he saw was the wide-eyed expression on the driver's face. He heard the sound of the horn, but it was too late.

CHAPTER 33

THE cell phone on the side table rang, and Sam rolled over and groaned. It was five in the morning. He squinted at the display on the phone. Aiden. How long had it been since they'd talked? More than a week?

"I'm glad you called," he began. "I—"

"Is this Sam?" The voice was clipped. British.

"Who the hell is this?"

"Cam. Cameron Sherrington. I used to—"

"What the fuck are you doing, calling on Aiden's phone?" Sam was sitting up now, wide-awake.

"Look, it's not what you think. Aiden was with me and… well… it's my fault. He was very angry when he came to my office."

"And this surprises you? Put Aiden on the phone."

"I tried to calm him down," Cameron continued, "but he was so angry. He didn't believe me, that I'd never… oh, shit. I followed him downstairs, out of the building. I don't know if he even heard me, he was so angry. And then he walked out into the street and…."

There was ice in Sam's veins. He could barely breathe. "Aiden. What's happened to Aiden?"

"I knew you'd want to know. I—"

"Tell me what happened to him, Cameron." Sam's throat felt tight, and his heart beat so hard against his ribs, it almost hurt.

"He was crossing the street. The taxi didn't see him. He stepped in front of it."

Oh, God.

"What… I mean how—?"

"They took him by ambulance. The Royal London Hospital. He's alive, but I don't know how badly he's hurt…."

"I'll be on the next flight."

SAM hadn't even realized there was an early morning flight to Heathrow from Philadelphia. He'd tried calling Cam back on Aiden's phone, having forgotten to get another number from him. He'd also tried calling David Somers, although he had no idea if the conductor was even in London. Neither had answered.

Aiden.

They'd been pulling away from each other for months now. Sam knew it. Worse, he'd *let* it happen. They'd talked, but they hadn't been honest with each other. He'd blown it off when Aiden had told him he wanted to help out with expenses. He figured that Aiden spent enough money flying back and forth between Philly and Europe. He also hadn't listened when Aiden had tried to tell him he wanted to help around the house. He'd told Aiden he didn't need his help, that the least he could do for him was to wash the laundry, vacuum, and dust. But Sam knew at least in part that he *wanted* to do the chores on his own—that he liked the way he'd been doing things for the past eight years and didn't want Aiden to do them *his* way.

He knew Aiden hadn't been truthful when he said the rehearsal schedule had changed, and he hadn't called him on it. *He lied, and you knew it. You just found it convenient to ignore the lie.* Why? Because he'd been lying to himself, telling himself that things were fine, that they would work things out, when really he was silently terrified they wouldn't survive this. He couldn't help but wonder if not asking Aiden about Becca, or the time he'd called Aiden "Nick," were the stupid mistakes Aiden said they were. He'd finally realized that the long-distance part of their relationship wasn't the easily surmountable obstacle he'd said it was months before. It had been so easy to rationalize it all. Now, he could lose Aiden forever, and how had he left things? He hurried into the A&E, the British equivalent of an ER, after asking for directions at the front desk.

When he found the right curtained-off cubicle, he nearly knocked a nurse off her feet as he barreled inside.

"I'm sorry," he panted, out of breath, terrified of what he might see. "I'm here to see—"

"Sam?" Aiden was sitting up in the bed, dressed, his arm in a sling.

"Thank God." Sam strode over to the bed and hugged Aiden as gingerly as possible. "When I got the call, I thought…." His voice trailed off as he realized they weren't alone. Cam was standing near the bed, watching them. He looked as uncomfortable as Sam felt to see him there.

"Thank you for calling me." Sam reached out his hand to shake Cam's.

"*You* called him?" Aiden's eyes were wide.

Cam's jaw tensed visibly. "I should be going." He turned to Sam and added, "I'll check in with you later. See how he's feeling." Sam knew it'd be polite to protest and tell Cam to stay, but he didn't want to be polite. He'd spent his whole fucking life being polite. And he didn't give a shit if Cam knew he was jealous.

"He called me on your phone." Sam fought to keep his voice from breaking.

"Cam did?"

Sam nodded but remained silent. He didn't want to know what Aiden had been doing with Cam. He'd ask later.

A nurse pulled aside the cubicle curtain. "Mr. Lind? Mr. Somers's car is downstairs."

"Thank you."

"David?"

Aiden smiled—Sam thought he looked exhausted—and tapped his head. "Concussion. David's in town. Said he'd play nursemaid. They wouldn't have released me otherwise."

"Oh."

"If you can stay. I'd much rather have you play nursemaid."

"I'd like that." As if he'd have said no.

THE sun was already setting outside the window of Aiden's room. Sam felt a surge of guilt at the realization that this was Aiden's second home, and that he'd never even seen the place until now. The room was lovely, with its antique bed, carved wooden chest of drawers, and the small table at the bedside. The drapes were floral but not overly fussy: the bright botanicals of an English garden with a pale-sage background, tied back to let the light inside. The windows were open, letting in a soft breeze that carried the light fragrance of flowers from the courtyard.

Sam helped Aiden into the bed over Aiden's weak protests. Sam guessed Aiden liked the attention, in spite of his obvious embarrassment. And no wonder he craved Sam's touch—they'd been so distant the past few months.

"Pain meds?" Sam asked.

"Yes, please." Aiden yawned and rubbed the bridge of his nose. "Headache's pretty bad, and the room keeps spinning."

A few minutes later, having downed two of the pills with some water, Aiden was propped up on the pillows and smiling at Sam, who was seated on the side of the bed. "I'm really glad you came."

Sam's gut clenched at the implication he heard in Aiden's words: that he might have chosen *not* to come. Had things between them gotten so bad that there was a question?

Yes. It pained him to admit it to himself.

"Listen, Sam," Aiden began, "I'm sorry."

"For what? This wasn't your fault." He knew exactly what Aiden meant, though.

"Not for the accident. That... that was just stupid. I was distracted. I meant that I'm sorry. About not coming home."

"You were working. I didn't expect—"

"I didn't come home, Sam. I didn't want to."

Oh, fuck. It wasn't a surprise, but he hadn't wanted to hear the truth, either. He'd known Aiden had been staying away, but he'd done nothing. He'd let Aiden go.

Sam took a deep breath. "I know."

For a minute or two, neither of them spoke. Amazing how long a few minutes could feel when the weight of the world hung on them.

When they spoke again, it was both at once. They laughed—uncomfortable, nervous laughs—and then Aiden said, "I missed you."

Sam was sure Aiden could hear the breath he released from between his lips. "I missed you too."

"I know I fucked up." Aiden spoke in an undertone.

"You? No. *I* was the one who fucked up. I let you go."

"I lied when I said I didn't have time to fly home. I'm sorry." Aiden yawned. In the dying light, the dark circles under his eyes seemed more pronounced.

"No apologies. We said no more apologies, remember?"

The edges of Aiden's mouth turned faintly upward. "Yeah. I remember." He laughed. "We do a shitty job at that, you know."

Sam got up and walked over to the window. There wasn't much to see: other rooftops, some old tile roofs, others newer. "I don't want to lose you, Aiden.

"I had some time to think," Sam continued. "On the plane. Not like I was going to sleep, worrying about you. What might have happened to you…." He took a deep breath. A couple of pigeons flew off a roof and into the darkening sky. The clouds were a thick, nearly solid gray, covering any stars.

"It was like I was back there again… in New York. And I wasn't sure if Nick would live. I kept hoping, but something inside of me knew. It was happening all over again." Sam's eyes filled with tears. "There was nothing I could do. Nothing. Just wait and not know.

"I realized how I'd gone and fucked it all up with you. Treating you like you were second best. Like Nicky was still there, in my heart. Doing things like he and I used to do things. Expecting you to *be* like him." Tears coursed down his cheeks. He didn't want to look at Aiden as he spoke the words—he didn't want Aiden to see him this vulnerable—so he kept staring out the window.

"But… on the plane… I realized I didn't want him. Not that I didn't love him—I don't mean it like that, because God, I loved him—

but that I wanted *you*. That if anything happened to you, I didn't think I could survive it."

Sam wiped his eyes with his hands. "I was so afraid to lose you like I lost him that I pushed you away. I didn't understand I was doing that, all these months. I wish I could take it all back... show you how much I love you... how much you mean to me." He inhaled slowly and said, "I love you so much, Aiden."

He'd expected to see forgiveness on Aiden's face, but when he turned around, he realized Aiden was sound asleep. How long had he been sleeping?

It doesn't matter. You'll tell him again when he's feeling better. Aiden would understand too. Sam was sure of it. He'd probably always understood; he hadn't wanted to burden Sam with it.

Sam settled into the large chair by the bed and rested his head against the high upholstered back. For more than an hour, he watched the steady rise and fall of Aiden's chest as he slept. It was nearly sunrise when he heard Aiden's voice from the bed.

"I don't want to sleep alone. Come lie down next to me?"

Sam nodded and, bleary-eyed, slipped between the sheets with Aiden after making sure that Aiden's broken arm was supported by one of the pillows. It only took a few minutes this time for both of them to fall asleep.

CHAPTER 34

"HEY." Sam walked out into the small garden behind the flat. There was a tiny fountain in the middle—a lovely modern design with colored stones and mirrors that reflected the little rays of sunshine that managed to peer through the usual clouds. "How are you feeling?"

"Sore." Aiden forced a smile. Every muscle in his body ached. Even smiling hurt. "But I'm fine." His head still pounded, and the dizziness lingered. The doctor had told him it might be like that for a while, with the concussion.

Sam motioned to the bench. "Mind if I join you?"

"You don't have to ask, Sam." Aiden was painfully aware of Sam's discomfort. *I'm the reason for it.* He repressed a sigh.

"Look, Aiden, I—"

The glass doors to the garden opened. "Cam."

"I'll come back later." Sam got up abruptly.

"Sam—" Aiden tried to follow, but the world spun and Cam rushed over to steady him. Sam was gone.

"I'm sorry. I didn't mean to chase him off." Aiden shot him a look of keen irritation, although Cam's regret appeared genuine. "Should I go after him?"

"Why are you here, Cam?" Aiden didn't even look at Cam. He was staring at the doors Sam had just walked out. He didn't care that he was being rude.

"I came to see how you were."

"I'm fine. Now please leave." *I don't need you here to make things any worse.*

"Not until I tell you what I found out." When Aiden responded with a frown, Cam added, "About the contracts. You know. I—"

"Later, Cam," Aiden said as he opened the doors that led back inside. He needed to find Sam. He needed to talk to him, and something told him he'd better do it now.

"WHAT are you doing?" Aiden steadied himself against the doorway of his room. Sam was packing his bag. The cold feeling in the pit of Aiden's stomach became one of panic and nausea, and he was pretty sure it had nothing to do with getting hit by a car. This was far worse.

"I should go," Sam said without looking up from his suitcase. "I'm only in the way here, and Cam—"

"What the hell are you talking about? You just got here, Sammy."

"It was a mistake. I should have realized—"

Aiden gritted his teeth and grabbed Sam by the arm. "Look at me," he demanded. "Will you look at me for a minute?"

Sam turned and met Aiden's gaze. Sam looked hurt, as if he were steeling himself for the inevitable. "Aiden, you look terrible. We can talk about this la—"

"Stop, Sam. Stop and listen to me." Aiden hadn't meant to raise his voice, but the feeling of helpless dread had only intensified when he saw Sam so rattled.

Sam nodded, then helped him sit down on the edge of the bed. He looked perfectly miserable.

"Please, Sam. I need to say this."

Sam sat down next to him on the bed. His shoulders were visibly tense.

He thinks I'm going to tell him it's over.

Aiden knew he needed to say something and that he'd better make it good. "I don't want you to leave." Could he make it any clearer? Shit. He was so bad at this! Give him a fucking aria and he was the king. Ask him to talk to someone—really *talk* to someone—and he became Little Aiden Lind. Insecure, awkward, unable to string two words together to make a sentence.

I love you, Sam. Don't leave me.

"But I thought—"

"What are you afraid of, Sam?"

Did I just say that? Aiden cringed inwardly. Sam looked so lost, so pathetic, so… defeated.

Sam blinked in surprise, and Aiden saw something like guilt on his face. *Hell, this isn't what I wanted to do. I wanted to make it better, not worse!*

"I…." Sam's voice sounded rough with emotion. "You're right. I'm an asshole."

"No." Aiden put his fingers to Sam's lips. "No, you're not. It's what you said last night. You're afraid of losing me like you lost him… like you lost Nick." There. He'd said it.

"You… you heard me?"

"Some of it. When I woke up this morning, I wondered if I imagined it. But you *did* say it, didn't you?"

"I did." Sam inhaled audibly.

"I don't want you to go. Talk to me, Sammy. Please."

"I didn't want to bother you with it. It was so long ago, and I didn't think it mattered anymore." Sam rubbed his face with a large hand.

"It matters to me. I need to know. I need to hear what happened with Nick. Whatever I think about what happened, it must be a hundred times worse, and I want to understand. I love you, Sammy. I won't lose you to his ghost."

Sam's eyes were wet with tears. Aiden felt like the biggest dick. Why the fuck did he have to go and say that? "Shit. I'm so sorry." His voice came out in a hoarse whisper. "I didn't mean—"

"No. It's okay. I said it myself last night." Sam got up from the bed and went over to the mirror. For a moment he seemed to stare at himself, although Aiden wondered what he saw there. "Last night, I said I'd been treating you like you were second best. And it's true." He turned and faced Aiden. "I wanted you to *be* him."

Aiden tried not to react to the sting of Sam's words, putting on his best acting face as if he were donning armor for some battle. He forced himself to smile like he meant it. "It's okay."

"No. It's not," Sam said. "I tried to pretend that it was all right, doing things the way I'd always done them with him. 'House rules', I said. I cleaned up after you like I used to clean up after him. He was such a slob. But you're not like that, and I knew it, but I couldn't help myself." Sam's laugh was bitter. "Maybe I was scared of change. Maybe I was scared that if I let you in, I'd forget about him, and I didn't want to forget him."

"I'd never want you to. I mean it."

"I know. Shit, do you know how many times I told myself that?" Sam ran a hand through his hair. His face was tear-streaked. Aiden fought the urge to comfort him—but he knew Sam needed to say this.

"On the plane, I thought...." Aiden could see him steeling himself. He saw the pain in Sam's eyes, raw and pulsating there. "I thought I'd lose you like I lost him. It was the worst thing.... Even now, it hurts so much. Remembering him like that."

This time Aiden held his good arm out to Sam, but Sam hesitated. "Please. Let me help. I love you, Sam."

Sam drew a ragged breath and sat down beside Aiden.

Aiden drew Sam close and felt him shudder at the memory. "Tell me about Nick. About what happened to him. If it's okay, I mean."

"Are you sure?" There was a surprising note of relief in Sam's voice.

"Yes. I'm sure." He reached out and put his hand on Sam's thigh.

Sam took a deep breath and nodded as if steeling himself. "You already know the basics." He turned to look directly at Aiden. Aiden squeezed his thigh and smiled back at him. "We'd been together since we met in undergrad. We bought a place together—a loft in Brooklyn." Sam put his hand over Aiden's. "He was selling his work, getting the recognition he deserved. I was looking at a job working for a small employment law firm on the lower east side. Plaintiff's firm. It would have been a pretty big pay cut, but we'd worked it out. It'd mean a few years of vacations close to home, that sort of thing. I'd planned on resigning from the law firm the next week....

"I got the phone call on a Friday morning. They'd taken him to the hospital. The woman at the gallery said he'd been complaining his head hurt. And then he just collapsed.

"They said there was nothing they could do for him, that the bleeding in his brain was too bad. They couldn't operate." Aiden could tell Sam was fighting back tears. "He lingered. They told me he wouldn't wake up from the coma.... I remember thinking that it wasn't fair that he could live like that. He wouldn't have wanted that. Nicky was so full of life...."

Sam popped up off the bed and strode to the window. "I *wanted* him to die, Aiden. God! It was horrible. And when they told me that I could end it, that he wouldn't live without the ventilator.... I knew it's what he would have wanted. Hell, I knew it before they even told me there was nothing they could do for him. But I waited. I kept thinking—hoping—that he'd wake up. I knew it's what his family wanted even though they kept telling me what I wanted to hear... that he might wake up and be fine. He was their *son*, and I was the one who could end it for him. Put him out of his pain and suffering. Let him go."

Aiden stood up and walked over to Sam, put his good arm around Sam's waist, and pressed his face to Sam's back.

"Shit, Aiden. I felt so selfish—wanting him to die so I wouldn't have to make the choice. Knowing it was the right thing to do for him...."

For nearly a minute, Sam said nothing. Aiden wasn't sure what to say, so he held Sam tighter and waited. Finally, Sam laughed. "Nicky always told me I took forever to make decisions. He was right. But I knew that this was for him and that he'd trusted me to do the right thing.

"So one day, after they'd all said their good-byes, the doctor turned off the machines. I sat there holding his hand. Knowing I'd just let the only man I'd ever loved die...."

Aiden closed his eyes as hot tears ran down his cheeks.

"I told myself I couldn't do that again." Sam pulled away and met Aiden's gaze. Then he laughed again, a bitter, self-loathing laugh that made Aiden's gut clench. "So here I am, like an idiot, running away from you. As if that's any better."

"I'm not going anywhere. Not if I can help it. And Cam... he and I've been over for a long time."

Sam shook his head and smiled. "I know that. I've known it from the very start."

"Then why were you packing your bag? Leaving? I thought maybe you thought—"

"God. You're going to laugh at me. It's so juvenile."

"What? What's so funny?"

"I wanted you to come after me."

"Seriously?"

Sam nodded, looking shamefaced. "I know. It's about the stupidest—"

Aiden kissed him.

"Why did you do that?" Sam asked a moment later.

"Because I love you, Sammy. And yeah, it's stupid. But it makes me feel good to know you wanted me to come after you. Maybe that makes us *both* stupid."

Sam laughed, and this time, for the first time that day, it was the laugh Aiden remembered he loved so much. "I don't get you sometimes. But I guess that's okay."

CHAPTER 35

"SO WHAT now?" Sam asked. "Since I've acted like a complete fool and you haven't told me to go home, I'm thinking maybe you're not so keen to dump me?" He felt shaky, having just spilled his guts. Vulnerable too. But for the first time in a long time, he felt at peace. He'd been avoiding telling Aiden about Nick for too long.

You've been avoiding thinking about what happened for even longer.

"As if." Aiden took his hand and squeezed it. "But we need to talk. About how to make this thing work. Because I want it to."

"I know. I want it too." Sam wondered if he looked as fragile as he felt. Still, he'd spent the entire night before thinking about making this relationship work, and he knew he was ready to talk about it.

He took the suitcase off the bed, then lay down and gestured for Aiden to join him. It was awkward with the cast on Aiden's arm, but Sam helped him so that he rested on his uninjured side, his broken arm against Sam's chest.

"I feel like a baby," Aiden admitted. "I can't even lie down without help."

"I like taking care of you." It was true, and he knew that was one of the things he'd been missing so desperately during the long separations. He wanted to feel needed. Useful.

Aiden smiled. Sam was struck by the difference between that smile and the one he'd come to expect when Aiden didn't want him to know how he felt about something. He resolved not to let Aiden pass off the other smile again. *Never again.* Not if he could help it.

"I like it when you do."

Sam kissed him on the nose, and Aiden laughed. "I also like to hear you laugh like that."

"So what do we do now, Sammy? How do we make this work?"

"I've been thinking about that. I thought about it on the flight over," Sam said. "That and the fact that I couldn't lose you."

"And?"

"And I know I'd probably get in your way, but I was thinking maybe I could come with you when you travel."

"You'd do that?" Aiden looked genuinely pleased. Surprised too.

"You'd want me to?"

"Are you kidding? I've wanted to ask you to travel with me. I didn't think you could manage... I mean, what about your job?"

"Which one? The law firm? Or the magistrate job I turned down yesterday?"

"What? But the job was perfect for you."

"Perfect for my career. Not perfect for me."

"But you said—"

"I said it was a great career move. That doesn't mean it's the right thing for me." He smiled reassuringly at Aiden.

"I don't want to hold you back, Sam."

Sam carefully pulled Aiden back against his chest. He closed his eyes for a moment, reveling in the feel of Aiden's body, warm and solid against his own. "You aren't holding me back. You never could." He paused for a moment, then said, "I like my job. A lot. Stace and I have worked our asses off to make the firm what it is."

"But that's the problem."

"No. It's not. The firm is doing what it's supposed to do. What we *intended* it to do—run itself. It doesn't need me to make things work on a day-to-day basis. It's why we've worked hard to hire good people, and it's why we pay them well." When he saw the look of confusion on Aiden's face, he continued, "But I've gotten into the habit of having my fingers in everything even though I don't need to. But that's all it is: a habit. It's time to step back a little. I'm not saying I could give up practicing law like Jason did, but—"

"I'd never want you to."

Sam's fingers brushed Aiden's cheek, and Aiden shivered. "But I can still practice law, and I can do it when and how I'd like," he continued. "I'm the boss, remember? Honestly, I'd have been traveling with you months ago if I hadn't been such an idiot. Stace kept telling me I should ask you if you'd want me to come, and I kept telling her I'd be in your way. I should have asked." God, he was such a fucking idiot! He knew two-year-olds who were better at communicating than he'd been.

"Shit. We're a pair!"

"I've got a few other ideas too. But we can talk about those later." He would talk about them too. He wasn't going to screw this up again.

"They'd better include letting me do some of the work around the apartment when I'm home."

"I think I can arrange that."

"And you'll stop pretending you're my butler and unpacking for me?" Aiden kissed Sam's cheek.

"You really hate that, don't you?"

"Makes me feel like a guest in my own house," Aiden explained.

"You got it. I like that you call it your house, though." He really did. The warm feeling it gave him reminded him of how he'd felt, years ago, living in Brooklyn. Aiden's presence made the place in Philly feel like home.

"I do too."

"Although I was thinking we might look for something together. A place that's *ours*," Sam said. "Maybe even a row house."

"You'd do that? Move?"

This time Sam kissed Aiden. "Yeah. Not that I don't like the apartment, but I was thinking it'd be nice to have a little backyard. Maybe something along the lines of what David has here. Where we could have dinner in the spring and maybe plant flowers and—"

"I love you, Sammy," Aiden interrupted, rolling over and wincing when he put too much weight on his arm.

"How long before that stupid cast comes off?" Sam asked as he pulled Aiden back onto his side and arranged the pillows behind him again.

"Too long." The smile Aiden shot him was wicked. "But that doesn't mean you can't take care of me."

"What about Cam?"

"Who?" Aiden shook his head in mock reproach. "I'll talk to him later. He'll be back anyhow. He always comes back."

"I'm going to have a little talk with him."

"Jealous?" Aiden's tone was playful, and Sam let out a theatrical sigh.

"Damn straight. But don't you dare tell him that," Sam warned.

"So I'm waiting, Sammy." Aiden's eyes flashed with heat. "Are you going to take care of me like you promised?"

"I... yeah, but...." He didn't want to hurt Aiden, but God, he *wanted* him.

"It's just my arm." Aiden bit his lower lip. "There are plenty of things you can do to the rest of my body."

"Tell me what you want me to do." He wanted Aiden in charge.

Aiden grinned. "Strip."

One word and Sam's cock filled. *Like magic.* He laughed with the thought.

"Nothing funny about this, Mr. Ryan. I gave you an order." Aiden's smile belied the stern words.

Sam had already hopped off the bed with his shirt half-undone by the time Aiden finished speaking. He didn't need to be told twice—he wanted this so badly he ached. The shirt fell to the ground a moment later. As he unbuttoned the waist of his jeans, he watched Aiden. Aiden's gaze was fierce. Hungry.

Sam unzipped the jeans slowly, teasing. He knew full well Aiden knew what he was up to, though Aiden didn't let on. Sam pushed down the heavy fabric and stepped out of the legs. His boxers were tented, but instead of giving in to the familiar embarrassment, he forced himself to look Aiden directly in the eyes.

"Nice." Sam knew Aiden understood the significance. Aiden waited a moment, then said, "Turn around."

Sam complied, all the while swallowing hard and sucking on his tongue to keep from moaning. His nipples hardened, though he doubted the slight chill in the room was to blame.

"Now take those boxers off. Nice and slow."

Sam shimmied—slowly—out of the cotton boxers, keenly aware that with each movement, Aiden was studying his ass. He was leaking now. He felt a drop of wetness on his thumb as he nudged the material over his hard cock.

"No," Aiden said as Sam began to turn around to face him. "Stay like that."

Sam bit his tongue hard enough that he tasted copper.

"And don't fidget." Sam heard the smile in Aiden's admonition, but he forced himself to remain still.

"Better." Another pause, then: "Now turn around and face me." When Sam was quite literally pointed in Aiden's direction, Aiden said, "Touch yourself, Sam. Pretend it's me touching you."

This time Sam couldn't bite back the moan. The sound was pleading and pathetic to his own ears. *Holy hell!* Sam grabbed his cock and squeezed with one hand, then ran the other over the tip to wet his fingers.

"That's it, baby. Squeeze it for me. Does it feel good?"

"Fuck, yes" was all Sam could manage to say. He closed his eyes and imagined Aiden's hands on him, making their way up and back down again, caressing him, working him. His gasps and groans broke the silence from time to time. He heard Aiden's breathing become more labored. When he opened his eyes again, he saw Aiden shift on the bed to accommodate the bulge between his legs.

"Now put a finger in your mouth. Slick it up good." Aiden's nod of approval sent shivers up Sam's spine. "That's it. Now I want you to put it inside yourself."

Sam's breath caught in his throat. For a moment, he was unsure if he could do this—not that he hadn't touched himself there when he'd been home alone, wanting Aiden. But this way? Exposed—vulnerable?

"Do it, Sammy. You know you want to."

Aiden was right. He wanted this. Just the thought of it had him aching to come. He pulled his dripping finger from his mouth and, opening his legs slightly to accommodate his hand, skirted his hole.

Aiden smiled and nodded. "Do it, baby."

Sam pressed at his entrance until the tip of his finger breached the muscle. "Fuck." He pushed it farther inside, then realized he was no longer looking at Aiden. He forced his gaze back upward. Aiden's mouth was slightly open, his breath audible. Seeing Aiden so turned-on, Sam moaned again.

"Put another one in."

No hesitation this time. Sam withdrew and spit on his fingers, then, as Aiden watched, he worked himself open, hissing and groaning with the pleasure and the pain, all the while stroking himself.

"I want you to come now, Sammy." Aiden's eyes were dark, his jaw visibly tense. "I want to see you come. Come and stand at the edge of the bed so I can see you better."

A minute later, Sam stood next to the bed, stroking himself as he shoved his fingers in and out. "Fuck, Aiden."

"That's it. You know you want to come. Let me hear you come. Tell me what it feels like."

"Feels amazing… with you watching me… makes me want to… ah, fuck!" He spurted so hard he shot onto the sheets and all over his hand as his body shuddered. "Aiden!"

He was too far gone to remember when Aiden had moved from the head of the bed to the foot, but he was there, catching Sam's spunk with his hand and rubbing it over himself. Sam tried to recall when Aiden had pulled down his pants to expose his cock. It didn't matter. Because a moment later, he settled onto Aiden's cock and began to fuck himself on Aiden.

"Christ. Aiden. You don't even know how much I've missed you. Missed this." More than that, Sam missed the way he felt when he put his trust in Aiden. Unquestioningly. Wholeheartedly.

Aiden just laughed and supported himself with his good arm so he wouldn't fall backward with the effort of their sex.

"Aiden. God, Aiden. So good. So fucking good."

"I'm coming, Sammy. Hold me tight. Tell me you love me. Say my name."

Sam's eyes never left Aiden's. "I love you, Aiden. God, I love you. More than you'll ever know. You, Aiden. Only you. Forever, Aiden. I love you forever!"

Aiden's face was transcendent as he came with a shout. "I love you too, Sammy. So much. Only you."

CHAPTER 36

New York City
September

AIDEN walked to center stage and bowed deeply, doing his best to catch his breath and settle the rapid beating of his heart. The air around him and the floor beneath his feet vibrated with the din of applause. Even now, after six weeks of rehearsals and opening night behind him, the expansiveness of the place overwhelmed him. The Metropolitan Opera. The pinnacle of success for any red-blooded American singer.

He smiled and bowed again before picking up several bouquets adoring fans had tossed onto the stage. The crowd got to its feet, and he heard shouts of "Bravo!" throughout the hall. He looked up at the highest balcony—to the Family Circle seating affectionately called the nosebleed territory. He couldn't make out faces from this far away, but in his mind's eye, he envisioned himself seated there as a young singer on his first audition trip to New York. Back then he'd believed that his happiness lay in his career alone. He understood now that it wasn't enough and never could be.

Having offered the last of the bows, he headed back through the opening in the curtain, where already the stage crew had begun to break down and move the set in preparation for the next day's performance. Don Giovanni's chambers would soon be transformed into the gardens of Lammermoor Castle for the matinee performance of *Lucia di Lammermoor*.

"Mr. Lind." A stagehand shined a flashlight at Aiden's feet to guide the way off the stage in the semidarkness. "Please follow me."

The sheer exhaustion of an evening spent under the intensely hot lights dulled the reality of his accomplishment. He was costumed in a blue-and-gold brocade jacket with a high ruffled collar, tights, and heavy velvet pantaloons. The thick pancake makeup on his face had begun to melt, and sweat ran down his cheeks in rivulets. His scalp itched beneath the dark wig, and he had been forced to bite his tongue to moisten his mouth.

The dressing room was filled with flowers and cards. He grabbed a bottle of water off the table and chugged it down while he read quickly through them. He stopped and reread the one he'd pulled from the bouquet of irises.

> *Aiden—*
>
> *Congratulations! We wish we could have been there to cheer you on. Looking forward to seeing you in Paris at Christmas. Jules promises to bake a bûche de noël if you'll sing "O Holy Night."*
> *Bises,*
> *Jason and Jules*

He smiled as he inhaled the fragrance of the flowers, adding the card to the one from his sister and his high school drama teacher. He would keep those.

Three dozen roses in a crystal vase caught his eye. He pulled out the card.

> *Aiden—*
>
> *I hope you'll forgive me for not being there tonight. I have no doubt you're in good hands, although I rather wish they were mine. You will always be in my heart.*
> *-Cam*

Aiden rubbed a thumb over the card. He had Cameron to thank for more than just his freedom—he had his career back on track. He'd finally met with Cam a few days after the accident.

"I know you don't believe me," Cam told him as he handed Aiden a folder with a few pages of bank records and some other documents, *"and I understand. But I wanted to make this right for you."*

Aiden stared at the records. *"Alexandria's husband?"*

Cam nodded. *"I spoke with him, you know. He admitted Alexandria told him nothing ever happened between you two, that you told her you didn't date married women."*

"He was the one?" Alexandria's husband had never crossed his mind.

"Bit of a jealous prick, it seems. She told him the truth, but he chose not to believe it. I still don't think he believes her, but it doesn't matter," Cam added with a sad smile. *"We've taken care of it."*

"We?"

"David Somers and I. We've put out the word that if François Gilman tries to interfere in your contracts, we'll take care of it."

"What do you mean, 'take care of it'? Sounds like a mob hit or something."

Cam laughed. It reminded Aiden of why he'd been drawn to Cam in the first place—his sense of humor and love for life and adventure. *"Not a bad idea. But I only meant that we've put out the word that any donation he can make, we can double."*

"You can't—"

"It's not a matter of paying for you, Aiden. It's simply a matter of channeling my already generous contributions where they're most needed. Honestly, it was David's idea. Not that I think anyone would dare cross David and break a contract with you—the man's too big for anyone to play around with."

Aiden realized he'd get nowhere arguing with Cam over how he spent his money, though he added, *"If I find out that you're putting pressure on anyone to hire me or pay me more...."*

"You're more than good enough to get your own work, darling. You don't need my help or David's. Not anymore."

For once, Aiden actually believed Cam. *"Thank you."* Aiden swallowed hard. *"I owe you."*

"No. You owe me nothing." Cam paused for a moment, then pursed his lips and blinked his eyes a few times. Was he fighting back tears? No way. *"I'm the cause of this whole fiasco."*

"How do you figure that?" Aiden almost laughed as he spoke these words.

"I'm the one who fucked things up with you. If I'd realized... if I'd not been such a fucking bastard, maybe you'd still be with me. I... I'm sorry. Truly, Aiden. I know you don't believe it, but I'm truly sorry. And not only for myself. I'm sorry I hurt you."

Aiden blew air from between his lips as he fought to school his expression. This time he was sure Cam was telling the truth, and it nearly took his breath away. *"I appreciate that,"* he said at last. *"And I'm sorry I accused you of—"*

"Of something I actually considered doing myself?" Cam laughed. *"Don't give me too much credit. When I told you I'd make you regret it, I meant what I said."*

"But you didn't do anything."

"No," Cam admitted. *"I didn't."*

Aiden smiled and put his hand on Cam's shoulder. *"There's hope for you after all, my lord. Just don't fuck it up."* He kissed Cam on the cheek. *"Thanks, Cam."*

The wig master knocked on the door and set to work, bringing Aiden back to the here and now. "You were amazing." She beamed as she removed the heavy pins that held the wig in place.

"Thanks."

She gently worked the wig off of his head and set it on the wig stand, then removed the cap and pin curls beneath.

"God, that feels good." He laughed as she scratched his itchy scalp with her long fingernails. "The way to a man's heart is most definitely through his head."

"I wish." She winked at him knowingly in the mirror and shook her head. "I'll get Charles to send the flowers over to the hotel. Do you need me to call you a car?"

"No, thanks, Cecilia. I'll walk."

"What? Not going to the opening night party?"

"Not this one. I've got someone I need to meet. Would you please give Maestro Somers my regrets? Tell him I'll make it up to him."

"Someone important, then?"

"You could say that." He smiled and picked up the note that had been stuck to the mirror when he'd gotten back to the dressing room after the first act. *Meet me at Battery Park after the performance*, it read.

He and Sam had planned on meeting after the performance, though Aiden had expected they'd join David and Alex for the party. *Battery Park?*

Sam had been staying in New York for the past two weeks of rehearsals, working remotely from their hotel room. For the past few months, he'd been traveling with Aiden as promised. When Sam couldn't come, they scheduled nightly chats by Skype or telephone. Over Sam's protests, Aiden had also cut back on his performance schedule. It was rare that they spent more than a few weeks apart now, and when they were home, Sam and Aiden hosted regular get-togethers at the apartment, with Becca joining in. Aiden had started to get to know Sam's friends. He'd even made a few of his own. Philly was beginning to feel a lot like home.

An hour later, showered and dressed in casual clothes, Aiden headed south on the No.1 subway to South Ferry. It was warm in spite of the late hour. He loved this time of year in the Northeast: one day it was cool and the leaves had begun to turn; the next it was like summer again and everyone headed for the beach.

There were still people in the park—some on their way home to Staten Island by ferry, others tourists, Aiden guessed, wanting to view New York Harbor and Lady Liberty at night. The sound of steel drums rang throughout the park, calling to mind a tropical island. At first, Aiden had found the sound strange for the southernmost tip of New York, but later he'd come to associate it with the city. He'd often come here when he lived in New York. The ferry was a cheap date, and the view was nearly as good as the more expensive tourist lines that headed across the water to Liberty and Ellis Islands.

Aiden ran a hand through his hair, took a deep breath, and headed farther down the path, toward the water.

SAM stood at the water's edge, looking out over the harbor. The air was fresh and cool, with a faint scent of salt from the ocean beyond. Above, stars were visible between the light dusting of clouds. On the horizon, the moon had risen orange and full. How many nights had he come here with Nick and watched him paint? He'd lost count—it was never a chore. Each time had been a new experience, an inspiration for Nick's creativity. He'd learned so much listening to him describe what he saw in the clouds and the water.

He'd arrived early after stopping at the hotel to change his clothes and grab the backpack he'd left. He took a cab downtown because it was faster. He'd wanted a little time by himself before Aiden got there. For the past half an hour, he'd watched the boats—tiny points of light on a dark background, like stars—as they traveled across the harbor toward New Jersey and beyond. Several ferries had come and gone. People had begun to leave, headed to clubs and restaurants or making their way home. People laughing, talking, enjoying the last gasp of summer before the leaves began to fall and winter threatened.

Hey, Nicky. It's been a while.

Nearly eight years. It still took his breath away how much it hurt to think about Nick, even after so long. He hadn't told Aiden, but he'd gone to Brooklyn Heights that afternoon to see the loft. He'd even knocked on the door, hoping he might be able to look inside, but no one had answered. He'd decided it was the universe's way of telling him to move on. Only he'd already moved on. He'd just now realized that it was okay to look *back*.

S'only your fault it takes you forever to accept that things change, he could almost hear Nick say. Almost. The voice was fainter now, but it was still there.

You're right, Nicky. It's only my fault.

He pulled the backpack off his shoulder and sat down on a bench. He unzipped it and pulled out the battered cookie tin. The lettering, *Macadamia Chocolate Chip*, had faded, and the paint was scratched off in spots. He'd almost forgotten where he'd put it when he'd moved to Philly. Almost. He put the tin on his lap and ran his fingers over the surface. He didn't fight the tears but closed his eyes and let them spill over his cheeks. He tasted the salt on his lips and held the tin tighter in his hands.

The phone in his pocket vibrated. *Where are you?* the text message read.

Sam wiped his eyes, smiled, then typed, *Benches by the water. In the middle.*

Be there soon, Aiden answered a moment later.

Sam took a deep breath and set the tin back down.

AIDEN spotted Sam standing near a bench. They embraced in silence, holding each other before kissing. Sam brushed Aiden's hair from his eyes. "You were incredible tonight. I've never heard you sing better."

"Thanks. I'm glad you were there."

"As if I wouldn't have been." Sam brushed his fingers over Aiden's cheek, and Aiden let out an audible sigh. "You're probably wondering why I asked you to meet me here."

"Thought had crossed my mind. How did you know I didn't want to go to the party?"

"David's idea. He said you hated them—the donors' parties. He thought some time alone might be more up your alley."

"He's right." Aiden laughed.

"He said you owed him but that he'd figure out some 'suitable penance' for you."

"Probably an extra aria at his next soiree. Something high and fast. Figaro, or something else I sing like shit."

"Somehow I think what you think is shit sounds great."

"That's only because you're tone-deaf," Aiden teased as he pulled Sam close and kissed him again.

"Let's sit down." Sam motioned to the bench.

"Sure."

Sam slipped his arm around Aiden's shoulders. "I came here the night I met you, you know," Sam said after a few moment's silence. "Before I went to the bar."

"You worked near here, didn't you?"

"Yeah. I used to love this place. I still do, I guess. I'd eat lunch here when I could manage a break from work. But mostly Nicky and I would come here when the weather was nice. He'd set up his easel over there." Sam pointed to a spot to their right. "Sometimes he'd face the water. Sometimes he'd face the park and paint people."

Aiden wasn't sure what to say, so he leaned into Sam. He also wasn't sure where this was leading, but Sam rarely talked about Nick, and Aiden really wanted to know more about him. It still scared him a little to hear about Nick, but he no longer worried that he couldn't live up to Nick's ghost. He knew Sam loved him, and that was good enough.

"The night I met you, I came here to say good-bye. I'd been holding on to what was left of him." Sam looked out at the water, but Aiden knew he wasn't seeing the harbor anymore. "I spread his ashes here."

"That must have been hard."

Sam drew a long breath and released it audibly. "No. It was easy, really. I just opened my hand and he was gone." He paused, then said, "The hard part comes in bits. Like when I let you go to Europe, and I realized part of me was ready to move on, even though I wasn't ready yet. Or when I was in Paris and something reminded me of him. Or when I thought I'd lost you and I knew I couldn't...." Sam turned to face Aiden. "When I knew I couldn't let you go, so I had to let *him* go."

"Sammy, I'm so sorry you had to—"

"Shhh. I don't want you to be sorry. Remember what we said?"

Aiden nodded. "I remember."

"So I asked you to meet me here"—Sam's voice was once again bright, even hopeful—"because I'm ready." He reached to his left and pulled something off of the bench. A cookie tin, scratched and dented, coated with paint spatters. In answer to Aiden's unspoken question, Sam nodded. "This was Nicky's. But what's inside is for you."

Sam opened the tin and placed the top next to him, then withdrew a smaller box covered in velvet.

Aiden's mouth went dry. He took the box and his hand trembled.

"Open it," Sam said. "Please. And if you don't want it—if you don't want this yet—then just leave it in the box and maybe someday—"

"Shhh." Aiden touched his fingers to Sam's lips. He met Sam's gaze and held it for a moment, then reached down and opened the box. "God, Sammy, it's beautiful." He pulled the platinum ring out and held it up so it caught the light of the nearby streetlamp.

"There's a matching ring—for me—if you want this."

"Yes. I want this." Aiden wished the lump in his throat would stop getting bigger. Or maybe that was his heart, ready to explode? Unsure what to do, he replaced the ring and handed the box to Sam with slightly shaky hands. "Can you put it on me? Please?"

Sam nodded and pulled the ring out, then slipped it onto the third finger of Aiden's right hand. "I want to put it on your left hand when I marry you," he said in an undertone as he rubbed his thumb over the top of Aiden's hand in slow, sensual circles. "We can figure out the when and where later. David's offered to throw a party for us."

Sam's touch was making it difficult to focus. "You told him?" His voice sounded far away, even to his own ears.

Sam looked a bit sheepish. "I was afraid you might say no. He convinced me you wouldn't." Sam leaned in and brushed his lips over Aiden's.

"I need to thank him." Aiden brought Sam's face back toward him, then kissed his nose, his cheeks, and finally his lips. The kiss deepened, and Aiden moaned when their lips parted. "But first I need to get you somewhere private, where I can spend the whole night showing you how happy you make me."

"I'm liking that idea. A lot." Sam stood and offered Aiden his hand, pulled him up from the bench, and slung the backpack over his shoulder.

"Did you forget something?" Aiden glanced over at the bench and the cookie tin.

"No." Aiden saw a mixture of pain and happiness in Sam's expression.

I'll take good care of him, Nick. I promise.

Aiden kissed Sam sweetly on the lips, then went to retrieve the tin. He handed it to Sam, who smiled at him in silent wonder.

"Keep it." Aiden wrapped his arm around Sam's waist and drew him closer to kiss him. "So you can remember."

In her last incarnation, SHIRA ANTHONY was a professional opera singer, performing roles in such operas as *Tosca*, *Pagliacci*, and *La Traviata*, among others. She's given up TV for evenings spent with her laptop, and she never goes anywhere without a pile of unread M/M romance on her Kindle.

Shira is married with two children and two insane dogs, and when she's not writing, she is usually in a courtroom trying to make the world safer for children. When she's not working, she can be found aboard a thirty-foot catamaran at the Carolina coast with her favorite sexy captain at the wheel.

Shira can be found on Facebook, Goodreads, or on her website, http://www.shiraanthony.com. You can also contact her at shiraanthony @hotmail.com.

The BLUE NOTES series

BLUE
NOTES

SHIRA ANTHONY

http://www.dreamspinnerpress.com

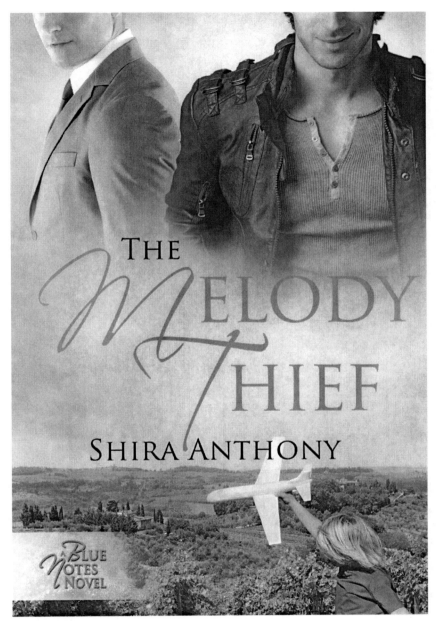

Also from SHIRA ANTHONY

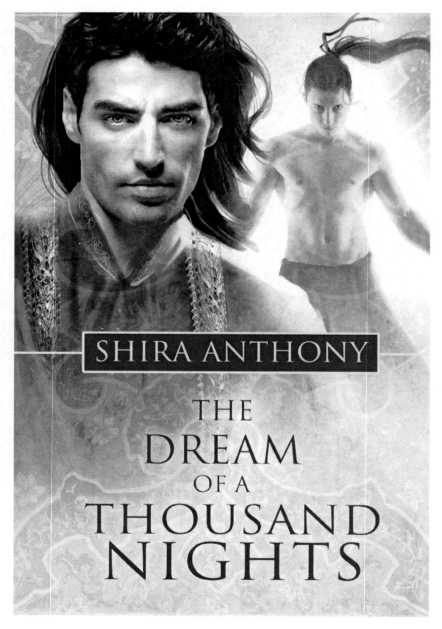

SHIRA ANTHONY

THE
DREAM
OF A
THOUSAND
NIGHTS

Also from SHIRA ANTHONY

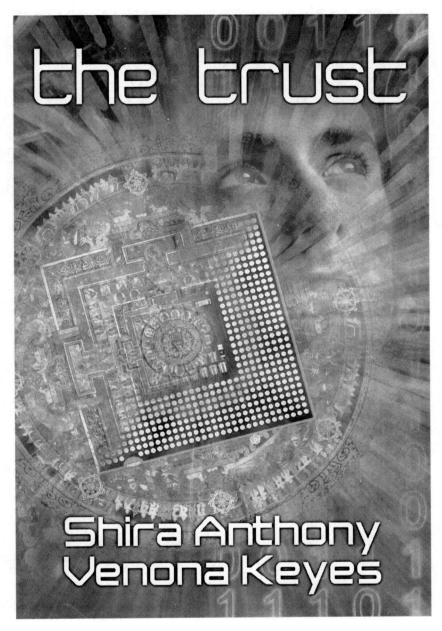

the trust

Shira Anthony
Venona Keyes

http://www.dreamspinnerpress.com

CPSIA information can be obtained at www.ICGtesting.com
Printed in the USA
LVOW05s2344240414

383062LV00003B/368/P